JESSIE'S HAREM

GHOULS JUST WANT TO HAVE FUN

MANDY ROSKO

Cover Design by Melody Simmons

Gordon, Saleena Chamberlin, Ramona Cabrera, Dusty Weller, Terri Eaches

Daria Donnelly, Kayla Reindl, Clare Parrott, Patricia Cassar, Sheryl Tegtmeyer, Lori Martin, Anne Rindfliesch, Stacy Ittersagen, Megan Mills, Christina Morgan, Monica Lynn Emery, Leanne Ede, Cassandra Hyden

Anne Samson, Pauline Dixon, Rachelle Binkley, Rebekah Snyder, Michelle Chantler, Thomas Werner, Kaer Baer, Sharron Anthony, Roxanne Johnson, Rachel Morse, Karen, marlene eaton, Julie Spencer, Wendy Custer, Annette Alex, Shelia Deal, Carolyn Lown, Mellissa, Jill Micklich, Confused child, Samalee Johnson, Sandy Folz, Janet Rodman, Jeanne Clark, David Friend,
Lizzy, SoshanahLila, Alexandra Smith, Virginia Robinson, Donna Hogel, Nanci Quinn, Janice Richmond, Stacey F, Barb Sands, Marcy Schwendiman, Charlotte Brincat, Sharon Manning-Lew, Teresa Albarran, GerryAnn L., Denise Holder, Gail Powell, Rose Allen,
Opal Carew Lori Trask, RetiredHsMom, Maria T, Rachel Barckhaus, Laura Furuta, Angela Cowen, Diana Mason, Beth Wolfe, Toni Mcconnell, Valerie Cobb, Valerie Jondahl

Tiffany Villeda, Iona Stewart, Charz Moore, Samantha Quinones, Seen Cassell, Melissa Carlton, ugo, Amanda Barker, Tricha Fely, Corrina Mayall, Ellen Swindall-Bailey, Alexis Abbott, Selena Kitt, Essie Munro, Anna Garcia-Centner, Biggi Ziegler, Jill Morrison, Alexia Falco, Kerrin Brittain, Ruth Roberts, Carol Ingham, Cynthia Powers, Tanya, Yolanda Pedroza, Belinda Jarrell, Miriam Loellgen, Pam Van Veen, Tammy Francis, Valerie Marshman

JESSIE

HAVING HAD ENOUGH of men's shit, why shouldn't Jessie use them to do her bidding for once?

Jessica Anne Gerolf watched idly from the tops of the trees as the wolves and the dragons fought with each other. Always ripping each other up for territory, always fighting over some such little thing. She hated that. Such wasted blood and effort over rock and dirt they had no rights to as far as she was concerned.

But, here they were, and though the sight and smell of their blood was making her mouth water, all that testosterone and aggression could be put to better use. She knew someone who really deserved to have his face ripped off and fed to him. Why not let one of these wolves or dragons do it for her?

Better yet, why not all of them?

Oh, ho! All right, this suddenly seemed like a much better plan.

Jessie slipped from her spot on the branch and started to move.

She needed to find their alphas. They would be the

bigger ones—at least Jessie thought they would be—so she didn't think she had to look all that hard.

There were more wolves than dragons. Maybe it was more than one pack? Or just an oversized pack? Didn't matter to her so long as they all bent the knee and decided she had a better target for their super up and sweaty rage.

The dragons were big but not huge. Maybe slightly larger than a grizzly bear each. It was their wingspans that made them seem larger, more frightening.

Hopefully, frightening enough to kill a man.

The idea of killing a man who deserved it was too delicious for her to pass up. There was a time in her life when she wouldn't have thought herself capable of purposely going out of her way to have a man killed, or to do what she was about to do to innocent people, but here she was. Things changed, and these guys might not be as innocent as she thought. Dragons and werewolves? Right. There was no way they were any better than she was. They had killed innocents in their lifetimes. Had to have. There was no shifter Jessie had ever met who didn't have the innocent blood of some poor fool on their hands. It was the way of things. If anything, they could consider this to be their penance.

And who didn't want to help a gorgeous damsel in distress anyway?

Jessie hugged the treetops. Just because she was up here didn't mean she was safe. Those were still dragons down there. Some of them might even be able to use those wings. They could come up here and see her hiding, assume she was the enemy, which she kind of was, and then attack.

Jessie had to be careful.

Luckily, she found the alphas.

Well, she *hoped* they were the alphas. They looked

pretty alpha as they fought each other. One-on-one, which was pretty ballsy of the alpha wolf down there as far as Jessie was concerned. He was a bigger wolf than the rest of his friends, but that still didn't compare to the dragon that continuously waved his tail at the shifter.

The wolf barely dodged out of the way, and when his tail smacked against the nearest birch tree, it exploded the base in a rush of splinters and leaves as the tree went down. Jessie's brows lifted, and the wolf still went back for more, jumping on the back of the dragon, right between the wings where it could not reach.

The dragon lifted its spiny head, mouth opening, fire bursting from those scaly lips that lit up the night.

Holy shit. All right. Now she was convinced. These were the alphas. They were the ones in charge, and all she had to do was get close enough to both of them, without getting tackled, and she could work her magick.

How to do that when both creatures looked as though they were ten seconds away from killing each other? She couldn't just jump down there and infect one, hoping the other would stand back for a few minutes and do nothing about it.

Then the dragon crouched, roaring as it launched itself into the air, the wolf still on its back, teeth digging into the neck of the dragon as it flew up, and up, and up into the stars.

Well, fuck. Maybe she wasn't going to get her chance with both after all. Now she had to hope at least one of them came down alive so she could get something out of this.

Jessie was done walking away empty-handed.

Now, she was leaving here with something.

Someone.

3

PATRICK

PATRICK GUNNOLF WAS SO FUCKED he could feel it. The higher they went, the more fucked he realized he was as he let himself shift back into his human shape just so he could have something to hang onto. The fact that he had to hang onto one of the damned dragon's horns didn't exactly make Patrick feel secure with his position on the back of the beast's long neck.

"Carlton! Stop!"

It was getting cold up here, too cold even for a dragon to handle, and it seemed as though Patrick couldn't take in the air he needed anymore. Too high. The bastard was flying too high, and he was going to kill them both. Patrick was all right to die, but he was not all right to leave James behind...

Finally, Carlton leveled out his wings. At least Patrick thought he did. No, he dipped down, diving back towards the earth and sending Patrick's guts hurtling into his stomach. Then the asshole decided to do a few barrel rolls. The prick. If Patrick survived this, he was going to have a good time ripping out each and every one of this cocksucker's scales.

As it was, he needed to survive first to do that. Patrick clenched his thighs around the dragon's neck, held tighter to the horns as the wind blew in his face so hard he thought his eyeballs would fly right out of their sockets, and he was blinded with the wind and tears that came. Maybe that was what Carlton had been waiting for. It seemed Patrick could just make out how close he was getting to the ground again when the dragon suddenly spun him around, flinging Patrick off his neck to be impaled on the trees below.

Shit. Sorry, James.

He crashed through the branches of the trees. He waited for one of them to stab at him as they slapped and scratched at his body.

He thought he felt it as he crashed against something harder, but no, he was still falling, and he wasn't dead. At least not yet. The hard smack against the back of his skull seemed to have something to say about that, but just before the black tunnel closed in on him, Patrick made out the perfect swell of breasts in front of his face.

A woman, kneeling in front of him. Her mouth was puckered with concern, and her eyes...

Her eyes glowed gold, and she smiled something wicked when she realized he watched her. Then her claws came out, and she scratched herself, revealing something dark and oozing before she brought it to Patrick's mouth...

Black blood. Oh fuck. He knew what this meant.

Goddamnit. Why this right now? It couldn't be more inconvenient.

Maybe he should have hoped for death over this.

5

CARLTON

CARLTON PANTED for breath as he dropped down for a sloppy landing. His wings trembled, but he shook the frost from them and felt infinitely better. He still felt like shit, but one step at a time. He was working in tiny chunks here.

He had to find the body. With his luck, there was a chance that stupid wolf was still alive, and Patrick needed his head if he was going to stop the fighting.

For now.

Just because he was exhausted from the battle, and the flight, didn't mean he needed to let his enemies know.

He was sure Patrick had landed somewhere over here. Carlton had watched how the man had fallen, and he could see the broken tree branches as he went deeper into the darkness of the woods. He could smell Patrick's blood, the sweat of his body. Then, Carlton spotted the man. He lay slumped against a crooked pine tree, looking almost as though he'd simply sat down for a rest. Blood trickled down the side of his head. All in all, his body looked good, considering what Carlton had put it through.

He stepped closer to the other man, watching him, waiting for any sign of life. There was none. He listened for a heartbeat; there wasn't one — just a waste of flesh and life.

"Should have walked away, idiot."

Carlton was sorry to have done it. Patrick had been an exceptional challenger. It was just a shame he couldn't see that this was dragon territory. Things could have worked out so much better if he'd simply given in and found another place for his pack of fur balls to get off to.

He'd always kind of liked wolves. Not just the natural ones, but the shifters as well. They were an interesting breed, to say the least, and their ability to stick together and protect one another was respectful from a dragon's perspective.

Satisfied the man was dead, Carlton got to one knee before him. He pressed his hand to Patrick's shoulder, as he would for any fallen soldier, though it had been years since Carlton had been in that sort of uniform.

"You fought well. Thank you for an honorable fight."

He stayed like that for a moment, not looking away from the male before him, but he could only keep that position for so long before it became impossible.

Carlton swung around, his claws at the ready, barely stopping himself before he could slash open the exposed throat of a young woman.

A beautiful young woman.

Her eyes stared defiantly back at him. She tilted her head back, as though inviting him to make the killing blow.

Carlton retracted his claws and pulled his hand back quickly. "Woman, what are you doing here?"

She stared at him, her eyes narrowing harshly. He

didn't have to look back at the dead male against the tree to know this had something to do with her.

"Are you his mate?"

Some of the female wolves were known to run out and fight with their men. It was not something Carlton approved of as a dragon, especially when she barely looked dressed for any sort of fight.

Her clothing hardly seemed fit for a battle. A loose-fitting black dress, one shoulder exposed. She carried a red shawl looped around her arms. She wore no jewelry, though her eyes were dark, and her lips bright red. She looked as though she were getting ready for some sort of formal function.

And she was not answering him.

"Woman?" Those dark eyes turned golden. They glowed. Her blood red lips pulled at the sides in a sort of smirk. Carlton stepped back from her. He didn't sense a heartbeat, and now his defenses were up, suspicion and caution catching him far too late. "What are you?"

She continued to smile at him. "Just someone who needs your help."

Carlton frowned. He backed up another step. Tried to. He could not. He backed into the chest of Patrick, who was now standing tall and strong. The other man said nothing as he wrapped his arms around Carlton's body, holding him tight.

"Hurry up!"

"Get off me!"

He tried to summon his wings, to bring them forward and push Patrick off him from behind. He did not get the chance as the other man held firm, and the woman came closer. Her nails, looking as though she'd just come from a salon, changed color from bright red to black, her eyes

8

still glowing that demonic golden color as she pierced the flesh of his throat with those claws.

The strength to fight drained from him. He could still move, still stand, but only with great struggle.

"Sorry, Carl," Patrick said, and oddly enough, he sounded as though he meant it.

Not that Carlton cared as the woman sliced one of those black claws down her wrist, black blood pooling from the wound. He knew what that was. He'd heard the stories, knew a curse when he spotted it.

"Get away from me," he growled, turning his head away when she brought her wrist to his mouth.

It was Patrick who grabbed a fistful of Carlton's hair, forcing his head back into place while the woman pressed her wrist to his mouth. He kept his lips shut, but the woman tsked at him.

"I promise this won't hurt a bit. If you're good," she said, pinching his nose, "I might even let you go when you're finished."

He couldn't breathe! Carlton was normally adept at holding his breath, but after the battle he'd had with Patrick, the instant the woman pinched his nose, it was as though he'd already closed his lungs for five minutes. He couldn't do it! He couldn't let her curse him!

He could taste the blood in his mouth. Black blood. The blood of demons, of witches, the cursed, or all three. He felt it sliding down his throat, but he refused to swallow. His body demanded he breathe, but even through his mouth he could take in no air with the way the woman forced her wrist between his lips. There was no gap, no chance for him to take even a sip of air, and a dark tunnel closed in around his eyes.

"Stop making it so hard! You know if you just make

yourself pass out, I'm going to force feed it to you while you're out."

"She will, too," Patrick said, growling a little under his breath, as though he didn't much like what she had done to him any more than he liked what they were doing to Carlton.

And they were right.

It was better that he be the one to decide, that if this had to happen, he let it happen while he was still on his feet. He would not let this bitch put him on his knees. He would drink her dirty blood, and then he was going to find out how to kill her quickly to get back at her.

So he let his tongue work. He pulled her filthy, sewage-tasting blood into his mouth and swallowed it down. And again, and again, until she was satisfied and stepped back. When she did, Patrick immediately released Carlton, and he doubled over, sucking in the hard breath he desperately needed.

Patrick stayed close. He put his hand on Carlton's shoulder. Carlton growled and shoved the man back, stepping away from him.

Patrick looked honestly glum about what he'd done.

"Motherfucker," Carlton spat, approaching the man, his claws at the ready. "I'll deal with you first."

"*Stop.*"

Carlton did. He didn't want to, and it wasn't as though his feet were glued to the ground beneath him. Patrick stood right there. Almost within reach. Carlton could swipe his claws out right now and take the bastard's nose off.

Yet, he could not.

Because the woman had commanded it.

He looked back at her, though he couldn't bring

himself to so much as growl at her. A light glare seemed taxing on his body.

She had one arm crossed beneath her perfect breasts. Her other hand lifted up, finger pressing into her cheek, as though she was thinking about something.

"The both of you will do very nicely. Yes, I think this will work."

"What will work?" Patrick snarled.

Based on the terrible twisting in Carlton's gut, he got the feeling this was not something the wolf wanted either.

"What did you do to us?" Carlton asked.

She shrugged. "I made you stop fighting."

Carlton clenched his hands into fists, though he could already feel there was nothing he could do in retaliation. "What *else* did you do to us?" He was now under the impression that was not red lipstick on her lips. Patrick's blood? Someone else's?

"There's no need for you to be so defensive. I just need a little help with something, and when I'm done, I'll send you on your way."

"What do you want done?" Patrick asked.

The woman would not stop smiling, but she suddenly looked a little less evil about it. Now, she seemed genuinely excited, even pleased. "I want you to kill a man for me."

4

JAMES

JAMES HAWKE KNEW there was a problem when he lost track of Patrick. His alpha had gone off to fight against the dragon leader, Carlton, and it felt like an eternity before the battle was called off.

First, with a triumphant dragon roar, calling the dragons to stop what they were doing. James' heart sank, terror gripping him until he heard the howl of the wolf that followed, and only then was he able to breathe again.

That was Patrick. He was alive. They were both alive.

Weird. Why would they both still be alive? Patrick had been adamant that he would kill Carlton for what he'd done to their home. For the terror and damage he'd caused, some of which was irreparable, but they were both alive. James didn't care for the dragon to still be breathing, but as long as Patrick was all right, James could focus on his duties.

The dragons around him shifted cautiously back into their human shapes, all of them looking more confused than the other as to what could cause both their leader and the alpha wolf to call off the battle at the same time.

"I'm going to find him," James said, looking back at Roger.

Roger growled and snorted. "Make it quick. I don't want to be hanging out around here longer than we need to if we can be gone." James didn't think the other man noticed when he started scratching at the scar on his face. Although, maybe he was genuinely itchy. Roger wasn't the sort of wolf who would want to give away if he was uncomfortable or scared at the idea of sticking around the dragons for too long.

"I'll be back."

James turned and shifted. He ran quickly, ducking and weaving between the confused dragon shifters, needing to find Patrick before the lizard brains realized something was amiss, or changed their minds and started fighting again. James didn't trust them. Not for one Goddamned instant.

Soon, the smell of his alpha caught his nose, and it became stronger as James followed after it. The smell comforted him, but that did not mean all was well or that they were entirely safe.

James slowed to a trot when he started to make out the voice of...a woman?

What the hell?

He was soon close enough that he could see his alpha through the many trees and various shrubs, but there was something off about it. Something not right. For starters, Patrick stood in front of the dragon shifter, Carlton Dreng. They were both in their human shapes. Both of their clothing had been torn up from the fight, but they stood almost relaxed in front of each other, Patrick with his fists on his waist, and Carlton with his arms crossed.

Between them, a petite woman stood, chatting with them, smiling, as though the two males on either side of her weren't growling at her like they wanted to put her over their knee and each give her a spanking.

James shook the thought from his head, but he came in a little closer.

"Does that sound fair to you boys?"

"Do we have any other choice?" Carlton asked, his voice a low hiss.

The woman tapped a brighter manicured fingernail against her cheek. "No. Now that I think about it, I don't think you do have much of a choice, do you?" She laughed. It was sweet sounding, but the more James heard from her, the more he started to think she wasn't exactly a sweetheart. "It really was rude of me to ask when you know the answer I want, wasn't it?"

Neither man answered her. They both narrowed their eyes, however. She continued to laugh and smile. James had to admit, she did have a nice laugh, but his guard remained up. Something was happening here, and he wasn't about to let himself get pulled in.

She'd *done* something to them. To both of them. She wasn't entirely human. James could smell it on her. He growled low in his throat.

Her gaze snapped up, and she finally noticed James' approach, red lips pulling back into an even wider smile. Her attention was all it took for both Carlton and Patrick to notice James standing there.

Carlton growled at him. Patrick looked as though the floor dropped out beneath his feet. "Stay back." He held his hand out, and though they were still many feet away from each other, James halted as though he'd been physically shoved.

James glanced at all three of them. "What is this? What happened?" He looked at the woman. "Who are you?"

"Is he one of yours?" the woman asked, looking to Carlton.

Carlton snorted, glancing away. "Mutt isn't one of mine."

James growled low in the back of his throat at being called a mutt, but he had better things to attend to.

"Patrick, what happened? Why did you stop fighting?" He tried to think of something possibly innocent that this could be. Not much came to mind. "Did you agree to a peace treaty for the land?"

Both men growled at each other, suggesting that wasn't what had happened.

The woman, however, continued to smile that innocent, pixie grin. "I made them stop fighting! In exchange for helping me."

"You made..." James couldn't wrap his brain around that, and suddenly, he was sick of trying. "Patrick, who the fuck is this woman?"

Patrick shook his head, his lips curling. James had known the man for decades. He was James' mentor, best friend, and confidant, and James had never seen that *look* on his face before.

"She is...she is going to be working with us for a while."

James was disgusted to hear such a lie from the mouth of his alpha. He's thought Patrick respected him more. "Horse shit. Who the fuck is she? What did you do to them?"

"How do you know I did anything? I'm just a little girl."

"Yeah? Well, you stink like something that crawled out of a cemetery."

She tensed, blinking those long lashes at him before the wind flew, and a hand latched around James' throat. The woman was right there, up in his face, so fast he

15

barely had time to register anything was happening before she had him slammed into a crooked tree, dragging him off his feet.

"Cemetery?" she hissed, her eyes changing color, glowing, golden.

Right, he knew something was off with this bitch.

Patrick ran to her, but to James' surprise, he didn't try to stop her from strangling James to death. Instead, he stood off to the side and started begging, like some desperate little pup.

"Let him go. You don't need to do this. He doesn't know."

"He insulted me," the woman said, still sneering at James as though he was something she just finished squishing beneath the heel of her shoe.

"Let him go, or I won't help you. Let him go!"

"You'll help me anyway. You have to."

All right, this was getting annoying because now James really couldn't breathe.

While the bitch had her attention turned onto Patrick, James slammed his fists down onto her elbows. He was stunned with how difficult it was to break her grip. Hitting someone there should have been enough to make her drop him immediately, but he had to slam his fists down again before she did so, backing up a step while James coughed for breath. He was pleased he managed to stay on his feet. He stumbled a little, but he still proved himself to be the better warrior by remaining upright.

"You fucking bitch, what the hell are you?"

"I don't think you want to know that one, little wolf," Carlton replied.

James didn't take his eyes off her. She, however, looked down at her nails, as though making sure none of them had broken while she'd manhandled him.

"What are you? Patrick? What did she do to you? Why do we have to help her?"

"You don't have to do anything, James. Get the hell out of here before she makes me do something I regret."

Make. All right, this was getting ridiculous.

"She a witch? What did she do? You're both not trying to kill each other anymore, and she looks like she's got the both of you on a leash."

Carlton growled. Patrick looked...holy shit, he looked worried. Patrick, a warrior James had witnessed kill his enemies with his bare hands...he looked honest to God concerned.

But not for himself. Not with the way he was staring at James.

James backed up a step.

"Patrick," said the woman. "Grab him for me, if you please."

"James, run."

James was loyal. He knew his alpha, and he knew to do what he was told, even if it was humiliating... like retreating.

So, yeah, he ran. Not that it did much good.

17

PATRICK

"JESUS CHRIST, you leave him alone! Leave him alone!"

Jessie came to stand beside him. She had one finger to her cheek, observing Patrick as he stonily walked in the direction James had rushed off in.

He couldn't summon the strength to stop himself, but he could force himself to hold back. He wasn't running after James, the way Jessie wanted him to, but he was still moving.

"You're stronger than I thought," Jessie said, her tone the sort that made Patrick unsure if it impressed her or not. And why the fuck was he interested in impressing this bitch when she had him by the balls here?

Finally, she seemed to come to some sort of decision, sighing and snapping her fingers. "Carlton, bring me back that wolf."

"What?"

Patrick looked up just as Carlton formed his wings, crouched down, and jumped into the air, the whoosh of his wings flapping as he flew after James.

"No, no, you don't need him."

"That's where you're wrong. Honestly, I am sorry about this. But I need all of your wolves, and I need all of his dragons for this."

"I'm not killing one damned person for you, and I'm not killing James!"

She rolled her eyes, suddenly seeming less confident and more annoyed. "For God's sakes, you shifters are such babies. I don't want him dead. I just wanted you to bring him to heel for me."

"I won't do that either." Patrick's muscles twitched with each step he took. With each forward push, a new bead of sweat formed on his face and the back of his neck.

Jessie walked backwards in front of him, smiling. "You really are trying here, aren't you? This is good, honestly. This is really good."

"Fuck you."

She mock shivered at him. "So scary."

A scream sounded above their heads. James. He wasn't a fan of heights.

Thankfully, the idiot dragon didn't drop him. He did land hard, however, hard enough that the ground beneath Patrick's feet rumbled, and because he was still working under the command of this woman—witch, demon, whatever she was—the instant his gaze locked onto James, Patrick's body changed direction against his will. He started moving towards him.

James shook his head, his body wobbling as he pulled himself to his feet. But then he spotted Patrick heading for him, and he backed up. "Carlton, grab him. Patrick, stop. You don't have to bring him to me. He's already here."

Patrick stopped, relieved, but that relief was short-lived as he watched the dragon grab James by his arm and the back of his neck. A grip James could easily get free of if there were not claws pointing dangerously at the delicate, pulsing spot of his throat.

James looked worried. He was a proud warrior. He didn't like showing his concern, not even to Patrick, and Patrick knew him the best.

Jessie walked over to them, circling. Her eyes remained trained on James, however. She seemed to be paying no attention to Carlton. "You're not as tall, definitely not as broad in the shoulders as your alpha. Are you a beta?"

James glanced at Patrick. Patrick nodded.

"Yes. What did you do to them?"

Jessie continued to smile pleasantly. She half turned, looking back at Patrick. "You can let him know if you want. I have no use for him. That doesn't mean I'll have him killed. Believe it or not, I'm not that bad."

Her smile brightened. Fuck, why did she have to be so fucking beautiful? She was a demon in an angel's body.

"Well, I am bad, but I'm not evil, let's say."

"That's debatable," James replied. "What did you do to them?"

"Stubborn. I like it, but I need strength more than I need someone to get mouthy with me. Patrick, you can explain it if you want, he's your beta."

She waved her hand as though it was of little consequence to her who explained it, but Patrick was glad for it. James would understand. He would lead their pack in Patrick's absence, and James trusted him to help keep the betas and omegas away from this woman.

"She wants us to kill her maker."

James blinked, his head jerking back a little, which was more than enough to make Patrick nervous since that bastard dragon's claws were still pointed at the soft spot of his throat.

"She...you want them to kill your father?"

Jessie refused to look at him as she crossed her arms. "Don't be an idiot. I would never force anyone to kill my father."

"Not her father, her maker, you fool boy," Carlton hissed. "She's a...a something. A ghoul. A succubus. She's got us, and you're lucky she wants nothing to do with a scrawny runt like you."

James growled, fur coming in around his throat as his claws took shape.

Patrick put a stop to that shit immediately. "James, focus. Right now."

James did, though his mouth was still pursed with annoyance.

Patrick inhaled a deep breath. Jessie was no longer smiling. Now, she watched, as though this entire thing was something that had piqued her interest.

"The dragon is right. She did something to us. We have to obey her. There's no getting around it." Might as well rip that Band-Aid off right now. There was no hope of getting out from under her claws. No chance of escape until her commands were brought to fruition, so he wouldn't put that hope in James' head either.

James' face remained stoic. He looked from Patrick to Jessie and back again.

"I know what you're thinking, and I don't think killing her would help. I don't think we can kill her."

"I made sure of that," Jessie said with a smile.

James continued to stare at her. Torn between two loyalties, Patrick knew where his thoughts had gone off to.

So did Carlton. "You won't kill her either. Much as I wouldn't mind seeing it, we would stop you."

"He's right," Patrick said. "I can see it in your eyes. I know you're thinking it, cut it out."

"Why?" James asked.

Carlton tightened his claws around James' throat. "Because if you try it, I'll kill you, and I don't need her telling me to rip your throat out to do that all on my own."

Patrick looked to Jessie. "Don't let him do it. I will fight you to the end if you let him kill anyone in my pack."

"Anyone? Or just him?" Jessie walked up to James. She got in close, a little too close, leaning in so their noses could have been touching. All Patrick could do was watch her fingernails. They stayed red. They did not transform into that inky black they had become when she had taken him and Carlton as her servants, and she didn't seem all that interested in opening the wound on her wrist back up. But that didn't mean she couldn't move quickly if she really wanted to. "You like him, don't you?"

James held his breath. Everyone seemed to be holding their breath.

James didn't dare look at Patrick, but he didn't need to. Patrick knew what the other man felt for him. It had always been unsaid between them because Patrick was not only James' friend, but his alpha. And Patrick never wanted to confront James with those feelings.

"Not just as a friend, or a mentor, or even a brother."

"Jessie, that's enough," Patrick snapped.

She looked back at him, that mischievous look in her eyes.

Patrick just wanted this to end. "Enough. Please?"

James still refused to look anywhere near Patrick, and Patrick hated that.

"All right then. You help me, your pack helps me, and I'll keep your little friend out of it. Then you won't fight me. Deal?"

"Deal." Patrick was taking it and not asking any questions.

"No, fuck off, that's not a deal!"

"James, shut the fuck up, you are taking the deal."

"No, I'm staying with you. Lady, whatever you want him to do, I'm in."

Jessie tilted her head to the side.

Patrick wanted to murder his best friend.

"James—"

"Patrick, close your mouth."

Patrick did as he was commanded. It felt as though there was something invisible over his lips, forcing them shut, preventing him from speaking.

Carlton smiled at him, the pecker head, as if he thought the whole thing was funny. Patrick was going to turn his face inside out when he had the chance. He swore he would.

Jessie, meanwhile, ignored them both and observed James, as though he might just have something interesting to give to her after all. "Why would I want any help from you? He already offered to stop fighting me if I let you go. I've got his entire pack behind me, and the clan of that dragon. I can spare one omega."

"Because if you take me with you, you don't need to do to me whatever it was you did to them. I'll be loyal. I'll get the job done if, for whatever reason, they can't."

The confidence, the arrogance on Jessie's face almost seemed to melt away, but Patrick couldn't be entirely sure of that. He didn't trust any expression she happened to make. Not where James was concerned.

"You want to make sure that I give him back to you alive, is that it?"

James hesitated. Then he gave in. "That's exactly it."

"You don't trust me?"

"Not for one second."

23

She smiled at James, glancing back at Patrick. The smile didn't quite reach her eyes, as though she was...

No. Patrick didn't give a shit if she was sad. He didn't care if she looked and sounded as though her entire world was falling apart. He didn't trust her. He just wanted his friends and family untouched.

"All right, deal," she said. "Patrick, you can open your mouth again if you want."

He did. "James, you stupid son-of-a-bitch, you dumb piece of shit, I never asked for you to back me up and I don't need you to, so take that shit back!"

"No."

"*Idiot*! Take it back! I don't need you!"

James would not look at him, though. He only had eyes for Jessie, and it made Patrick fucking furious. "Whatever you want them to do, I'm in. So you don't have to infect me or curse me, or whatever it was you did to them. I'm in."

"You really want to stay with your friend, don't you?"

"I do." James seemed to get a full inch taller as he observed Jessie, as though he was trying to make himself look like a better candidate for what she wanted. "I can fight. I can be quick and quiet, and I can move in and out of places that alphas can't get to."

"Yes, you are tall, and you've got muscle, but not so much that you would stand out. You could pass for human. I bet that comes in handy, doesn't it?"

"It does."

Patrick shook his head. His entire body trembled with the heat of his fury. If he didn't love James so damned much, he'd break the man's head open.

"I will be loyal to you. You don't have to worry about me."

The fool. The stupid fool thought that sort of begging

would actually work.

Jessie nodded, then she sighed. "If only I could bring myself to believe that." She moved with inhuman speed, her hands, like talons, grabbing either side of his head as she brought James' face down to hers, forcing him to kiss her.

And as much as Patrick wanted to stop her, as much as he wanted to force the two apart and prevent this from going on, there was nothing he could do but watch.

James did give her a little trouble. He pulled back, apparently stronger than she, which gave Patrick some hope, but it wasn't enough. Patrick wasn't sure how she did it. Did she have blood somewhere in her mouth that he didn't know about? Either way, she made James drink it. Wherever it had come from, James drank down enough of it with just that kiss.

Yanking back from each other with a heavy sigh, James blinked wildly, shaking his head. Black blood was on his lips. Perhaps all the woman had to do was think about having her blood appear outside of her body and it would materialize. That was something terrible to think about in and of itself.

James wiped the blood away with the back of his hand, but it was too late. Patrick could tell there was nothing to be done about it now.

"What..." James wobbled on his legs. "What did you..."

Patrick didn't want to watch. He forced himself to because to look away would be cowardice. This was his friend. Patrick knew what he was feeling, and he knew it would be over soon. "Give it a minute, James. You'll be fine in a minute."

"I will, God." James pressed a hand to his stomach and a fist to his mouth. The nausea hadn't stayed with Patrick for long, and very soon he'd felt nothing but the need to be close to the woman before them, to obey her above anyone and anything else. James would be feeling that soon. Patrick wished the stupid son-of-a-bitch had stayed away like Patrick had ordered him to. He supposed he couldn't have everything he wanted in life.

James sank to his knees. Even the dragon seemed to be staring at him with a pitying expression on his face. Patrick normally would not appreciate that, but there was nothing to be done about it now other than wait for it to be over.

After about a minute or two of coughing, and even a bit of gagging, James seemed to breathe in deep, and then come out of the side effects Jessie's blood had on him.

James stood. He looked at Carlton, then at Patrick, then at Jessie. He didn't say anything, but there was an expression in his eyes that spoke loud and clear.

He should have left well enough alone.

Jessie smiled at him, scratching under his chin. "Right, now you'll be loyal for sure. I hope you don't mind, but I didn't want to take the risk. A girl can't be too careful around multiple men she doesn't know, right?" She almost sounded apologetic.

James didn't swear at her, and he didn't growl or snap his teeth. He seemed almost...unsure. Of himself, of her, and Patrick didn't want to think it, but he even seemed unsure of him.

"What did you do to him?" Patrick barked.

Jessie shrugged, alarm filling those golden, inhuman eyes. "I didn't do anything to him that I didn't do to you or Carlton. Hello? Are you all right in there?" She snapped her fingers in front of James' face. He frowned, turning away and batting her hand away from his face.

"I'm fine. I just...that was really weird."

"Oh, well, don't scare us like that. Your alpha already

wants to rip my head off, the last thing I need is for you to look like I've put you into some sort of waking coma. Got it?"

"Right." James finally looked at Patrick, and Patrick was able to sigh with relief.

At least he could see James was all right, but now that left behind the other problem where the stupid fucker had allowed himself to be taken as a slave by a succubus for some sort of revenge plot.

"What do you want us to do?" James asked, looking back at Jessie.

"Eager. I like that." Jessie pointed a red fingernail at James' nose, her other hand on her hip. "You and I are going to get along just fine."

"Well, the sooner I get this over with, the sooner Patrick and I can go back to our pack. And make sure we have a place to live."

Carlton growled low in his throat. "The second this is over, Patrick and I are going to finish what we started. This land belongs to the dragons, and there's no way in hell I'll let him take it just because he wants it."

Patrick growled back at the man, but before he could say a word, Jessie snapped her fingers again, and his mouth snapped shut.

She sighed, rubbing at the bridge of her nose as though fighting off a coming headache. "Men. You always want to fight." She shook her head. "Whatever. Let's get out of here. Time to tell the rest of the boys that they'll be working for me for a little while. Then we can get down to business, and the three of you can go about your way." She snapped her fingers again, allowing Patrick and Carlton to speak again.

"Sounds good to me," Patrick growled.

"Can't wait to get back to business," Carlton replied,

making a show of cracking his knuckles.

Big boy thought he was tough. Whatever. If he hadn't cheated like a bitch, Patrick would have won that fight.

"Hmm." Jessie looked to James again. "Maybe it was a better idea than I thought to bring you on. You're the only one who doesn't stroke your own dick in front of me trying to show off."

James sputtered, his face transforming to a bright shade of red that didn't belong on a warrior. Patrick rolled his eyes. "Can we just get this over with?"

"Of course. Move out, troops," Jessie said, waving her hand as she commanded Patrick, Carlton, and James to follow her.

Which they did, because of course they did. They were compelled to.

"Hey, boss? You want me to step in yet?"

Patrick frowned. That didn't come from James, and the way Jessie looked around made it clear she didn't know who was there either.

Her perfect manicure once more turned into something that looked as though it could be used to slice open steel if she really wanted it to.

She put some of those nails to Carlton's throat. "Show yourself now, or your friend gets it!"

Carlton just smiled.

A dragon dropped from the tops of the trees, shifting into another male. He was bare-chested but still had on jeans and the sort of shit-kicking boots that had probably busted a few heads open.

He was definitely a warrior. The scars on his inkless chest were all the evidence Patrick needed of that. The man crossed his arms, as though he didn't have a care in the world. "Kill him for all I care. If you do, I get to lead the clan."

6

DRACO

"Great, who in the hell is this guy?"

Draco was honestly amused by this. "Not sure if the guy who just gave himself up like a sucker should be moaning and complaining about anything right about now."

The wolf flushed again. He really didn't look like he belonged on a battlefield. Not if he couldn't sufficiently hide his emotions.

"You want to tell me what you're planning on doing with my clan leader right there?"

The woman eyed him. She was beautiful. Stupidly beautiful. She looked like she'd just come off the cover of the swimsuit edition of literally anything, and better than all that, she'd managed to take these three idiots for a ride with little effort.

And she was holding her claws to Carlton's throat, and he was a cunt when he wanted to be.

So Draco might be in love here.

The woman tried to act as though his words hadn't

surprised her, but Draco could see they had. "You would let me kill your clan leader right in front of you? No love lost there, is there?"

She looked up at Carlton, as though waiting for him to confirm it.

Carlton's mouth set in a firm line.

"Would he really mind if I killed you, or is this a trick?"

"Honestly? Sometimes I can't tell."

That got Draco right in the chest, but he ignored it. There were better things to be worrying about.

Of course, the stupid werewolf, the smaller one, had to open his mouth and comment about how brittle a dragon's loyalties were, under his breath, like a little bitch.

"You're not one to talk about how anyone's loyalties work when you put yourself under the spell of a...what should I call you, sweetheart?"

He expected a teasing smile in return for his banter. She watched him with suspicion. "Jessie. Carlton, does this man really want you dead?" To Draco's shock and relief, she removed her hand from Carlton's throat.

"Not really. He's just my idiot second. Always bitching about the way I run things. He probably wouldn't mind it if I did die, but he doesn't want you or anyone else to do the deed."

"He wants to kill you himself?" Patrick asked. Draco recognized him. "A member of your own clan?"

"Shut up. He doesn't want to kill me, right, Draco?"

"Not at all. I was just hoping to see the lady thrown off her guard. Though I would run the clan much better than Carlton ever could." His leader growled at him, and Draco was forced to raise his hands in defeat. "All right, all right. So what am I going to do with the lady?"

"Nothing," Carlton snapped, which was not the

command Draco expected to hear from him. And he knew it was not the command he wanted to give either.

Draco laughed a little. "Wow, huh, holy shit. You're the real deal, aren't you? So, what happened? Did you steal their souls or something?"

"Or something," said the woman, Jessie, with a smile.

The sort of pleasant tingling Draco got whenever he knew he was about to get lucky hit him, and it hit hard. He wanted this woman. He wanted her for himself. He was getting all kinds of vibes from her, maybe mating vibes, maybe not, but he definitely wanted her body.

And that was just as good as mating in some respects, wasn't it?

She kept smiling at him. "Do you want to join us, too? This one decided not to fight me too much about it." She pointed to the beta wolf, who rolled his eyes and still looked ashamed of himself.

"You know what? I do, but you're not giving me that black blood of yours. I want to do this right."

"Hmm." She seemed to think about it, then shook her head. "Nope." She lunged for him, just as quickly as she'd done for the beta, but Draco had seen that coming a mile away and was prepared. He ducked out of the way, enjoying the shocked and irritated expression on her face.

Not so easy if your prey knows you're coming.

She might not have been able to take out Carlton, the alpha, or that beta if she hadn't gotten so massively lucky. When Draco arrived, she'd had her wrist to Carlton's mouth, and then he watched, fascinated, as she tricked the beta and made him her servant, too.

Draco let his wings out. They fluttered behind him, ready to pull him into the air if needed.

"You want me to think you're stronger than you really are. That's cute."

She lunged for him again, but Draco enjoyed being faster than his opponents, and he made absolutely sure that there was no one else who could beat him as far as speed went. He worked hard to make sure things stayed that way.

She lunged for him again, moving so quickly his eyes briefly lost sight of her. That didn't happen often, and had he not had a feel for the wind, she might have actually caught him if he didn't get out of the way.

Instead, he got another laugh when she appeared again, her hands empty as she realized she had missed her target.

And Draco was loving this too damned much. The flush of her cheeks, the heaving of her perfect breasts as she tried, again and again, to grab onto him.

"I love you, too, sweetness, but I don't think I want you putting those nails anywhere near me. We're not in that kind of relationship yet."

"Shut up!"

Draco took a risk. It was one of the things Carlton said was the reason why he wouldn't make a good leader, but fuck Carlton right now. Draco had his sights set on something a little better. So he came in a little too close, taking the woman by her wrists in a tight grip with one hand. Her golden eyes bulged as she realized she was trapped, and Draco leaned in a little too close to her red lips. "We can be in that sort of relationship if you want."

Roaring, Jessie pushed him away, staggering back several steps, and this time there was definitely more anger flowing through her than he expected. He could almost feel the heat as it flowed from her.

"Don't touch me!"

An angry woman was a beautiful thing. This woman,

however, looked ready to tear his head off, and if she really was a succubus, she might actually have the power to do it.

Raising his hands in surrender, Draco decided to give her this. "All right, sweetheart, I'm sorry."

"Stop calling me that!" She pointed a finger at him, her arm trembling, but there was no spell of any kind that stemmed from her hand. Instead, hands from behind grabbed Draco before he could spread his wings and jump back into the safety of the trees.

Draco looked back. Carlton, Patrick, and the beta male all had their hands on him, all looking apologetically at him.

"Did I ruin your fun?" Jessie asked, suddenly in his face.

Draco smiled. "Not really. Not if you make me your slave the same way you did for the runt back there."

She frowned. "What—mmph!"

Never one to be outdone, Draco leaned forward, crushing his mouth to hers, beating her to the kiss. All right, so he was going to be the servant of a succubus, demon, whatever she was, but at least this way he could make sure she knew he was the one choosing it. That he was going to stick out from the rest of the pack of losers behind him.

And then, it happened. He felt it. She might have bitten her tongue, or she might have just summoned the liquid forward, but he tasted the black blood as she slid her tongue into his mouth.

He couldn't decide whether it was sexy or weird, but fuck it! He was an adventurer at heart, and he was going with it. He tilted his head to the side and met her tongue with his own. He tasted her blood, felt the little noise of surprise she made, and he enjoyed the fuck out of that, too, as he pushed his tongue back into her mouth, tasting her, licking her deep as she threaded her tendrils through him.

Jessie grabbed him by his hair, her grip tight enough to hurt, but fuck it. He felt something inside him clench and pull towards her, and not just his cock either. And then he really felt it. He was hers. Whether he wanted it or not, but she wasn't his in the same way. He couldn't feel anything pulling her to him in the same way he was being yanked to her.

She ended the kiss way too soon, gasping for breath when they were apart.

"Independent woman?" Draco smiled, finding it difficult to hide how dazed he felt. "I like that."

She smiled at him, reaching out and scratching at the bottom of his chin. "I think I'll like you, too."

When the other three growled at her for the comment, Draco felt an intense possessiveness settle over him. "Don't be jealous that she likes me more than she does all you. Only makes sense she'd want a man."

"I think they're more interested in ripping my head off than wooing me," Jessie replied, amusement in her voice.

That's what she thought.

Sure, Draco could understand the annoyance of being turned into a servant against his will, but he could also spot a gorgeous creature when one happened to be placed in front of him. The fact that she was also a powerful damsel in distress only made Draco want to serve her. She thought she was capturing him for whatever plan she had. Yeah, right. He wanted to stick around.

"You look a little too pleased with yourself," Jessie said, clearly suspicious.

Carlton growled at him. "Yeah, you do."

Draco shrugged. "I'm just eager to get to work and help out a beautiful lady. I see nothing wrong with that."

"She's forcing you to do this," said the beta.

And now everyone was looking at him as though he'd lost his mind. Whatever. That was not his problem, and he wasn't going to pay much attention to it. Draco had two goals. Get this spell or curse, or whatever it was, off him, and see if he couldn't get the lovely lady's phone number before his three rivals behind him, which might be harder than it appeared since they were all clearly hiding their lust for her beneath their growling exteriors.

Draco presented his arm to her. "If you would, I'd like to walk you back to the wolf pack, and our clan, so we can let them know plans have changed."

Her red lips continued to pull up in that lovely smile. "You would like that, huh?"

He shrugged, ignoring the heat of the glares on the back of his head, and trying not to make it too obvious whenever he glanced down at the perfect swell of her breasts. "Why not?"

She shook her head, but then lightly rolled her eyes before accepting his arm. "Very well, but don't think that just because you get cute means I'm willing to trust you."

"Wouldn't dream of it," Draco said. "I'm probably more untrustworthy than you are."

"I doubt that."

"Just tell us who exactly you want to kill," Patrick said with a growl. "I want to know precisely what I'm going to tell my pack about this bullshit arrangement when I see them."

"Same here," Carlton replied.

The beta said nothing, but that was only because all betas happened to be enormous pussies.

"All right. I want you all to kill my husband."

Aaaaaand there went his hard-on.

Draco tended not to get involved with married women. He'd learned his lesson on that decades ago, and she wanted them to kill her husband?

Right. This romance was fucked from the start.

7

JESSIE

JESSIE EXPLAINED, but only as much as she needed to. These were servants, not friends. So she told them what they needed to know, leaving out anything that would make her appear smaller or weaker than she actually was.

Because she was not small, and she was certainly not weak. Not anymore, and a servant was never going to respect the master if they thought the master to be ill-suited to lead, or thought them to be scared and shivering.

So Jessie stood tall, chest out, shoulders back, and declared she needed her husband murdered for cheating on her. No way in hell she was going to explain the rest, and fuck these boys if they thought for one second she owed them any more than this.

"So, for cheating on you, you want to murder your husband?" James sounded a little too horrified for her liking. She wanted them to fear her, not look at her as though she was the monster. But, then again, she had made the decision that this was the part she was going to play. She might as well not get shy about it now.

"Of course. What else am I expected to do about it?"

"How about a divorce?" James asked in a way that irritated her.

"What? You were ready to kill each other over land a minute ago. Don't pretend to get all prissy about murdering someone for hurting me." She said a little too much with that one sentence. She didn't want them knowing he'd hurt her, but maybe they weren't paying attention as well as she would have liked them to, because they skipped over that part and started talking about everything else.

"What's the guy's name?" Patrick asked.

"Valbrand the Almighty."

"What?" Draco snorted. "Really?"

Jessie had to smile a little herself. "Yes. Whenever a lunatic names himself, he usually gives it a flourish."

"Like Lord Voldemort?" James asked.

"Yes, and you should read another book if that's the only example you can come up with."

James growled at her. Jessie could see she wasn't about to make friends with him any time soon, but it wasn't as though she'd been trying to make friends with him anyway. She just needed them to do as she told them and to keep their pretty mouths shut about it.

Draco thought it was funny, James was barely concealing his disgust, but Patrick and Carlton...

They watched her. Their eyes were knowing in a way she didn't like, in a way that made her feel a little too undressed for the occasion.

She was fairly certain she was older than the lot of them, but that did not mean these were young men. Werewolves could live to be well over a hundred, and some dragons made it to a thousand.

Some.

She should have looked in on them a little before

making her decision. Checked in on age and experience, because these men looked at her in a way that suggested she wasn't putting anything past them.

She didn't like it.

Still, it wasn't as though she had a resume for any of the males standing in front of her. They'd sort of fallen into her lap, and she had to act fast. Otherwise, these idiots would have killed each other before Jessie could force their cooperation.

Draco cracked his knuckles. "Well, I'm game."

"Of course you are," Carlton snarled. "Killing a man we know nothing about other than what she's told us? That sounds like a marvelous idea."

"Stop pretending like you're not itching to help her get her revenge," Draco said, still managing to look at Jessie as though *he* was the one who'd snagged a real bargain here. "A beautiful woman enslaves you, and all you do is bitch about it."

Carlton huffed. "Of course I'm complaining about it! I don't want to be anyone's slave!"

"But we're not exactly her slaves, are we?" Patrick asked, eyeing her.

She didn't know what they were talking about and didn't care to find out. The speculation was enough. "Don't get any thoughts in that perverted brain of yours. This is strictly business."

"Sure it is," Draco said, still smiling.

She was not going to smile. Jessie bit her lips to make sure there would be no smiling for this stupid foolishness. Draco saw right through it, and she wasn't sure how she should be taking the flirting.

Draco was open to it, James was clearly irritated, and Patrick and Carlton seemed to be...planning. She would rather James' reaction than all the others, even though it oddly stung to feel that irritation from James, and she found herself flattered by the attention.

Stupid. Stupid and foolish for her to be allowing these sensations within herself. She knew exactly where they led, and she didn't need those sort of thoughts in her head, or the sort of attention Draco promised her.

Not when he smiled at her like that.

It had been years since she could look at a man's smile and see anything other than plotting, and her own pain.

Draco stopped smiling, realizing she wasn't about to rise to the bait of his flirting.

This was *business*. The fact that these men happened to all be...exceptional was beside the point. Even the beta was easy on the eyes, and despite his irritation, she could see the reluctant interest whenever he looked at her.

Because that was her curse. Men couldn't help themselves around her. It was how she lured in Valbrand's prey. It was how she'd survived for just over two hundred years.

"You are all going to help me kill my ex-husband—"

"*Ex*-husband now, is it?" Patrick asked with a jealous growl.

She ignored him. "Do this, and you will all be released to fight and kill each other as you please. It doesn't matter to me what happens to the lot of you after I'm through. Do you understand?"

"It's not like we have a choice anyway," Carlton said, rather unhelpfully.

"I'm in," Draco replied, beating a fist to his chest. "Any male worth his salt wouldn't harm a lady such as yourself. You can believe I will be there to protect your honor."

Did he talk like that when he wasn't trying to get laid? It was difficult to tell, and one of the few things Jessie still struggled with when it came to the men she ensnared. They often behaved in ways they usually wouldn't when they were working on getting their rocks off with whoever happened to hold their fancy.

She didn't want that. She didn't care how good-looking these males happened to be. The lust they felt for her wasn't real. It had never been in any man. Regardless of what spell happened to hold him, their lust was never real to begin with. It was a chemical reaction and nothing more, so there was no point in entertaining these thoughts.

"You all know what needs to be done, and I am through discussing the details with you. If you would all please get a move on, I would like to get this over with as soon as possible."

"Why? Does he know where you are?" James asked.

"I do."

Jessie pressed her lips together, clenching her neck as she turned and looked at the one man she hated more than all the others.

Valbrand stood there, barely twenty feet away, arms crossed, white robes fluttering around him, and he smiled at Jessie as though this was all some sort of amusing stunt.

"Darling, shouldn't you be at home right about now?"

8

PATRICK

THERE WAS NO WIND, so it was clear the man was making his robes sway like that around himself. It really did look like an image out of *Harry Potter*, but recalling what Jessie had said about reading more books, Patrick decided to move onto a different reference.

"Gandalf the White here is your husband?"

Jessie glared at the other man as though he was the one holding reins. She looked very much as though she wanted to break those reins.

And break his bones.

She spoke through clenched teeth. "Yes."

This was more than a cheating husband. Patrick should not be giving her that sort of benefit of the doubt, but something was clearly wrong here that had more to do with infidelity. There seemed to be no actual love lost between the pair of them to begin with, so he couldn't see how cheating was the reason for her hatred.

Of course, Patrick had come across a woman or two who had enacted a form of revenge so heinous that it made him debate the words "gentler sex."

Jessie was a...well, she was something. He wasn't sure if she was a succubus or a ghoul. Christ, she could be a banshee for all he knew. Being beautiful didn't mean she couldn't also be a monster.

Valbrand, on the other hand, looked like an angel. An actual angel. He had an honest to God glow about him, his jaw chiseled, his long hair neatly groomed about his shoulders. The only thing missing was the wings.

All this made Patrick distrust the man even more.

After all, what sort of guy just wandered around glowing like that? And what sort of man married a demonic woman?

Valbrand smiled at her, as though they were getting ready to meet for lunch. "My love, we talked about this—"

"Fuck you. I'm done."

Jessie stepped back. Patrick wasn't entirely sure if she was aware she'd done it. He caught Carlton's eyes, and it was clear the other dragon had noticed it as well.

Valbrand sighed. "Will you please listen to reason? We have a wonderful arrangement. Beneficial to us both."

"The lady told you to fuck off, pal," said Draco, stepping forward to fill the space Jessie had vacated. Patrick would admire the man's commitment to getting laid if it wasn't so unnecessary at the moment. And annoying. The guy was already acting as though he had competition. Just because Patrick thought Jessie was a looker didn't mean he was going to go out of his way to impress her.

Wanting to fuck a succubus, if that's what she was, wasn't exactly unheard of, and Patrick had more self-control than that.

He hoped.

Valbrand ignored Draco. He seemed to be looking through him, as though his entire focus was only for Jessie.

Patrick, along with James and Carlton, stepped up to be beside Draco. Standing as a unit, with two dragon shifters, would have been strange had it not been for the already strange situation of being Jessie's slave.

Valbrand nodded as though he was pleased. "Right, I told you these skills would be useful, didn't I?"

"I'm not taking anything from them."

Taking from them? What could she be taking from them?

"Then what do you want them for?" Valbrand seemed confused.

"To kill you."

The command was unsaid, but Patrick's body reacted to it as though she had screamed it in his ear. He lunged for the other male, Carlton, James, and Draco acting as one with him, their claws, teeth, fur, and wings becoming known as they aimed their fury at the man.

Valbrand smiled as they flew at him, watching them descend on him before he finally vanished.

Patrick's claws sunk into the dirt and rock, irritated to have missed his target. His other senses picked up the slack as he gauged how the wind blew. He spun around, Carlton keeping up with him as they rushed back to where Valbrand suddenly appeared.

Less than a foot away from Jessie.

Enraged! That was the heat and hatred swirling inside that he could have let that fucker get close to her. Valbrand snapped his hand out. Jessie narrowly avoided being grabbed, stepping back and slapping Valbrand's hands away from her. He kept coming, his smile faltering, but he didn't seem to notice Patrick and Carlton rushing him. Not until he turned.

They both moved as one, their fists pulling back and

punching forward. Patrick caught Valbrand on his left eye, and Carlton got him on the right.

He flew. Literally. The guy went up ten feet in the air, but before he could come back down to earth, he seemed to just stop.

He hovered there, his hands covering his eyes before he removed them. And then he looked a little less angelic. The glow around him appeared more blue, even black.

"Christ, what's wrong with him?" James asked.

Carlton snorted. "Demon in disguise, pup. Keep up."

Patrick snarled at the man, but he said nothing. For now. Had to keep his eyes on the prize, and that prize had red glowing eyes and fangs protruding from his mouth.

"You simple little fools," he said, his voice straining, though it sounded as though it echoed deep in Patrick's ears. It sounded like it was coming from someone else's mouth, something way more monstrous than any succubus.

"Come near her again, and we will kill you, demon," Patrick replied.

Valbrand looked back down at Jessie. Patrick didn't need to follow the demon's eyes to know Jessie was quickly padding her way behind him and the others, using them for protection.

Interesting. This really wasn't for revenge. There was no way in hell Patrick could believe that now.

And great, knowing that made a protective instinct he did not want rise up within him. He was getting protective over the bitch that had enslaved him.

Perfect.

"You think they'll do anything? You think they'll give you the protection I can?"

"I don't want their protection," Jessie replied, suddenly

sounding so much more passionate and out of control. "I want you dead!"

"Say the word, princess, and I'll get his head for you," Draco sang, snapping his claws together as he watched Valbrand like he was prey.

Patrick didn't want to say anything, but he felt the same way.

Because of the spell they were under, he was positive the same could be said for Carlton and even James.

Jessie vibrated with the emotion that seemed to surge through her. Patrick could have sworn he spotted flickers of lightning jolting across her body, her hair, and her hands.

"Do it. Bring me his head, right now!"

Patrick ached to obey the command. A result of the spell, he didn't doubt that for a second. But he could not. Valbrand was high in the air, and he seemed too pleased to be there to bother with coming down to fight.

Fucking coward.

But his simpering little smirk weakened when he realized two of his opponents were growing wings, and he looked actually panicked when Carlton and Draco launched themselves into the air after him.

James whimpered. "I want...I want..." He scratched at the back of his neck with both hands, watching the scene.

Patrick knew what he wanted because he felt it, too.

"We have to wait."

Though he ached at having to stand there and do nothing.

Patrick didn't think he or James would be getting any relief from Jessie over this matter. She seemed too preoccupied with the sudden battle happening in the sky to bother with relieving Patrick or James of a command they clearly couldn't obey.

So Patrick watched, waiting for the right moment.

Valbrand produced an actual sword, another item that would have made him appear even more angelic than he already did by the silver blade and golden handle, but Patrick had already seen the man without the mask on, so there was nothing he could pull out of his ass that would make him look like a saint anymore.

Draco seemed more eager to get closer to Valbrand than Carlton did. The dragon leader circled Valbrand, searching for the right moment to make his move, and when he found it, during a moment when Valbrand struggled to keep out of the way of Draco's claws, he dove down on the other man.

Valbrand must have given himself a sort of tunnel vision in the battle, because he didn't see it coming at all when Carlton made his move, ducking down, and the look on Valbrand's face when Carlton slammed into his body was hilarious.

Cartoonish wide eyes and mouth opened wide. If he stuck his tongue out, it would have been perfect, but that wasn't the thing that had Patrick's attention.

He was coming back down within reach.

"Let's go!"

He shifted, keeping to hind legs as he let his wolf partially take over. He wanted to remain upright, and opposable thumbs would be more helpful than his claws could ever be, so he didn't plan on keeping those back.

James shifted fully, getting down on all fours in his grey wolf shape as they charged their target, preparing to meet him when he landed.

Valbrand roared, righting himself in mid-air just before he could reach the dirt, throwing Carlton off him and right into Patrick's and James' path. Being struck with a dragon shifter while in his wolf shape was hardly pleas-

47

ant. The bony parts of his wings hurt, and the clawed tip that got right in Patrick's face, narrowly missing his eye, really pissed off the wolf side of his brain.

That, coupled with the rage of missing the real target, caused the beast to lash out in ways Patrick hadn't experienced since he'd been a fourteen-year-old boy.

He grabbed Carlton, attacking and clawing at him, his teeth coming down, intending to rip away the man's face, but Carlton grabbed his snout before his teeth could make contact.

The man struggled to hold Patrick back, and Patrick couldn't stop himself either.

In the back of his mind, he heard Valbrand laughing, and James shouting, but he couldn't pull back. He wanted blood. He wanted flesh. He wanted to tear anything and anyone into pieces for putting him in these chains and preventing him from getting his hands on the real prize.

He would kill everyone in his way.

Something slammed hard against the back of his head. White flashed in his vision, blinding him, enraging him. He would kill whoever dared to attack him with his back turned. Rip their faces off, eat them in front of them!

Patrick spun around.

Jessie's golden eyes narrowed at him as she stood with her hands on her hips. She grabbed him by his muzzle, showing little to no fear of his teeth.

Mistake.

"What the hell do you think you're doing? You're supposed to be—hey!"

She yanked her hand back when he snapped his teeth at her. Ignoring the dragon on the ground, he got to all fours, stalking the woman in front of him. For a hair of a second, he thought he could feel her nonexistent heartbeat, but he could taste the blood flowing through her veins — different blood. Delicious blood. He wanted it. He wanted it on his tongue and teeth, and now, her fear spiked, he could almost lick the air and feel what he really wanted on his mouth.

Valbrand laughed out loud, staying a safe distance away on the ground as Draco came to land between Patrick and his prey.

Mistake. He growled low in his throat. This woman belonged to him. Him and only him, even if he had to eat her to get her.

"This is what you choose to protect you? You think this mutt can save—*oof*!"

The man in white suddenly moved, drawing the attention of the wolf. His companion, James, had gotten close and punched the man in the jaw, sending him stumbling back before he pushed himself into the air again.

He held onto his mouth, glaring down at the beta.

James glared back up at him. "You talk too much."

Patrick shook his head, blinking, focus returning, but it was difficult. Like wading out of muddy water.

They weren't out of danger. They were surrounded by enemies, by dragons, and he couldn't leave James alone to fight off this male and the two dragons by himself.

Control. He was a fucking alpha, and he would have his control back!

Snarling, growling, fighting through the itch for the beast to maintain its control, Patrick forced himself up and out of the wolf skin he'd put himself into. He panted for breath, sweat forming all across his body, and even with his clothes still on, he felt as cold as if he was naked.

That didn't stop Carlton, James, or Draco from tackling him down to the ground like the idiots still thought he was out of control.

"Control yourself, man! Control yourself!" Carlton shouted.

"I am in control, you fucking lunatics!"

They were on top of him, and he couldn't fight them off. They struggled with him, assuming he was still about to lose his shit and attack. Maybe they thought he was going to attack Jessie, but right now he wanted to go after them more than anything.

The stupid fuckers tangled themselves up with him the harder he fought.

"I'm fine! I'm fine, you morons! Get off me!"

"You filthy, lowly, pitiful animals." Valbrand didn't yell the words. He said them as calmly as though he was asking for a coffee from Starbucks.

Patrick didn't care if that was supposed to be some sign of how really pissed off the guy was, because he was still furious that he was stuck beneath Carlton, James, and Draco. James pulled himself back first, and Draco caught his balance next, the two of them helping Carlton, making more of a spectacle out of themselves than anything.

Not very warrior like.

"You think these animals will kill me? Are you serious?" Now he sounded angry as he turned his attention back to Jessie.

Patrick growled. "You don't get to talk to her."

Valbrand ignored them.

Jessie faced him, her back straight, her chin up, but the way she slowly backed away from the man showed just how fearful she was.

She didn't want to show it. She must have known it would put her at a disadvantage, but there were some things that couldn't be helped. Some instincts that couldn't be ignored.

Patrick shoved Carlton off him. He and the dragon

barely spared a glance to each other before they were standing again. Carlton kept his wings out, and though they were folded back, Patrick noted they gave him an added height, or the illusion of such.

Lucky bastard.

"We don't know the particulars," Patrick snapped.

"But you're not taking one step closer to her," Carlton finished.

Valbrand looked less than impressed by the show. "After you lot just finished playing a game of Twister, you really expect me to fear you?"

Draco stepped forward. "You'll fear us when we start peeling the skin from your face and make you eat it."

James' claws were still at the ready as he pointed them up at the male. "We'll give your ex here a fancy seat to sit on so she can watch. I think she might like that."

Jessie continued to back up, into their fold, allowing Patrick, Carlton, Draco, and James to step between her and the threat.

And now they were one, and not because they were playing a stupid game of Twister.

Patrick needed to make sure this idiot got the message. "It's time for you to cut your losses, princess. The lady doesn't want to go with you, and she's not gonna."

Valbrand started to glow that disconcerting dark glow again. "You dare think you can speak so casually to me? I've walked the earth since your kind were savages and the humans liked your heads onto sticks. They wore wolf pelts and cut the wings off dragons for sport."

James growled, taking that more personally than anyone else in their group. "Yeah, and you're the bitch who doesn't get to do that. Now fuck off."

Patrick was proud of him in that moment; his chest seemed to inflate with it.

Valbrand looked at the four of them. Wizard or not, he was clearly weighing how much trouble this was worth. He might be able to take them, considering Patrick and James were not in line with Carlton and Draco, but they could still do a lot of damage, and Patrick doubted Jessie would just be standing around doing nothing.

The five against one odds were clearly enough to make Valbrand decide against his plan. His mouth pressed together in a thin line as he backed away one step. "Jessica, my love, at one point, your animals will not be looking, and when they're not—"

"Yeah, yeah," Jessie muttered. "Will you go away already? You're a creep, and no one likes you."

It was such a casual thing to say to him, and perhaps that was what stunned him the most. Valbrand's eyes popped wide open. He fell back a step, his mouth dropping open as his nose scrunched.

Jessie, meanwhile, continued to glare defiantly at him.

Valbrand sputtered for something to say in response. He did that for a painfully long amount of time. Then he seemed to give up as he decided it wasn't worth the effort.

"They'll stop watching you eventually. You'll go to sleep, eventually. I'll pike all of their heads onto my mantle, and it will be on your hands." He pointed menacingly at Jessie.

Draco shook his head. "He really is trying to give the Lord Voldemort thing a go, isn't he?"

Valbrand shrieked, his arms coming up above his head as the bright, heated flames enveloped his body. He was consumed by them, and then there was nothing. He was gone.

Patrick stepped forward, reaching out with his other senses to determine where he'd gone. He didn't appear behind anyone with a blade. His scent wasn't high in the trees, still watching them.

He really was gone.

And that left him, Carlton, James, and Draco to look at Jessie, wondering what the hell had just happened.

And who she actually was.

She sighed, and finally decided it was worth her time to look at them. She smiled as if that whole fucked up situation hadn't just happened. "Now, gentlemen, should we go and explain things to the rest of your men? They'll all be wondering where you are."

9

JESSIE

JESSIE COULD FEEL the eyes of every dragon and every wolf on her as Patrick and Carlton explained what was going to happen. They left out a good number of the details. Mainly how there had just been a fight between the man Jessie wanted dead and themselves.

A not very hopeful fight.

Maybe Valbrand was right. Maybe this was a stupid idea, and she should be putting her time to better use somewhere else.

With someone else.

Perhaps it had been a mistake to use both dragons and werewolves, especially ones who had been in the middle of fighting over land. Of course they wouldn't work together at an optimal level. Of course they would not get along with each other, and of course their fighting styles would be different. There would be misunderstandings, like the one that left Patrick appearing more animal than man while the others tackled him to the ground, as though they feared he would come after her.

Perhaps the real problem was these men in particular.

54

They might not be strong enough for what she had planned.

They might die.

Jessie shook the thought from her head. What did it matter to her if they died? The last time she'd cared about whether or not a male died had been…

Well, it was no matter. That was then, and this was now. Jessie hadn't thought of him in years. She couldn't believe that being in this position brought up *those* sorts of memories. A month ago, she never would have thought she would be worrying over the health and well-being of another male. She'd promised herself she would never put herself in that sort of position again. And yet, now here she was.

Ridiculous.

"You've got to be fucking kidding me."

The hissed words, spat as though they were filthy on the tongue, jerked her out of unpleasant memories. Jessie paid attention once more, looking up at the male who spoke. His face was scarred, and the sneer on his mouth made him appear even more crooked than he already did.

He stared at Jessie as though she was the devil herself. He wasn't all that far off.

"You can't seriously expect—"

"I do, Roger," Patrick said, standing strong and firm, his arms folded across his chest, which made his perfect muscles look that much bigger.

She should not be noticing his muscles.

A succubus was not supposed to feel this sort of lust for her prey, but she wasn't a true succubus either.

"And you're going to keep your damn mouth shut about it."

Jessie clenched her teeth, fighting back against the groan that threatened to bubble up and out of her throat.

Patrick was getting all growly and protective to one of his own over the man's tone with her. It didn't mean anything. He was only doing it because Jessie had forced him into this situation. He wasn't defending her honor for any noble reasons.

And she didn't want him to anyway.

That wasn't what this was.

"You don't order us around, furball," said one of the other men with a sneer.

The oversized group of testosterone seemed to be split into two different camps. The dragons were on one side of the clearing, and the wolves were on the other with at least five feet separating them down the middle. As if they couldn't bear to be any closer to each other than absolutely necessary.

Men. Stubborn no matter what age they were born into. She loved it, and she hated it about their ilk. If only she could rip out everything inside her that pulled her towards men like these, she would be one happy woman.

But she needed Valbrand dead first. That was a big step towards her happiness.

"Carlton, come on, are you fucking serious with this?" asked another of the dragons, just as horrified and shocked as Roger had been.

Most, if not all, of the dragons glanced to the side from time to time, watching the werewolves, waiting for one to attack, or thinking about doing the attacking themselves. The only things that held back both groups were Patrick and Carlton, both standing in front of their respective groups, strong and proud, as though they were forming a wall to hold back the mob. It seemed to barely be working, even with James and Draco there to back them up. The two groups were getting snappier and louder with each moment that passed by.

And there was already some hardcore suspicion that they might be under some kind of spell.

They neither confirmed nor denied this. Jessie's spell wasn't preventing them from lying to their own men, and the fact that they chose not to wasn't something she was going to dwell on.

"This is going to happen, no matter how much you all choose to bitch about it!" Carlton roared, his scales appearing across his arms and throat, as though he was having trouble holding back the beast inside now as much as Patrick had been less than an hour ago.

His anger silenced the dragons, but it didn't quiet the wolves.

He was not their leader, and they felt no loyalty to him or to his anger.

So when Patrick opened his mouth, bared his fangs, and roared at the lot of them, they did silence themselves quickly. They looked at their alpha, none with fear, but with a renewed sense of where their loyalties lay. Their alpha was telling them to do something, so they were going to do it, whether they wanted to or not.

"All of you will keep your fucking mouths shut about this arrangement and do as you are told. The lady needs help, and we are going to offer it with the dragons. That is to be the end of it. Do you all understand?"

No one nodded eagerly. There was still quite a lot of grumbling about it, but the wolves rocked from foot to foot, resigning themselves to their fate of having to work with a group of dragons none of them particularly liked.

There was still a lot of glaring on both sides, and Jessie was pretty sure the distrust Patrick and Carlton sent to each other every time they so much as glanced at each other had something to do with it.

Jessie rolled her eyes. She was going to have to do

something about this. She loved stubborn men, but this was the part of their nature she hated. If they didn't learn to work together, Valbrand would have a better chance of bringing her back than she wanted to admit.

That and, as much as these two would deserve it, she didn't want them getting killed because they were unwilling to work together. It seemed a little unfair to James and Draco.

James was adorable, and Draco was flirtatious in a way she enjoyed. For now, she would rather they not die. They would be innocent bystanders in the whole situation.

More or less.

She stepped forward, coming to stand between Patrick and Carlton while both men spent their time snarling and snapping at their own men, pushing them into submission. She hoped this would work. She could ensnare a few men at a time, but this was a small army. Nothing short of convincing them to help her would do the trick if they refused to be swayed by their own alphas.

At the sight of her stepping forward, all the men quieted down.

They watched her with equal parts suspicion and anger in their eyes, but that was all right. Only an intelligent male would look upon her with suspicion, and a man with any sense would be angry with her because if she was acquainted with them, it was only because she wanted something out of them and had forced their hand into giving it to her.

Or Valbrand, but that was no more.

She observed every male before her. Some were fully dressed, some shirtless, others entirely naked. A talented shifter could shift with their clothes still on, but there were those who preferred the feeling of being *free* when they ran in their animal shapes.

She hoped there were none in this group who were lacking in talent. She needed everyone she could get.

"My name is Jessica Anne Gerolf. I am...not entirely a demon, but I am something of that nature."

There was a lot of frowning, some muttering to each other, but all eyes remained fixed on her.

"You can call me a succubus if you like, or a ghoul. I have eaten the dead, I have killed many men, have seduced many more, and have taken their souls."

"You want our souls now, too?" someone shouted. Most likely a dragon since it was Carlton who growled at the man, whoever he was.

Jessie didn't need him defending her from his own men. She needed him to defend her from Valbrand. "I don't want your souls. I would like to have mine. I am not going into the particulars about it. It's not any of your fucking business as far as I'm concerned. I just need this one man killed, and when I am free, your alphas will be free, too."

Though she wasn't looking at them, Jessie could feel Patrick's and Carlton's angry eyes on the back of her head for ratting out their situation. Off to the side, she could see a little of Draco's smirk, as though he thought the whole thing was hilarious. She couldn't even bring herself to be amused by it. Jessie hated that she had to give away as much as she was now. It was too private, too personal, but what else was she going to do about it?

"Help me be free from this man, and I will set your alphas free to fight and kill each other as much as you please."

There was a soft throat clearing beside her. Jessie looked up and realized James had come to stand next to her.

"Not the best way to rally the troops."

She glared at him, but he shrugged and didn't seem interested in what she thought about the matter. It wasn't the best way to rally them. She'd basically told them all to get over it and shut the fuck up.

She was the outsider here. They wouldn't want to listen to her, and none of them knew or liked her, so of course they wouldn't care if she was in trouble.

Jessie had learned long ago not to expect strangers to care for anyone but themselves and their immediate group. She didn't even blame them for it anymore. After all, she cared nothing for these men here, or their alphas, or their friends. They were a means to an end. She was just hoping they would see a small, skinny woman, and their inner white knights would come to the surface to protect her from danger.

It seemed to work.

Carlton and Patrick came to stand on either side of her. Draco and James weren't too far behind her, circling her from the back.

A protective wall meant to keep out any who would do her harm.

For a split second, she allowed herself to think it was real, that they cared, and it warmed her insides to believe it.

"This is happening," Patrick said. "Like it or not, you will all follow where we lead. We are doing this. We will kill this man. End of discussion."

"Any of you got something to say about it, walk away now," Carlton finished. "You can all find another clan to live in."

Jessie wasn't so sure that was a valuable threat to dish out. These all looked like healthy young men. Of course, looks could be deceiving. She knew, for their species, many could live well into their hundreds, but they were all still very clearly in the prime of their lives.

Would it be that difficult for them to find another clan or another pack to live in? Perhaps the threat was more for any family they might have. Jessie ignored the painful clenching she felt in her belly over that. It wasn't her business what these men and their families did with their lives. She would keep to her goal.

Ultimately, no one left. There were still more than enough suspicious glances in her direction, but nothing that would suggest to her anyone had plans to walk away. Carlton and Patrick were either excellent leaders, or the threat of being removed from their homes was greater than it appeared.

Maybe it was a little of both.

Because no one left, Patrick and Carlton took the time to round up any strays, any of the wolves or dragons who inched their way closer to each other in an attempt to start a fight. It was…interesting to watch, to say the least, and the unpleasant clenching in her belly left her when Patrick or Carlton happened to glance her away.

But with the both of them at a distance, it left Draco and James as her protectors, standing at each of her sides while Carlton and Patrick worked with their men, giving them their instructions, and seeing to it that no one would disobey them. Some of the men looked unhappy about the ordeal; others sucked it up. A few argued privately with Carlton and Patrick separately.

Their body language set off all kinds of warnings in Jessie's head.

"Is there going to be a fight over this?"

"Most likely, at least from the dragons," Draco replied, sounding pleased. "We like to fight for the things we believe in."

"So do werewolves," James replied. "We just know when a fight is worth it as opposed to a waste of time."

Draco snorted. "Look, little man, you don't have to be snippy with me. You got something to say, then say it. Don't hide behind your passive aggressive horse shit."

James growled. "I can be aggressive if you want to see it."

"Oh, will there be something to see?"

"Both of you shut up right now." Jessie was getting a headache from this entire thing, and because James and Draco were both required to do as she commanded them, their mouths immediately snapped shut. She sighed at the peace, though it was a little less fun than she thought it would be. Forcing them to do as she wished in absolutely everything...kind of took the life out of it.

Even when she was attempting to steal a few souls for Valbrand, it had been interesting enough to let the humans she'd been preying on backtalk her, flirt, or make their threats. Their words had been the one thing she'd been able to give them since she had ensnared their bodies so easily.

"Never mind, if you both want to argue, then feel free." Jessie waved her hand, and as though she was yanking the tape off their mouths, they both opened up, inhaling deeply as if they couldn't breathe a moment ago. "I don't care what any of you do."

"Where are you going?" James called.

Jessie wrapped her arms around herself, unsure why she felt so cold. "For a walk."

"You know that's an incredibly stupid thing to be doing right now, right?" James called.

Jessie stopped, embarrassed and insulted for almost making such a simple mistake. She glanced back.

Draco was already trotting towards her, an eager

expression on his face. "Don't worry, sweetheart. I'll keep you safe if you want some privacy."

"Having you around would literally prevent me from having any kind of privacy," she said.

"We can keep to a distance if you want," James said, coming forward, though with less spring in his step than Draco, but still with a determined air about him. Right. Jessie had not only asked for this, but she'd also literally forced these men into her business.

And because of the nature of her...condition, it was only natural they were going to want to stay close to her. They were going to want to bed her, and considering they were all handsome men, and she might want the relief that came with a good romp, Jessie wasn't so certain she was capable of denying them.

"All right, just try not to speak so much. I'm getting a headache."

Draco snorted a laugh. "Right, said by every lady when she's playing hard to get."

James groaned.

The headache didn't worsen. Jessie was amused, and she felt herself relaxing for the first time since she'd thought up this ridiculous plan.

JESSIE

THE TWO MEN followed her like they were puppies. They wagged their proverbial tails as they went. Draco refused to allow her out of hearing distance from the pack and the clan, though she suspected he allowed her to be somewhat out of sight of them because he wanted to be alone with her.

As alone as he could be with another male, but this wasn't the first time she'd spelled more than one male at the same time. She'd been with men and women, and sometimes more than one at a time, so there was nothing to be concerned about now that she had more than one male following her. Four at once was new, but for now, only James and Draco were with her, and James didn't seem like the sort of man to act on any lust he might be concealing.

Not that she suspected he didn't play for her team.

In fact, she was under the impression that he enjoyed playing for *both* teams, but that didn't mean he was going to enjoy being attracted to her. Especially since she'd spelled Patrick, the one whose affections she was more than certain he really wanted.

"Are you only following me so you can make a move?" she asked, turning back to Draco since she didn't think it was James who would be giving her much trouble. He was going to suppress the lust she'd inflicted him with for as long as possible, probably until this whole thing was over, so she didn't see the need to bother with him. Even though she did feel the itch to rise to the challenge he presented.

Draco, however, smiled at her as though they were already on the same wavelength. This male was, as the ladies and gentlemen of her day would have put it, a scoundrel, though he did still manage to come across as being adorable about it.

"You were the one who wanted to be alone. I couldn't exactly leave the lady to wander off all by herself when there's a dangerous man out there who wants to do her harm, could I?"

James crossed his arms, shaking his head and muttering, "Whatever."

Jessie barely spared him a glance. She kept the majority of her attention focused on Draco since he was the one determined to be a flirt. "I know what you want and what you're feeling, and I can give you exactly what you want without you having to go through all these cute little hoops. I'm not a genteel lady, you know."

"Oh, I know, you're a demon, succubus, something-or-other, but every woman likes being treated like a lady anyway, don't they?"

He had her there.

"Draco, don't be an idiot, you're only attracted to her because of whatever spell it was she put on you," James said, still looking distrustfully at Jessie.

She might have had him wrong this whole time. He was a beta male, but he wasn't weak, and he was no fool. He knew what was up.

"Few men have ever been able to see through their lust and put that together."

Draco rolled his eyes and scoffed. "I knew that!"

Jessie wasn't so sure he did. Draco sounded scandalized, as though the idea that he could be tricked in such a base way was beneath him.

"Sure you did," James said. "You probably wake up all the time without your wallet after you're out all night fucking random women in bathroom stalls."

"Yeah, it's called being a man, short stuff. You should try it sometime." Draco reached out, as though to ruffle James' hair. James slapped his hand away with a growl, showing his teeth. Draco laughed. "Come on. Relax. I'm just playing with you."

"You can stop playing with him because you're not going to get the chance to play with me out here anyway. I really did just want to clear my head, and I might be a something-or-other, but even I won't lift my skirt when there are a hundred men forty feet away."

She scratched the underside of Draco's chin, watching the way he shivered helplessly. "You still have to earn it."

She couldn't believe those words were coming out of her mouth after just thinking how wonderful it would be to let herself be put on her back and enjoy having someone other than Valbrand take over. The man hadn't touched her in decades, and she'd been grateful for that. He was a handsome man, but he wasn't...whatever these men were.

She'd seen that spark in Patrick and Carlton, and there was something of that same flame flickering within Draco, even if he was a fool, and James, even if he was a prude, but it was still there, and she was drawn to it.

It had to be because of the spell. Had to be. She was not accustomed to falling under the control of such a spell when she was the one casting it. She knew what this felt like because of Valbrand, but no one else had ever...

She'd cast it wrong. Somewhere, somehow, she'd made an error, and now she was under the same lustful effects that these four warriors were. She could fight this. She was old enough and wise enough. If James could do it, then she could as well.

Unfortunately for her, Draco seemed to be a little more intuitive than she'd thought. The man tilted his head to the side. He eyed her, as though he could see right through her, and then his mouth pulled back in a wide smile. Jessie didn't like that.

Valbrand had done that a lot in the first few years.

While Draco had a plotting look on his face, similar to Valbrand, it wasn't sinister, and his face didn't suddenly become not handsome for having it either. He looked playful.

"What? Why are you looking at me like that?"

"You don't have as much control as you want us to think you do."

"What?" Better to act scandalized than admit the truth. She crossed her arms. "I have no idea what you're talking about."

"Yes, you do. You did something to us, but you're being affected by it, too."

James suddenly looked so much more interested now than he had a minute ago. "Jesus Christ, are you serious?"

"You kidding me? Look at her; she's starting to blush and everything."

Jessie didn't think she had been, but having him point

out that she might have, possibly, been blushing did make her feel a touch overheated. But she wasn't going to respect that with any sort of response. She was not blushing, the heat was just due to exertion from the recent battle, and she was not going to allow herself to be so easily manipulated by this scoundrel.

And yet, he was still smiling at her.

"Jessica!"

She looked away from Draco's bright and eager smile. Carlton and Patrick ran to her. It had been Carlton to use her full name, and both men looked on the verge of panic. Because they'd turned away from their men and realized she wasn't there.

Right. She faced them. They were her protectors now.

"I was just getting some air with Draco and James."

Patrick shook his head, coming to a stop in front of her, staring at her as though she'd lost her mind.

"You're outdoors right now. You're surrounded by fresh air. What the hell were you thinking?"

The ease Jessie felt at their sudden appearance vanished. "I thought I didn't want to be surrounded by so much testosterone."

"So you leave with two men?" Carlton demanded, ganging up on her with Patrick. "We have no idea what will happen to us, or to Draco, or James if you are hurt while you have us under your damned spell. Don't you ever wander off like that again."

Jessie narrowed her eyes at him. "Thought you were worried about me for a second. My mistake."

Carlton narrowed his eyes right back. "Don't think for one second that any worry I'd have for you would be because you're important to me. I doubt you're anything important to these hairballs here, either, and Draco just wants to fuck. You did this to us. We have no idea what will happen if we don't protect you sufficiently, and I'm not about to take the risk that something happens to my clan because of your bullshit revenge scheme."

The burn in the back of her throat, in the bottom of her belly, and her chest, was oddly out of place. Jessie wished it away, but it was still there. It clung to her like a rotting glue. "I perfectly understand."

"No, you don't," Carlton said, and right then, he established himself as the biggest bastard of the group. "These are our *lives* you're fucking with. You've thrown my men *and* their families in the path of some lunatic because you can't fight your own battles, and now you're fucking with my head, trying to make yourself look small and helpless, so I'll feel sorry for you. Well, guess what? I will never feel sorry for you, and the instant you release me from this spell, you'd better believe you've got as much running to do as that pretty boy you want us to kill, because I'll be coming after you next."

He got right in her face as he said that last part, leaning in, their noses practically touching as he bared his teeth.

She wasn't trying to make herself look small and weak, and she wasn't purposely trying to play with their emotions or their lust. She wanted none of their lust. She'd never asked for it while working with Valbrand and she sure as hell didn't want it now. But there was nothing she could say that would make these men believe her, so she supposed that left her a bit out of luck.

"Don't worry, I never assumed any of you would be my harem boys, so I have no intentions on any of your virgin bodies."

Draco sounded mortified and insulted. *"Virgin?"*

Jessie eyed the lot of them, trying to make herself loathe them since she couldn't bring herself to hate them. It was easy to be disgusted with the men she'd targeted previously. She'd had to bring about that emotion in order to keep her own sanity in check. After all, what sort of simpering, weak male allowed himself to be lured from the comforts of his home, usually his wife and children, for a woman like her?

In the end, she pitied them for having to take their souls, but she also made herself believe that, on some level, didn't they actually deserve it for being so easily manipulated?

"When this is over, I will set you all free. I will vanish, and none of you will ever see me again. Does that sound acceptable enough to you?"

Apparently not, because all she was left with were angry stares and scowling faces.

Carlton wasn't done. "The acceptable thing would have been to not bother any of us with your demonic shit to begin with, but seeing as how this is the only way to get rid of you, for now, I suppose it will have to do."

Her defense, not that she needed it, came from an unlikely source.

James scratched at the back of his neck. "Is it really that big of a deal to help her? We were all in the middle of trying to kill each other anyway. Why not just do this? It might bring your clan and our pack together. Give us a reason not to fight."

The slow turning heads as everyone looked to James, as though they were just as shocked by those words as Jessie was, was proof enough that he was preaching to the wrong choir.

"Never mind," he said, conceding though he did look at her with something of an apologetic stare.

Jessie did not feel a pleasant tightening in her belly. She absolutely did not, and she wasn't about to let herself think it meant anything either. Other than how pathetic she was for feeling so grateful for that morsel of consideration.

So she ignored him as well, pretending that what he'd suggested meant as little to her as it did to the rest of the men standing there.

"Kill Valbrand for me, and you all walk free."

"What if we can't kill him?" Patrick asked. "Much as I don't want to believe that to be possible, are you planning on keeping us for the rest of our lives if we can't end the man?"

Fair enough question, she supposed.

Jessie hadn't thought about it either. She was not going to admit that, but while she was…like this, she would have a long life span, and their long lives would ensure she could keep them under her command for a long time coming.

Carlton rolled his eyes. "Well, that silence says it all."

"No." She would not let him interrupt her and make her out to be even more of a villain than she already was. She'd grown to like being the villain, but there were those times when it got so old she wished the label would die already. Jessie took in a deep breath, feeling, for some reason, as though she had to gather her courage. "No, I will not be keeping you all for the rest of your lives. Valbrand is a demon, and his life is long, but he's impatient. He won't want to wait until you all die off to come for me. He will come. Give it a month, and it should be done with."

They all raised their brows. For being conflicting warriors, they were shockingly alike in some regards.

"A month? That's it?" Draco asked, a note of disappointment in his words.

"A month is still a long time, you fool," Carlton said, reprimanding his own friend.

71

Draco seemed a little helpless all of a sudden. "Well, not really."

Carlton rolled his eyes. James and Patrick whispered amongst each other, glancing her way from time to time.

"You know I can see it when you both stand there plotting like that, right?"

"We're not trying to hide it," Patrick retorted, going back to whispering to his friend.

Jessie pursed her lips. Thick as thieves, those two.

Draco got a little closer, still smiling at her like he wanted to impress her. "You know, just between you and me, I wouldn't mind sticking it out longer than a month if you still needed your little problem taken care of." He took her hand. She let him kiss her knuckles like a gentleman would. Her hand tingled when he pulled his lips back. "I wouldn't mind being tied up with you for a while longer than that."

"Tied up with me, is it?"

He shrugged. "We can do that, too, if that's your interest."

His flirting was so stupid, so utterly cringe-worthy that there was no reason in the world why she should have felt any amount of delight in having its focus on her. She should have been disgusted with him, and once, when she'd been very young, she would have been.

Not now. Now, he came off as charming and sincere, even though she knew he had an ulterior motive—to satiate the lust she had cursed him with the moment she kissed him. To be fair, of the four men she'd ensnared, he was the one she could look on with little guilt since he had basically asked for it, demanded it, when he initiated their kiss.

"I'll have to keep my eye on you."

He smiled at her, as though she'd just given him what he desperately wanted. "Looking forward to it."

"We've come to a decision if you're done flirting with her, Draco," Carlton replied.

Again, that careless shrug as he released her hand. "Whatever. I know you all want to. Not my fault you're all too stuck up to act on a good thing."

"That good thing most likely will eat your soul when she's done with you," Patrick replied, glancing at Jessie before darting his gaze away.

"So what did you decide?" Jessie asked. They still did not have a choice in this, but if allowing them this little meeting would be enough to make them more willing to cooperate, the better."

Patrick and Carlton looked at each other.

"We're in," Patrick said.

"One month," Carlton clarified.

Patrick pointed his index finger at her. "And you're not to use your power of seduction on us."

"Bad enough we can already feel it," James muttered.

Draco snorted. "Bad thing. Whatever."

She couldn't bother with being amused by their back and forth. She only heard one thing.

"You'll help me?"

All four men nodded, standing tall, firm, warriors— her warriors.

They would set her free from this miserable existence.

"We will."

Valbrand's death would literally kill her, but she didn't care anymore.

Jessie smiled at her knights, and for the first time in over a hundred and eighty years, she felt really and truly free.

11

JESSIE

She did it.

Jessie almost couldn't believe she'd done it. She didn't just have a dragon and a wolf. She had an *army*. She'd successfully managed to ensnare not one dragon, but two, and not just one wolf, but two, and with them, she now had the wolf pack and the dragon clan under her command.

And Jessie was awesome. There was nothing in the world she couldn't do, but for a little while, she'd started to think that maybe, just maybe, there was a chance she wouldn't be able to pull this off.

But she'd done it. She was fucking fabulous, and now she was riding on the high of her success.

Yeah, Valbrand could screw himself because he was going down. Jessie was riding around on big dick energy here, and she was going to make him eat it for all the shit he'd put her through.

She didn't even mind it that Draco was staring at her ass. Or that James was still glaring at her for what she'd done to his alpha, and to him.

She didn't mind. All would be forgiven when she got what she wanted.

As for Draco, he was an interesting case. He seemed to be completely under the spell of her more seductive side, but he was making no effort to hide it. It was as though he liked that he was being manipulated, that she was going to make him fight for her before throwing him away.

Jessie had come across her fair share of men in her life who had their own sexual pleasures tied to being commanded by a member of the gentler sex, but as for Draco...she wasn't sure. The vibe she got from him wasn't the same.

As though he saw her as more of a challenge.

If that was the case, he was in for a disappointment because she never lost those challenges.

James, well, he could pout all he liked. He was not special, and neither was his alpha. She wouldn't seduce either of them, not if she didn't have to, but if James made things difficult for her, then she knew what to say to make him back off. He was clearly in love with Patrick. He didn't hide it well, and Jessie felt sorry that he'd allowed himself to be so opened up to attack in this way.

The two alphas were where the real money was with this transaction.

They watched her cautiously, they clearly didn't trust her, but that was more than all right with her. She expected nothing less from them. No true leader would simply swoop in to scoop her up in their arms and offer their aid.

Jessie was a threat to their lives for the danger she put them in with Valbrand, and now she was a threat to the peace and security of both the clan and the pack. No one liked to be blackmailed, manipulated, or bespelled, and these creatures weren't going to be any different.

But that was too damned bad for them, wasn't it?

"So how do we find this guy?" James asked, his voice not quite sullen, as though he barely contained himself from pouting.

Cute.

They were still in the woods, in the exact same place where the initial battle had taken place. The wolves didn't wish to leave if it meant going to the dragon clan, and the dragons refused to be guests in a wolf pack, so staying here, on the land both sets of creatures had been fighting over, had seemed like the next best thing.

A camp had been made, dragons on one side and wolves on another, as though an invisible line had been drawn in the dirt when James made the fire, and he and Patrick sat down on one side of the fallen log with Carlton and Draco on the other.

Jessie found herself somewhere in the middle, sitting back straight, knees pressed together, and feet tucked to the side, a blazing fire between her and her new white knights.

It was almost poetic.

At least, she thought so. The wolves and dragons seemed to believe otherwise as they glared at her.

She ignored them, smiling at her new knights, knowing how much her lack of attention to the under-lings was annoying them.

Too bad, so sad.

"He can hide away for as long as he likes. He doesn't have to come out for the next three hundred years if he doesn't want to."

Even Draco lifted a brow at that, and his smile was tentative, unsure. "Uh, baby, you know that we don't have all that time to wait, right?"

"And you said one month," James added, narrowing his eyes at her.

The two alphas said nothing. They each sat next to their own, Patrick next to James, and Carlton beside Draco.

They watched her silently, as though they were still trying to figure something out about her.

Which was...unnerving.

Jessie sat a little straighter. She looked at Patrick, then to Carlton.

"Is there something on my face?" She glanced down at her chest, wiping away dust that wasn't there, casually touching her cheek, as if she thought something would be there.

Patrick growled at her, and Jessie noted, with some interest, how it looked when fur began to sprout from his jaw and the rest of his face. At first, it looked as if he was growing in a beard incredibly quickly. Jessie thought it was a neat trick until she realized exactly what was happening to him.

And then she was kind of impressed.

"I bet that's a scary look to get the kids off your lawn, isn't it?"

Patrick growled at her. James glared.

Draco snorted a laugh, and it was pretty clear to see that Carlton was struggling not to smile. They could smile all they wanted. She would get to them soon enough.

Roger still circled from his side of the camp, watching with narrow, suspicious eyes. She didn't get the same vibe off of him that she got from James. She didn't think there was that sort of connection between Roger and Patrick as there was between Patrick and James.

And even so, the more Jessie put her focus on James,

the more he stared back at her, refusing to back down, the more she was certain it was one-sided. But the lust for her was still there. He was harder to read as a paranormal creature of the night. He was no demon, and definitely no human. They were as easy to read as those large font books that took up a half shelf in the bookstores she visited.

Still, the lust was there, and he was not confused about it. He seemed angry about it, irritated. God, trying to get a read on people based on the looks on their faces alone was hard, and annoying. Jessie had almost forgotten about how difficult it could be.

James eventually looked away, but it was Patrick who decided to speak up.

"So if at the end of the month, your demon lord doesn't show up for us to kill, what then?"

"I'll release you from your promise, of course."

All four men looked at her, as though they were insulted she could treat them with such disrespect.

She didn't care.

Carlton remained as stony-faced as Patrick. "You really expect us to believe that?"

"I'm all right with her being a liar," Draco said, adjusting the way he sat until it appeared he was leaning forward, his expression eager. "Baby, you can make me your little manservant for all eternity, and I promise I will happily go about my duties in pleasing you." He actually winked at her.

The muscles in her cheeks and around her lips quirked. She was not going to smile at that stupidity.

But then Draco showed off his perfectly white teeth, smiling at her.

Oh yes, this was a male who was used to getting what he wanted.

"I think you're cute." Couldn't lie about that; he'd see

right through it. "And if you want me to, we can do all kinds of fun things, but I don't believe for one second that you actually want to be bound to me for life, and I doubt you do either, so please don't bother with the flattery."

"Flattery gets me everywhere with women, even with the ones who say it doesn't work, so I'll keep at it."

He shouldn't bother. If he wanted sex, she would give it to him. If it got Jessie closer to her goals and meant Draco would bitch as little as possible when the work needed to get done, so be it.

Otherwise...

Jessie shook her head, turning back to Patrick. "Valbrand will eventually try something. He might send his underlings tonight." Jessie watched the fire, searching in its flickering for any sign they might be spied upon right now. "He's impatient like that, and he won't appreciate the competition."

"But why?" James asked. "A guy would have to be stupid to do that when he literally has forever to be patient. A month would be nothing to him."

"It would be, if he wasn't certain I wouldn't find other men to take your place when I was finished with you."

She didn't mention when that was.

Jessie still wasn't so sure if she really was lying to them about releasing them from their servitude to her. She wanted to be telling the truth, so she channeled that. It helped her at times. Until she knew for certain where this went, there was no point in reiterating her promise again and again.

Not as though it mattered. With the exception of Draco, the lot of them looked at her with suspicion.

Draco tried to make light of the situation. "Well, if he's so determined to have you back, you must be something important to him." The light in his eyes dimmed, as though an unpleasant thought just now occurred to him. "If it's just a lovers tiff between demons, maybe hear him out? Or not. In fact, I'd prefer it if you didn't go back to him."

Jessie glanced down at the fire once more, searching. "I have no intention of returning to him, so that is out of the question."

As was giving more details than that.

The fire flicked just a touch brighter. Jessie could not look away from it. She couldn't see his face, but *he* watched her. She was certain of it.

"What kind of stupid fucking name is Valbrand the Almighty anyway?" James said, crossing his arms.

Jessie smiled, and because she was certain he listened, she decided to tell the tale as though he didn't.

Just to see what happened with the fire.

"There's an interesting story about that, actually. He didn't tell it to me until after we'd been together for fifty years."

The fire flickered. It always flickered, but the strength of it, the sudden bright embers that died back down to normal, confirmed everything she believed.

Of course, she ignored the flames as though there was nothing there.

She might be fooling these men, but she did not fool Val. He knew she was ignoring him, and it would piss him off all the more.

"I can't wait to hear this." Draco clapped his hands together. "All right, what's he compensating for? Mommy didn't love him enough? Or maybe she loved him a little too much?"

"I'm surprised you didn't ask if he had a small dick."

Draco shrugged. "Low hanging fruit. Everyone goes for the small dick jokes right off the bat. I want to get to the meat of the situation, the real heart of it, you know? His uncle touched him, didn't he?"

Carlton growled under his breath. "Draco."

"I'm being careful. I'm just trying to learn a little more about who we're working with. That's important in today's world, especially with a lady."

"She's not really a lady, though," James said.

Jessie struggled to not growl at him. "I am a lady. In every way. I'll thank you to remember it, or I will see to it that you'll be licking toilet bowls for the rest of your life."

James tensed.

"Can you really force him to do that?" Patrick asked, arms still crossed, gaze still calculating.

"If he continues to test me, he can find out first hand."

Most people didn't want to find out first hand. This would do it. This would ensure these men ate out of the palm of her hand and thanked her for it for as long as she needed them.

"You keep looking at the fire. Why?" Patrick asked.

That stunned her.

"A fire is a beautiful thing. Why wouldn't I look at it?"

James still wasn't finished with his childish pouting. "I suppose a demon would enjoy fire more than the average human."

"And considering how much humans already enjoy fire, that's a stupid thing to say."

He bristled. Had he been in his wolf shape, Jessie had no doubts that she would have seen his hackles rise up.

"Humans don't like fires!"

"Which is why all the ones who can afford it put fireplaces in their homes, right?"

His cheeks colored. James's mouth worked, as though his brain was desperate to come up with some sort of comeback.

He couldn't. Obviously.

"James, that's enough. Don't tire yourself out for her."

Considering all this was being said while Valbrand happened to be listening, Jessie weighed her options. She could let them continue to be angry with her, to bicker amongst themselves and give Valbrand the impression they were not strong.

Or...

Jessie rose to her feet. "Your alpha is absolutely right. Let's not quarrel." She walked around the fire, feeling the heat of its flames, and Valbrand's gaze, on her body. He liked to watch her, no matter what she happened to be doing at the time.

She moved towards James, who watched her with an expression of interest and suspicion. She could practically taste the lust on him. It vibrated from him. It was somewhat impressive that he managed to contain himself the way he did.

Though, men were often known to hide their affections behind a mask of disdain.

She reached out, touching his face, stroking his cheek.

He didn't pull away. Namely, because he didn't want to, but a proud male like this wouldn't want to give her the impression that she had discovered some weakness in him.

"I apologize. I would very much like to have your help in these matters. If you would consent to give it to me."

"I..."

She didn't give him the chance to respond. Jessie leaned in, kissing him on the mouth. She swallowed down his gasp of breath, and the rush of excitement that hit her as the fire behind her ass picked up in heat and intensity.

Valbrand was angry. James was stunned, and Draco was enjoying this a little too much.

Not just him, however. She expected his eyes would be as hot as the fire on her body, and they were, but she felt that same intensity, that same longing and desperate desire as Patrick and Carlton watched her.

An alpha wolf and a dragon.

Yes, they would do very nicely, indeed.

She pulled back from James' mouth when it appeared he was about to wake from the stupor she'd thrown him in, just in case he decided to push her away from him in a fit of stubborn male pride.

No, he stared at her, his face still flushed, and for the first time since she'd met him, he seemed to be at peace with himself, and with her.

"Can you forgive me?"

James blinked, and his expression soured. "I could forgive you if you weren't blatantly trying to manipulate me. Fuck off with your spells, lady. It won't work on me."

She blinked, standing straight, and for the first time in over a decade, Jessie...didn't know what to say.

It wasn't often she was put under this spell, that she couldn't bring herself to focus properly, but with Valbrand watching, and with this rejection that was not a rejection, she found she could not come back from it.

This was not what she'd expected to happen.

Was it just her, or was the fire behind her burning her ass a little hotter than what it should have been?

James glared at her. "Did you not hear what I just said? Stop looking at me like you're trying to influence me. It's not going to work!"

"All right," she drawled. "You made your point." She turned.

"Wait."

Jessie stopped short at the sound of Patrick's voice. She glanced back at him. "What do you want?"

A little harsher than she meant.

Calm. Easy. Maintain composure, and she would ultimately regain control of the situation. So, she smiled, willing herself to feel it, to know that she was the one in command here.

Patrick looked at Carlton. The two men seemed to share something between them that made Jessie uneasy. The only person who was meant to be in the know here was her.

"What was that?"

They looked back at her. She gauged the situation.

"Ten minutes ago, the two of you were getting ready to rip each other's heads off, and now you're sharing looks like you think you might know something. I'd like to know what you both are thinking of the situation."

Patrick nodded. Carlton tapped his fingers together. Jessie didn't think she liked this. How could they already be plotting against her? They were plotting against each other when she found them.

Patrick leaned to the side, getting a look at the fire.

Jessie didn't move. Her blood was made of fire, and yet today, in this moment, she felt frozen.

"Your ex-boyfriend is listening in on us, isn't he?"

Okay, now she was frozen.

The flames licked up higher into the air. Jessie looked back. Though it glowed, was red, orange, yellow and hot, it barely looked like fire anymore. It looked more like a tentacle monster, rising up out of the earth, clawing at the sky, laughing at her misery.

And it was laughing. The dragons and the wolves who had been keeping their distance just a few short minutes ago were suddenly coming a little closer.

Not what she had expected. Normal people would

have stepped away at the sight of something so out of place and strange.

But she didn't want normal people. She wanted warriors. An army.

This was her army. These were the people who were going to kill this son-of-a-bitch for her.

She could almost hear Valbrand laughing in the distance.

Then, no. She couldn't just almost hear it. She *could* hear it. He was *here*.

Draco rushed forward, kicking his foot out, sloshing dirt, rock, and dry sand all over the fire. It didn't go out, but the tentacle monster was gone.

The laughing continued for quite some time.

Jessie's skin seemed too tight for her body in that moment. Her spine tingled, as though a skeletal hand was touching her. She refused to shiver, but somehow, she knew she was giving away everything.

"Shut up with that pussified laughing, you little bitch! We're coming for you! And when we're done with you, you're going to wish you'd never fucked with our princess here."

Suddenly, she didn't feel like shivering in disgust so much as Jessie wanted to throw her head back and sigh at how ridiculous that sounded.

Except then Patrick and Carlton came to stand on either side of her.

James as well. He stood next to Patrick, of course, but he was still there, and in the moment, that meant a great deal to her.

The laughing did stop. It took Jessie a moment to realize it, but it stopped as Valbrand watched them. He made no effort to hide it now. She could see his eyes in the fire.

"We're coming for you for harming this woman," Patrick said.

Carlton stepped forward. "So you can get very afraid right about now."

"I would if I were you," James said, finishing their little speech.

It was the sort of thing that would have made her roll her eyes a few short years ago. The sort of jumped up, chest-pounding, testosterone show of dominance she would have detested on a normal day.

Except now…

This was her army. Her protection, and she did intend to kill Valbrand for what he'd done.

"I'm not coming back to you. So you might as well start hiding because I know exactly how you think and where you like to go and be. I will hunt you down to the ends of the earth. You got me?"

Valbrand said nothing. He was going to simper off any minute now, defeated, tail between his legs and afraid.

Except the sudden change in those eyes didn't give the impression he planned on skulking off to anywhere. In fact, it almost looked as though he was smiling.

Then the campfire exploded.

12

PATRICK

Debris and soot, rock and sand, flew everywhere.

Patrick was not the only one who reached for Jessie.

He shouldn't have. Even though James could take care of himself and he would despise the idea of being looked after in any capacity, Patrick had enough time to think that maybe he should have taken care of his own before he tried to play white knight to this woman who was hardly a lady.

Especially when Carlton reached out at the same time, grabbing her right hand just as Patrick snatched her left wrist. As he attempted to yank Jessie to him, so did Carlton, and both of them seemed to get nowhere as they pulled Jessie between them.

Then, ultimately, let her go.

Apparently, neither of them wished to be the reason behind why she had no protection, and so now they were both the reason why she had none as she was dead center in the blast.

It threw them all back. Even as Patrick attempted to ground himself and dig his feet into the earth, he could not withstand the pressure and heat that struck him like the hot hair of a plane engine running full blast.

When he opened his eyes, sitting up sharply and suddenly, he wasn't the only one on his back.

Jessie coughed for breath, pushing herself to sit up.

Patrick rushed to her, and to his annoyance, he made it to her side at roughly the same time that Carlton did. He glared at Carlton, who sneered back at him as they both looked over how injured Jessie was.

"Are you all right? Don't move," Carlton said.

Kiss-ass.

"I'm fine," Jessie choked, waving her hand in front of her face, as though trying to banish the dust. "You both suck."

It was such a mild insult, but it got Patrick right in the heart. A thin knife through his ribs that twisted all the way around before pulling out.

Sharp. Stinging.

Patrick grabbed her wrist, gently pushing down on the bones, working his way up her arm, eager to see if there was some internal damage he couldn't see.

Jessie yanked her arm away. "I'm fine!" She was positively pouting. "If you both hadn't been such idiots, I wouldn't have had my dress ruined."

"That's what you're worried about?" Patrick couldn't believe it. "You could have been killed."

"No, I couldn't. He does that all the time."

She made it out as though it was no big deal, as though there was nothing wrong with her, but she was bleeding. A scrape across her cheek, and one on each of her elbows from when she'd landed. Perhaps a normal explosion wouldn't have phased her, but that was no normal explosion. It had been brought on by something demonic. A warlock who practiced dark magick.

Jessie quite obviously looked unhappy to have been in a tug of war that put her right in the middle of the blast, but she was alive, and that was the only thing Patrick could think about.

Until his other instincts took over. The reminder of his responsibilities.

He looked to James. The other man was all right, and already seeing to members of the pack who had also been thrown back by the blast.

Roger blinked, shaking his head out as though trying to banish something rattling around in his head.

He, and many of the others, had their faces tarred in soot, and they walked as though the ground beneath their feet were slowly teetering back and forth.

The dragons, on the other hand, seemed to be faring much better.

One quick look was all it took for Patrick to see many of them melting out of their scales, skin replacing the multicolored, protective layers. Some still smacked their temples, trying to dislodge something stuck, or banish a ringing noise, but even if they were stunned by the sudden blast, they walked straighter.

Patrick was loath to leave Jessie with the dragons, especially Draco, but he couldn't sit by while his pack was in tatters.

So he walked away from her.

She was a big girl. He was sure she could manage.

Patrick went to Roger first. He put his hand on the man's shoulder, if only to make sure he was all right.

When Roger's eyes met his, Patrick nodded and went to the next brother of his pack who looked the most affected by the blast.

One was on his ass, nose bleeding and eyes wide. Danny. He was young, even for a wolf, and he wanted to be part of the team. He must have gotten real close when the fire pit exploded. It looked as though one of the rocks they'd piled around it flew and crash landed right into his nose.

Patrick knelt down next to him, along with his friends who crowded around him, showing their fingers and trying to get his attention, but Danny couldn't seem to hear them.

He looked around, dazed.

"Danny, hey." Patrick grabbed his knee and slapped him on the shoulder. "You awake in there?"

Danny blinked at him, then pointed to his ear before yelling. "I think my hearing's off!"

Patrick smiled, sweet relief yanking the weight off his back. At least he wouldn't have to explain anything too drastic to the kid's mother when they got home. "You're going to be all right." He looked up at the others clustered around him. Also all young, barely twenty. Now they could see what might be involved if they really wanted to be part of the team.

"You all take care of him, got it? No fucking around. Get his bandages ready and, if you find anyone in worse shape than him, they've got priority."

The others nodded, giving a good stiff upper lip as they got to work. They'd already had their first real battle with the dragons. Now they could get some experience with what it would be like to work after being dick punched like that by something other than dragons. Enemies weren't just with the dragons, or even other wolf packs looking to get in on territory that was not theirs.

Patrick glanced back at Jessie. She seemed to have brushed herself off well enough. Somehow, she looked as clean and pristine as though she'd come out of the salon.

And of course Draco was right there, kissing up and holding her hand.

Patrick couldn't tell if she was genuinely interested in his attention, or just flattering him.

The wolf inside didn't seem to care. It growled. Jealousy filled him up, and Patrick couldn't believe he was trying to squash down that feeling right now.

For a woman he barely knew, gorgeous as she may be, over his responsibilities.

Draco was clearly an idiot, but Carlton knew what his duties were. He dealt with his wounded as any leader would be expected to do, and that was at least something. If Carlton wasn't about to put his duties on hold over Jessie, then Patrick sure as hell wouldn't let himself be the one who was caught shirking first.

No, fuck that guy.

Patrick got to work.

So long as he had Carlton to compete against, it made things easier for him to focus on anything and everything other than the smell of Jessie's perfume and body.

And how irritating it was that Draco was still giving her so much attention.

Didn't that motherfucker have responsibilities to take care of? The dragons weren't as affected by the blast, but still, he was openly flirting while his alpha worked the scene.

Patrick wanted to punch his lights out for it.

"Sir."

Patrick snapped out of it only when James spoke to him. The other man seemed to appear right beside him without warning.

It wasn't normal for that to happen, and James knew it. "You're distracted."

MANDY ROSKO

He didn't have to ask why. The answer was right behind him.

"Don't let them get to you, sir. The dragons or the woman."

Every adult behaved like a simpering child at some point in their lives. For Patrick, he knew his time had come when he wanted to deny James was right.

"I'll get over it. This is only a spell. She'll be done with us, and then we'll go back to defending our land."

James nodded, the relief in his eyes evident.

"You don't like her so much, do you?"

James looked away from him, though the flush of color rushing up his neck made it evident what his thoughts were. "I don't dislike her so much."

Patrick grabbed James' shoulder and squeezed. "You don't have to worry too much. Bros before hoes, right?"

James snorted a laugh. He likely held it back because now really wasn't the time for laughing or joking, but all things considered, Patrick wanted to give his friend some relief.

He knew James' feelings for him. Patrick couldn't return them in the same way James wanted him to, but that didn't stop him from respecting the other man or enjoying his company.

"Let's get back to it. We can't rescue our damsel without taking care of this damage first, can we?"

"No kidding." James had a glance around. It seemed the pack was starting to recover well enough.

The shock was turning to anger on the dust-covered faces, and even Danny, who was being helped to his feet, was starting to realize there was a war cry rising above with the rest of the wolves.

His howl was a little more watered down, a little more tone deaf, but the howls and chest-pounding that happened were soon noticed even by those pompous dragons.

Pride swelled within Patrick's chest. His wolves might have been more affected by the blast, but they recovered the way warriors were expected to. They were ready to fight. They were easy to take up the mantel.

For their alpha.

And for their alpha's new woman, whose eyes danced at the wild show right before her gaze met his.

13

CARLTON

THE WOLVES RECOVERED SOONER than Carlton would have given them credit for. A few were bleeding. One needed help from his friends just to get to his feet, but then they were howling and jumping around like a bunch of fools. As if they couldn't wait to go out on the hunt.

It was impressive. Not that Carlton was suddenly going to be buddy-buddy with the wolves, but even he had to admit there was something honorable and right about a group of warriors ready to fight after a cowardly sneak attack such as the one they'd just suffered.

Jessie certainly seemed impressed. Carlton clenched his teeth at the rising jealousy that rushed up his chest and into his throat.

The feelings may not be real, they may be a product of her spell, but the lust clearly was.

Any man knew what a woman could accomplish when he was wrapped around her little finger.

He went to her, ignoring the smug expression on Patrick's face.

"It's not safe for you here. I think it would be best if we went somewhere else."

She looked at him, her golden eyes beautiful. Even now he could feel her spell taking hold of him. "Did you happen to have somewhere in mind?"

Draco, thankfully, made none of his idiotic comments. He also seemed to be waiting for what the commands would be.

"I think you should command Patrick to see reason. If his pack were to come to my land...it's better fortified there. More rock, and my kind can help to protect you better and hunt Valbrand."

She seemed to be thinking about it, which was not nearly good enough as far as he was concerned.

"Valbrand is a demon, is he not?"

"Warlock."

Carlton didn't think there was much of a difference. "Either way, his kind is drawn to creatures like me, like other dragons. If he knows you're with us, at our territory, then he might be more inclined to make another move soon."

"Not that we want you to go anywhere so fast," Draco said.

Carlton was going to beat the piss out of the man when he was done here. He really was.

Jessie just smiled at him, still willing to play into his game.

The game of letting him pretend he wasn't a fly in her web.

"Can I ask you something?"

"Anything you want."

Christ, that sounded a little too eager even for him.

"Why were you fighting over this land with the

wolves? If you already have your own territory, then I don't see the point."

It was a struggle to keep things hidden sometimes. A struggle to keep his cheek from twitching, his hand from clenching. Any little thing could give away something he did not want revealed.

"This is valuable farming land. It belonged to our ancestors before the wolves came and drove us out."

"Did they drive you out? Or did you both go to war and they won?"

Draco finally lost that stupid smirk that had been on his face. "It's not quite that simple, princess."

She shrugged. "You're right. I don't know, and I don't care, about your lineage, or the spoils of a war no one here was alive to witness. I care about killing Valbrand and freeing myself."

She smiled at Draco, scratching under his chin.

He didn't smile for her and thump his leg like a good dog, for the first time ever, but he didn't pull away from that touch either.

"Help me with this, and I will let you all go on killing each other as much as you want."

Draco seemed hurt. He really did wear too much of himself on his sleeve. "You wouldn't care if we were hurt or killed?"

Another careless shrug. "Men fight, kill each other, and die every day. As much now as they did when I was a girl, so I don't see the need to worry."

Draco kept right on smiling. Carlton could tell he was attempting to turn on the charm that pulled women into his bed every night. "Darling, doesn't that sound a little cold? You did want us for our skills, after all, correct?"

Jessie looked at her nails with the sort of boredom that came when attempting to pick out a new nail color.

"That is true, but be honest, you don't actually want me around here, do you? You hate that I'm manipulating your clan leader, even those wolves over there. You hate that I've interfered with your plans to kill each other and now you're going to hate me for dragging you into a battle you never asked for."

"Correct," Carlton said because he couldn't lie to her when he was being influenced by her spell, by her blood that ran through his veins.

"I don't mind," Draco said.

Carlton looked at the man.

He was...insane. He was actually insane. There was no other way to describe it, and he was definitely telling the truth because if Carlton couldn't lie to a question like that, then there was no way in hell he could either.

Jessie seemed just as shocked. She stared and at Draco, her eyes wide, though she recovered quickly.

Seemed to recover, anyway.

"Well, that's your fault for getting attached, isn't it?"

Draco tilted his head a little. A complete giveaway. Carlton had told him not to do things like that.

Jessie reached into her bra strap and pulled out a pocket mirror. She looked into it instead of staring at Draco. "If you wanted to get into anything physical, I'm more than all right to do that, but you're out of your mind if you think this is going anywhere else. I need you for a job, and you were the only one of the three who agreed to take it on."

Draco narrowed his eyes. "Yeah, you're right, I did."

Draco, however, in his usual state of being over emotional about everything, was missing something big here.

He was missing the big picture.

Namely, the embarrassed look of shame on Jessie's face.

She didn't blush, but she was avoiding eye contact, and there was something in her tone, a little too stony, that gave everything else away.

Carlton got her attention, standing in front of her and gently pulling down that little mirror. "I will speak with Draco and the rest of the clan about accepting the wolves onto our plot of land, how does that sound?"

She glared at him. "It sounds like you're trying to get rid of me so you can have a little chat about what to do about me behind my back."

Carlton looked at her, then he took her by the hand, lifting her delicate knuckles to his lips.

He felt her tense, then melt as he kissed her. "No. I am your servant, remember? I would not do that."

He couldn't be entirely sure if she believed him, but he was mostly sure he had her in his grasp.

She wanted to seduce her way to what she wanted?

Two could play that game. He had to do what she wanted whenever she wanted it? All right. But he was going to make sure she remembered this time.

Draco, however, fumed. He wasn't happy. Whatever, he would suck it up until Carlton could get him alone.

Jessie held still. She kept her hand in Carlton's fingers, and, dare he say it, he actually thought he did see something of a blush on her beautiful cheeks.

But then she yanked her hand back, putting a stop to the romance that had blossomed, and yanking the heat of her body away from his.

A heat that was not simply under her skin.

Carlton let her. He didn't need to keep holding her hand, or kissing her knuckles, because that was all it took for him to see that he had her right where he wanted her.

She could be chipped away at after all.

"Fine. You boys go and play, but don't even think about talking about getting out of my spell behind my back because it wouldn't work anyway. You're not free until I say you are, got it?"

He felt the command locking him to her orders.

Not to talk about escape. Got it.

"We understand perfectly."

"We understand," Draco said, sounding a little too much as though he was pouting.

Idiot.

Jessie looked at them both. She narrowed her eyes just a little, but, when she could see no signs of devious behavior, she walked away towards Patrick and James.

That was annoying, but Carlton had to remember the big picture here. He grabbed Draco by his arm, which irritated the other man to no end.

"What? What's the matter with you?"

Too damned bad for him. "Quiet yourself. We have plans to make."

Draco seemed stunned Carlton could speak at all. "I thought she said we wouldn't be able to—"

"We can't, and I have no intention to." There was no point in trying when the spell held him in its grip. "We're going to talk about something much better." He looked at Draco. They weren't best friends for nothing. Draco could read him, and Carlton knew Draco inside and out.

This was going to interest the other man greatly.

Draco put it together that something was up, so he shut his mouth, which was smart, and allowed Carlton to pull him deeper into their own group.

Carlton nodded to Tristan. He was third in command of the clan, and he tended to keep the warriors in shape during those few times when neither Carlton nor Draco could be there. Tristan would keep everything in lockstep for a few more minutes. He might be pissed off that they were going to do this, but he would soon come around as well.

They moved off to a little spot on the side, close to their men without being in direct hearing distance. Anyone who saw them so close would assume they were making battle plans.

Which was kind of what they were doing.

"So, what are you thinking?" Draco's entire body vibrated as though he was brimming with too much energy. "If it's what I think it is then you are a scholar and a gentleman."

"And you're an idiot, but yes, this is probably something you thought of just now. She wants to play with us; we're going to have a little fun with her. You've already started working your way in so it won't be suspicious."

"You want us to seduce that gentle bred lady and make her think our intentions are purer than what they actually are?"

Why was Carlton best friends with this guy again? "Yes, something to that effect. All's fair in love and war, right?"

Draco grinned as they grasped hands. "Abso-fucking-lutely right."

"Good." Carlton sighed. "Now to get Patrick in on this."

14

JESSIE

THEY WERE TALKING ABOUT HER. Even though she'd ordered them not to, but what could she do?

There was something unsettling about knowing this, however.

Jessie glanced down at her hands, as though she would find the answers she was looking for there.

Was her influence not working anymore? Was she losing her touch?

Jessie's heart pounded. She knew it wasn't true. She knew she was all right. She *had* to be.

But the doubt was there. Jessie sucked in a deep, soothing breath, though she didn't much feel soothed.

If her gift was gone…what would she do? Would Valbrand take her back?

And then there was the way Carlton had kissed her hand.

Her knuckles still burned.

Jessie clenched her fingers. She put her hands down and did a quick look around, making sure no one was looking at her. A few of the wolves were. They were still hopped up on testosterone and a clear need to go to battle, but they still looked at her as though she was a predator of some type.

She supposed she was.

But that one over there wasn't her prey. She didn't want to look at the wolf who happened to be bleeding, however. Though he seemed to be talking quite loudly to his friends, they didn't seem so happy with her. They looked at her as though trying to figure out how soon they could get their pack away from her.

Fair enough, but she wouldn't be here for long.

Where was Patrick?

Ah, right over there. He stood with James. A small circle of the wolves stood around them, including Roger, who seemed to be speaking animatedly to his alpha and the second in command.

Jessie really didn't want to deal with that.

She looked back to the bleeding wolf. His friends were focused on putting gauze around his nose and ear. It seemed to be annoying him.

This wasn't her normal skill set, but there were some smaller bumps and scrapes she could deal with. It was how she'd managed to stay so fabulous after Valbrand, the prick, made the nice fire explode in her face.

She didn't exactly have all the energy she wanted to be doing this right now; Jessie wasn't even sure how much she cared. This was a business transaction.

But did she really want to deal with everyone looking at her as if she was a parasite?

No, not really.

So, she went back to that bleeding kid over there. If only to make sure he was all right.

The boys around him tensed when they saw her coming. She projected her beauty onto them, willing them to find her more attractive, less of a threat. It seemed to work. They relaxed, although their air of distrust was still there enough that she could sense it.

Few people in the world who knew precisely what she was and what she was about could fully be put under the spell again.

"What do you want?" one asked, stepping in the way of his friend.

That was nice. It was always good to see people watching out for each other. Not that it always did them much good, but she enjoyed it all the same.

"I'd like to see if there's something I can do for your friend there."

The young man shook his head. He didn't have any hint of a beard coming through his jaw or around his mouth, which made him look way too young to be on any sort of battlefield.

In Jessie's day, boys of fifteen, even younger, went to fight and die in wartime. This was not a fifteen-year-old boy; none of them were. They all looked to be at least twenty or so, but still…

Perhaps after all the time she'd spent alive, people just seemed younger than they were, especially when they showed no signs of body hair.

"I have no interest in seducing him. This is to help him and nothing else."

The boy in front of her still seemed unsure, which either meant she was losing her touch, or he was stronger than average. Normally, he would have jumped out of her way by now.

So she turned up the volume just a bit, just enough to make sure he would get the message.

"If you would, please." The sweetness in her voice

dropped. If it was a literal dripping, he would have drunk it right up.

He definitely fell under her influence, because he stepped out of her way. He still seemed irritated about it, but the point was that he did it. Jessie held back a smile. It was important to not rub in her little wins too much, after all.

The boy with the blood all over his face stopped talking so loudly to the other young wolf next to him when he finally realized Jessie was standing right there, halting his story about how funny it was that his face had "survived the blast."

She didn't understand men in the least; she really didn't.

Jessie sat down next to him on the overturned log. He scooched to the side, watching her as though the local prom queen was finally giving him the time of day. She had to smile a little at that.

Yeah, she still had it.

The boy smiled. "Hi," he said loudly.

Jessie said nothing back to him. There was no point. Otherwise she would be yelling right back at him. Instead, she took him by the hand, holding it, threading her fingers through his. He tensed a little, which was an interesting response. She hadn't done anything else to warrant such a reaction, but there it was.

"Uh, c-can I help you?"

She adored it when they were shy.

Healing energy took so much more focus than bespelling the men she ensnared. It wasn't her thing, not the talent she had, and Valbrand had been a useless cunt, refusing to teach her.

Everything she knew of it came from her own self-study.

So, of course, she was terrible at it, especially with other people.

It did take pleasant thoughts, something which was difficult for her to pull off from time to time. It was not always easy to think happy thoughts when life was no so happy.

And she never really had that trick to use until she saw that play for the first time.

Flying boys, pirates, a ticking crocodile. She'd loved that play because it had given her the mantra to finally get some success in this practice.

So Jessie thought her happy thoughts.

She did not want to be thinking about Carlton's mouth on her knuckles, the warmth of it, how she'd shivered when he finished and looked her in the eyes. As though it was not her influence that was making him look at her like that.

If only.

How beautiful would it be to have a male look at her like that without her spells to influence them?

For it to be real.

Even Draco's attentions were flattering, but they were not real. He was simply being foolish.

It must have been a very happy thought, Draco's fool-ishness, Carlton's kiss; even James' standoffishness and Patrick's stubborn nature were pleasant to think about.

Because they belonged to her. They were hers.

She pulled her warmed hands back from the injured young warrior's. Jessie looked at him, and he stared back at her. He'd dropped the filthy cloth he'd been using on his face some time ago, revealing that his nose was no longer bleeding, not even shattered. It was perfectly healed, and even pleasant to look at. In fact, it turned him into some-thing of a handsome young man.

With a slight frown, the boy scratched at his ear be. losing patience and taking the bandage off. His ear wc now healed.

The illusion of him being a dashing young gentleman was thwarted when he stuck his finger right into his ear and wiggled it around. "Oh my God, I think I can...I can hear again. Holy shit, I can hear again! Guys!"

And that was enough for her. Jessie stood, backing away from the group of happy young men as they surrounded their friend, pulling him up from his seat and slapping him on the back. One of them yelled right into his friend's ear, testing how well he was healed.

They were all idiots, but it was still cute to watch, and Jessie did feel a little better when she finished.

Not that she planned on going back to Patrick and James, just to see them looking at her like that. She stopped, frozen. That tense feeling of being stuck seemed to happen to her a little too much when it came to these men. Patrick and James both smiled at her. There was a clear look of *gotcha* in their eyes. She didn't like that.

Keeping her shoulders straight and her chin up, Jessie went to them. "Find something interesting, boys?"

Patrick crossed his arms, but he still looked a little too pleased with himself, with everything around him. "Nothing in particular. I didn't realize you had such a soft heart."

That hit her in a way she didn't expect. Anger and surprise came at her at the same time and crashed into her in ways she didn't like. "I have nothing of the sort, and I'll thank you to never mention that to me again."

"Whoa," James said, though he was still smiling.

Patrick seemed more confused. "What's the matter with you? You did something good for a member of my pack. It's appreciated."

"And I do not care what you appreciate so long as you kill Valbrand. He is a soldier, and soldiers have their jobs to do, nothing more and nothing less."

They were still smiling! What the hell was the matter with them?

But she didn't lose her temper. She was close, but years of training had taught her better.

Keep control. Stay alert. Let nothing be revealed by her features.

So why did these men seem to see everything she did not want them to see? It was unnerving.

She crossed her arms. Even that was a tell she did not want revealed. "Please just ensure that you do your jobs. I healed one of your men so they would not look at me the way they do."

"We would protect you," James said, which was something she had honestly not expected to hear from him.

But she couldn't allow herself to feel any warmth in that. It was part of her own manipulation. He did not mean it.

"I know you will, that was the point of the spell."

"Not just for the spell." He sounded even more reluctant to admit to that now than before.

Almost as if…

No. No, it was not true, and she would not allow herself to believe it.

"Are you all right?" Patrick asked. "You seem confused about something."

She shook her head. "I'm not confused about anything. The dragons want me to convince you to take your wolves and move to their territory. That is all." She'd almost forgotten, but she wanted them to stop thinking about how she was nicer than she really was and get back to work.

Of course, they were not happy to hear the suggestion.

"No fucking way," James said, and he went back to glaring at her, distrusting her. "We can't just go and set up shop with a bunch of dragons. On *their* turf."

Jessie had to think about that as she looked at Patrick. "Are you really that afraid of dragons?"

"Afraid of betrayal, of death among my warriors? Yes, I am afraid of those things."

"You would have to agree not to betray them back, you know."

James gaped with his mouth wide open at his alpha, shaking his head. "Patrick, come on, you can't just—"

"I will make whatever decision is necessary for the safety of the pack," Patrick said.

Jessie was sure that was the first time she'd ever heard him snap at is second in command.

She didn't have the heart to smirk at the guy over her little win, because it didn't feel much like a win at that point.

"I can assure you both that I will make sure Carlton is on his best behavior. If I can make you both help me, then I can make him cooperate with you."

"She thought it was a good offer to make, that they would be pleased to hear it."

No. Apparently not.

"What's the matter? I thought you would be pleased with this. Is it not a good offer?"

"It's an excellent offer," Patrick said, though he shook his head softly as he said it. "But it's not your offer to make."

Jessie didn't understand.

Perhaps she left that a little too clear on her face. "You're forcing them as much as you are us," James clarified.

The way they looked at her, as if she was the one who should have known better, irritated her beyond all reason. A fire picked up in her belly, consuming her like the blaze of a witch trial burning. "You want to look at me like that? To judge me for making you idiots stop your fighting, is that it?"

James lifted his hands. "Now hold on, it wasn't supposed to be anything like that—"

"Well, that's what it sounded like! You were all ready to kill each other! Over land, and you don't even know who's the rightful owner of it."

"We are," said James and Patrick at the same time, as though their thoughts on the subject were perfectly in sync with each other.

She didn't care. She didn't care what their thoughts were about it, what they thought of her, and now she definitely didn't care about what they wanted out of this arrangement.

Jessie pointed a manicured fingernail at Patrick's nose. "You are going to command your wolves to go with Carlton to...wherever it is that he lives. You are going to work together. You're not going to fight, no one is going to kill each other or die except for Valbrand, do you understand?"

Of course he did. The command was strong, and he was still under her influence.

Patrick nodded. "I understand perfectly."

Even as he said it, he looked monumentally pissed that she'd forced him into this.

Jessie hardened her heart against that. Guilt came back to her. No. No, she would not feel that. She'd done this a thousand times before, more than that, and she was not going to develop a sad sense of conscience now. She dropped her hand. "Good. Now go."

Patrick clenched his jaw. He looked as though he wanted to say something to her, and Jessie honestly wasn't sure if it was her own influence that prevented him from speaking to her, or his own sense of self-preservation.

"We will get you back for this."

Jessie snapped her attention to James.

He glared at her openly, hiding none of his anger or his righteous indignation.

So she waved him off, wanting none of that. "You can go and give the news with Patrick if you want. Don't come back and talk to me unless you have something for me to eat. Something edible. And good."

Sometimes it was best to clarify these things. Otherwise people tended to get the wrong idea of what they could get away with.

James, still glaring at her, moved to do as he was told.

Jessie was left with that feeling of hungry guilt, and it wouldn't stop eating away at her insides.

What was wrong with her?

VALBRAND

VALBRAND HAD himself a chuckle as he watched the shit storm unfold.

The fire hadn't entirely been put out. Every small spark, every tiny flame, even the ones that were dying out on the shrubs or being stomped on by those monstrous dragons and the savage wolves were little windows he could see through.

And by little, he did mean little. It was almost as good as peeking through a peephole, and the sound was hardly better, but he was willing to take what he could get. Perhaps attempting to ensnare four men at the same time was a little too much, even for one as talented as Jessica.

She seemed so sad. Why was that? All she had to do was come home to him, and he would make everything right again. She had to know he would do this for her, and yet she insisted on staying right where she was.

With them.

Because she wanted to be away from him.

Valbrand pulled away from the flames. He sat back in his chair, watching the red crystal. It was a glass ball that he'd blown himself, and the smoke inside was of a mixture he'd smoked and blown into the ball before closing it.

Very old, and one of the first relics he'd ever created.

Just before meeting her.

With a wave of his hand, he banished the small, blurred images. He didn't need to see anymore.

She was struggling. That was all he needed to know to be pleased with his current state of affairs. She was struggling against her need for him, for his magick. And now she was surrounded by males who only thought of war and death.

She might complain from time to time about the work they did, but it was Valbrand who had given her those books to read, Valbrand who had taught her, who had changed her.

Who loved her.

He could be patient, but Jessica was right. He did want to move. He wanted to make his move and soon. He wanted no other men anywhere near her. Not unless he was the one arranging the meeting.

It was not the worst thing in the world to stomach the sight of his beautiful Jessica in the arms of another male, pulling them into her web when there were riches and knowledge to be gained from such a transaction.

So, he'd allowed it.

This was different. These dragons had nothing he needed other than perhaps a few ingredients for potions, and the wolves would do little other than make good furs for his library, and perhaps a rug or two at his hearth.

But he needed no ingredients from the dragons, and he had more than enough furs to satisfy him.

The unicorn skin hanging on his far wall was his most prized. Once he had that, everything else seemed a little too low class for his tastes.

No, this would not do. Those men had nothing he wanted, and there was no reason for Jessie to be in their company other than for to vex him.

And he despised it when she vexed him.

Standing, Valbrand moved to his fire, a real one, one in his office, that he could feel.

He leaned in close, proving to himself that he did not fear it.

Even if there was something watching him, there was nothing he could not handle.

Taking the small box off the top of the fire pit, Valbrand opened it, revealing the glass heart pendant inside. The thumping beneath the glass itself, the wet motion of the real prize within, was a reminder of what he already knew. She was his, and though she'd gone through her phases, she always returned to him with a smile when he finished teaching her the lessons she needed to learn.

Closing the box with a snap, Valbrand decided she needed to learn another lesson.

16

DRACO

Draco had to be the one charged with telling Patrick and that other wolf about Carlton's plans.

He didn't like it. He didn't want to do it. As far as he was concerned, he had better shit to spend his time on, like figuring out exactly what Jessie's secrets happened to be, and how he could get to Valbrand first so he could rip the man's face off and feed it to him for what he'd done to her.

Draco didn't have all the specifics, but what little he did know was enough to get his inner gentleman out to want to dust off the old fighting technique.

And killing. That was one he didn't often like to use unless he was in a battle, but when it came down to it, Draco wouldn't mind tying the bastard down and making him cry fat tears before killing him.

He was mean like that.

But, because Carlton was paranoid about these kinds of things, and because Jessie was sharper than she liked to let on, Carlton thought it would be a better idea if Draco was the one to get Patrick or James alone to let them in on the new plan.

If Carlton tried talking about this to Patrick, then it would look massively suspicious. Even Draco had to admit that much.

Both the alpha and the clan leader meeting up to have a friendly chat out of nowhere?

Yeah, that wasn't likely to make any sense at all. Unless they were plotting something, and Jessie was sure to put it together that something was happening she wasn't going to like.

So Draco put it off, just as he'd been told, he waited until the wolves were brought to their home base.

Which, now that Draco thought about it, was a pain in the ass to get to when he didn't have the option of flying.

Walking up the mountain, and at one point even climbing up it, just because the damned wolves didn't have any wings, was a pain in the ass. At one point, Patrick even made the offer to house the dragons back at his pack, where there would be less climbing and heights involved, but Jessie was determined.

Or stubborn.

She wanted Patrick's wolves on the mountain. She refused to hear of anything else.

There had to be a reason for that. Perhaps she really did believe what Carlton had said about the cluster of dragons being able to attract Valbrand for her.

Regardless, Patrick was forced to do as she commanded, and Carlton had to promise any one of his dragons would swoop in and rescue any of Patrick's wolves should they happen to fall.

Draco didn't think there was much of a worry. The mountain could be cold, and it was hard rock, and jagged angles, but there weren't so many steep drops. A man would have to be a clumsy fool to fall from any of them, lack of wings or not.

Still, he was stunned with how long it took them to return home.

A five minute flight turned into hours of walking, and for the first time in his life, Draco had an appreciation for those who were grounded on two legs when he got to his knees and kissed the floor of his home. Well, the shared garden just outside of his home, but it was the sentiment that mattered.

The sun was going down, so the first thing the other men did, aside from bitch about how long it had taken to return home, was start lighting the torches. Blowing fire from their mouths and bringing heat and light to the place.

"No, don't do that," Carlton commanded, drawing an immediate groan from the wolves, who complained of cold and aching limbs.

Draco couldn't believe it. "I thought you wolves never got cold."

"We just got finished climbing a fucking mountain at dusk!" snapped one of the younger-looking ones, the little fool Jessie had healed of a broken face earlier.

Draco flipped the guy off, but it was Jessie who had the final say.

"Light them, light every fire you can."

Even Patrick understood the folly of this.

"Your former master made a fire explode as though it was a grenade in our midst. All of these fires would be a hazard."

"I don't care. I want all of them lit."

Draco couldn't believe it. He went to her, taking her hand, pleased she allowed him to hold it. "Jessie, you have to know that's too dangerous."

"I can heal anyone hurt in any future blasts, and I don't think he would do it anyway. A physical reaction like that through a medium that's meant to be visual only takes a lot of energy, even for him."

Draco could feel the startings of a command getting ready to wrap around his body, to squeeze him tight and never let him go.

So he said the first thing he could think of.

"Baby, we have kids who live here. I get that you might be able to heal a few people if you concentrate hard enough, but I don't think ten-year-olds care so much. They just care when they're bleeding."

That seemed to do it. Draco saw the change in her eyes, felt that stirring of the command loosening its grip around him before it faded away.

And he smiled at her.

He knew it. He fucking knew it. She wasn't so tough to crack. She was a good, gentle woman beneath that hard exterior. He just had to help her shine a little, that was all.

"I want Valbrand to be able to see me. To know where I am."

"We'll think of something," Carlton promised. "But we can't have so many fires. I don't want to worry the parents that someone might be watching them or their children sleeping at night."

Jessie couldn't seem to find any argument with that. She opened her mouth, seemed to think better of whatever she was about to say, and then closed up.

Draco didn't want that for her either. He didn't want her to think she couldn't speak among them

"How are you guys going to see anything up here without fires to light the way?" James asked.

Draco rolled his eyes. The guy could be cute, maybe, but he wasn't the sharpest blade on the rack, was he?

117

"We do have electricity up here," Draco said.

James frowned at him. "I didn't know that. Why even bother with the fires then anyway?"

"To save money," Carlton said, answering a question he did not need to answer.

He didn't go into any more detail, but it was clear what he was saying.

Their clan didn't have the funds that Patrick's pack did.

It was an embarrassing thing to have someone else know about. Draco wished Carlton hadn't said a word, and he wasn't sure why the man bothered at all.

A few of the other dragons looked just as unhappy to hear it. Tristan didn't look at anyone in particular, but the expression on his face made it obvious what was going through his head.

Draco clapped his hands together, getting the attention off the subject at hand. "Anyway, welcome, you savage, flea-ridden wolves. This will be your home for now. Don't piss on anything. Tristan will show you around to some rooms. James, can I talk to you?"

James stared at him, clearly still pissy for being spoken to the way he had been by Draco earlier. "What for?"

Jessie watched them. They couldn't let her in on this.

"The second in command of the dragons needs to make a few things clear to the second in command of the wolves. Patrick and Carlton will do the same, eventually. Just come with me, I need to make a few things clear to you about living here."

Guilt caught him, speaking of Jessie like this behind her back. Well, of needing to speak behind her back. Either way, he didn't like it. He had no loyalties to her beyond the spell she'd cast on him, but there was something about her that ran deeper than any spell, and Draco didn't enjoy being the sort of male who tricked and manipulated his women.

Even when they were attempting to trick and manipulate him back.

James still gave him that look that suggested he didn't entirely trust Draco, but Draco didn't care. This was about business at this point.

James looked to his alpha, who nodded, but then he looked at Jessie, as though waiting for her to make some kind of command against him.

Draco's heart did a pulsing thing in his chest that it rarely did anymore.

If Jessie asked him precisely what he wanted to speak with James about, he would be forced to tell her, and this whole thing would be over with before it had a chance to start.

She nodded, her arms crossed, still less than pleased about the fire situation.

"All right, it's all good. Let's go. I can show you around and let you know what your duties will be while you're here."

"Why should I have any duties to a dragon clan?" Even as he asked the insulting, and ungrateful question, James followed. Like a good little dog. Maybe having the wolves around wouldn't be the worst thing in the world. Not with obedience like this.

"You're still going to have to work to earn your way. Now shut up and stop complaining. I'll show you where the pantry is.

"You are *not* getting me to do any cooking."

"No, don't worry, sweetheart. I've got other talents that I need you for."

James frowned, and he looked more than a touch confused at the pet name, but he kept his mouth shut otherwise. Which was perfect. The good doggy was catching onto something, as if he finally figured out the frequency was a bit off.

Draco got the man alone, in the darkness of the pantry. He shut and locked the door, making sure that even if there was a fire blazing somewhere, that asshole warlock wouldn't be able to even sort of hear what they had to say.

"You pulled me in a dark pantry with limited space to be alone with you?" Draco heard the smile in James' voice. "Didn't know you felt this way about me."

"Shut up, idiot. I don't do people I don't know. Not unless they're beautiful ladies with big tits."

"Uh huh, so you are interested in kissing men?"

Fine. He wanted to play this stupid game? Draco leaned in a little closer until James was forced to back up against the door.

Right, they were both second in command for their respective groups, but Draco enjoyed finding out he was the true alpha between the two of them.

Draco let his hands settle on either side of James' head. In the darkness, Draco could still see with near perfection. He could see James' annoyance with him, and the stubborn turn of his mouth.

"I'm not altogether picky about my partners, though I do have a preference."

"Clearly. You act like a horny twelve-year-old around a woman who forced your alpha into serving him. You make your dragon clan look ridiculous."

Draco shrugged. "Don't care, and I respect Carlton, but I saw a good thing, and I wanted to take it."

Confusion lit up those, admittedly, pretty eyes.

"Oh, come on. Don't look at me like that. You wolves have the concept of mates, don't you?"

James jerked back as much as he was able to while

pressed against the door like that. "You're saying that crazy woman out there is your mate?"

"She is, and I'll thank you not to call her crazy. She is a lady in distress, and I have every intention of helping her."

"So why are you and I in here?"

Draco grinned. "Because we're going to seduce her."

17

JAMES

JAMES FOLLOWED Draco back to the main assembly of dragons and wolves on the mountain.

His head was still reeling.

Really? The guy wanted him and Patrick to willingly partake in this? Was he serious?

He was. Draco had just admitted he thought of the woman as his mate, and not even his mate, but an innocent damsel in distress who needed their aid to be free from the warlock.

He spoke of her almost as though she was a helpless angel, on the run from an abusive ex-boyfriend.

James wasn't entirely sure that was the amount of credit he was willing to give to her, but there wasn't much he could do other than keep on going with this.

Because it was a good idea.

The more freedom he, Patrick, and even Carlton and Draco had, the more she learned to trust them, and the better they would be able to do their jobs.

"Think about it," Draco had said. "Carlton and your idiot alpha nearly got her killed or maimed because they couldn't let her go, and she needs to see reason whenever they do have a good idea together, so she doesn't fight them on it. She needs to trust us, and that means bringing you in on this, too."

James didn't want to be in on it. Even though he hadn't wanted her, and he was only here for Patrick, the spell Jessie had cast on him was more than enough to make him feel a sense of loyalty to her.

He didn't want to betray her. Even though he kind of hated her, he also loved her. He wanted to protect her.

Because of her spell. Because it wasn't real. That was it. Nothing else.

Besides, the way Draco framed it did make sense.

This would be for her own good, and theirs.

They would stop fighting her spell, give in a little, and allow her to see that they could be helpful.

James might hate the way she'd gone about seeking her help, but only a minute of careful thought was needed for him to know that she was indeed a woman in distress.

Someone was out to hurt her, and Jessie might seem as though she was the sort of woman who could more than easily take care of herself, but there was clearly something else going there.

A quiet vulnerability about her that pulled James to her, made him want to comfort and cradle her.

So, yes, he gave into Draco's request. He would do this.

Now to make Patrick see the light, which, he guessed, would not be all that difficult.

James eyed Draco from the corner of his eye as they returned to the sides of their respective leaders, listening to them arguing over the best way to fortify the land in case of an attack of the physical variety.

Draco was a fool, immature, loud, and he even seemed kind of stupid, but there was a charm about his own self-flattery. James could understand why Jessie smiled at the man's jokes, bad as they were.

Then he frowned, shaking himself from those soft thoughts that had come upon him.

Was there...no. That could not be possible.

Just because Jessie had ensnared the lot of them didn't mean there was any chance in hell there would be that sort of impact.

So he put the thought away for later examination, watching as Patrick's wolf hair started to grow out from around his neck and face, his eyes transforming into their bright shade of gold. James saw the claws that he tried to hide with clenched fists, but he wasn't the only one losing control.

Spittle flew between both men as they screamed each other raw, and Carlton's dragon scales were starting to form along his arms, throat, and even his face.

And, of course, because the alphas were at it, the surrounding dragons and wolves became restless as well, as though they were getting ready to pounce on each other at the slightest hint from their leaders.

As for Jessie, for the first time, James felt a swell of pity for her, standing between both men, her expression frozen, as though she was at a loss as of what to do.

Did she forget she could simply command them to bend to her will? To stop fighting?

James needed to do something before a fight broke out among the wolves and dragons, and they were on the dragon home base. That meant high enough up an actual mountain where, even though the air was still very breathable, they could be thrown off to their deaths.

James went to Patrick, grabbed the man's elbow, and pulled him back.

Of course, his alpha attempted to yank his arm away,

to get at Carlton, but thankfully, Draco had a similar idea, if only to prevent them from killing each other.

"It's my land! My mountain! You do not give the orders here, you mutt!"

"It's the better plan, you fucking coward! We proved ourselves! We came up here! You should do this!"

James wasn't sure he wanted to know what it was Patrick wanted; he assumed something to do with the fires.

At least Roger did his job. The man stood between the alpha and the rest of the wolves, holding them back. Though, in all fairness, if they charged towards their alpha's rescue, there would be nothing to stop them.

There were too many of them.

Tristan seemed to be doing the same for the dragons, some of which already had their wings out.

And James lost his temper.

He punched Patrick in the side of the head.

Patrick flew to the side, but he stayed on his feet, because of course he did. He was not the alpha of the pack because he could be taken down from one little punch.

Even though James severely wished to hurt the man right about then.

Patrick realized quickly where the attack had come from, and he glared at James, the fur and fangs all coming to the forefront even more so now than they had a moment ago.

"What the fuck was that for?"

"Because you're being a fucking idiot! Stop fighting! You want to start a war on top of a fucking mountain?"

Patrick was the alpha, but there were reasons why alphas had second in commands. Every once in a while, he was needed to beat some sense back into Patrick's stupid head.

Patrick growled at him. That didn't stop James from thinking he was an idiot, and he wasn't going to back down either. He looked at Jessie. "What the hell do you think you're doing?"

She blinked. "What? What did I do?"

"Don't play innocent with me now. I'm not in the mood for it! You could have ordered them to stop with a snap of your fingers, and you didn't. If the leaders lose control, then so does the rest of the group. They will fight to the death if they think it's what their alpha wants of them. Do you want that?"

Jessie glared at him, a guilty flush rising up her neck and into her cheeks and ears. "Of course not!"

"So why did you let them fight like that?"

She crossed her arms, and James could swear she was starting to pout. "That's not your business. Maybe I just wanted to see if they could."

He nearly flew at her. He wanted to rip into her, to make her pay for putting them all in this position, spell and lust be damned.

He stopped at the sight of Draco's glare.

The man had stopped holding his own leader back, and he looked at James with glowing golden eyes, the sort of eyes that could almost belong to a wolf.

He stopped. He didn't move another muscle, almost as though he was frozen in place. In fact, it took him a second to realize that he really wasn't, and James relaxed.

"If you care so little about the well-being of our people, then you could be good enough to keep it to yourself. We're only here because you are forcing us. This isn't a vacation, and you mean about as much to me, to any of these people here, as they do to you."

"Noted," she replied, not looking at him, arms still crossed. As if she had anything to be defensive over.

James snapped. "No, it's *not* noted. They will fight for you because Patrick will, because Carlton will," James said, hesitant to even give the dragon that much credit at all. But credit where it was due. "They will fight for you, and some might even die for you. Show some Goddamned respect."

She still wouldn't look at him, which drove James up the damned wall.

Until he took note of the number of times she was blinking, and the shine in her eyes.

Really? Tears? That was not going to work on him.

"I won't be guilted or manipulated by you. I'm under your spell, so I will serve you, but nothing more than that. Do you understand?"

She glared back at him. "Perfectly."

18

JESSIE

JESSIE WAS SHOWN to a room of her own, something small, clean, but it didn't have its own bathroom, and the tiny closet was a joke. Not at all what she was accustomed to whenever she snared her men. It was fitting for perhaps a guest of low importance, but not for someone of her stature.

Though the room was located one level below where Patrick slept, and his offer to have two dragons watch outside her door for her protection was not lost on her.

He thought he would turn the tables on her, to jail her as she had done to him, but in a more literal sense.

Jessie went to the bed. She sat down, settling her hands into her lap. She inhaled a deep breath.

James' words to her still cut. They shouldn't have. He was meant to be bound to her, not her to him, and yet the look in his eyes as he accused her of not caring...

He demanded she show some respect.

She would like to. The idea was not exactly repulsive. Jessie had always respected soldiers, men who fought and died in wars to protect the weak. The dragon warriors and wolf combatants were hardly the same as the soldiers who were trained to go into battle for their countries.

There was more of an old world, casual violence about the dragons and wolves than there was about two countries at war, but still, the idea was there, and she did not want to think lightly of those who may very well die for her.

She hadn't allowed herself to think of that when she'd searched for her own small army to kill Valbrand, but she was here now, and she could no longer hide away from the idea that someone would die for her.

For no one to die would be impossible. If only two men died, it would be a small miracle.

But one she would still have to live with.

And since she could not so much as prevent Patrick and Carlton from wanting to tear into each other's throats, how could she keep the casualties low?

James thought her entirely heartless. He was only kind of right.

Jessie had attempted to pull the two warriors apart. She'd commanded them apart. Told them to stop, but they would not.

Jessie inhaled a sharp breath as she realized she was scratching nervously at her thighs. Staring down at her hands, her fingers trembled. One of her nails had broken. When did that happen? When she'd put herself between Patrick and Carlton?

Jessie clenched her hands, willing the trembling to vanish, but it did not.

No. This could not be. Could she really be losing her touch?

How? She'd had this gift for so many years; she'd used it enough that she was aware of her talent.

Jessie swallowed hard, pushing the worry back into the

deep recesses of her mind. Now was not the time. She would get that fear out of her system. That would not be happening now.

Most walls had eyes and ears. Jessie would not be so bold as to assume she was not being spied upon. This room had been chosen for her. Somehow, they were watching. Listening.

Calm. She would be calm, collected, and in control.

Jessie stood, she moved towards the closet, sliding open the door. There was much inside. Spare sheets, towels, pillowcases, though no clothing to speak of.

Did they hope she would hang herself?

She moved to the dresser next, also filled with more bed sheets, and the bottom dresser contained a duvet.

Irritated, Jessie stood tall. "If any of you believe I will be hanging myself, you're out of your minds." She slammed the dresser shut, crossing her arms, pacing about the room, thinking of her next move.

Her next move by now would have been to go and seduce the male she had bewitched, but this was different.

Because there were four of them.

She'd done two at a time. Even three at a time before on Valbrand's orders, but four?

That was a little ridiculous even by her standards.

She was no whore, after all.

But still, James hated her; there was no getting around that. He was clearly drawn to her. The spell made sure of that, but he pulled against it more than the other three.

Draco was the one she had the best chance with.

He seemed to genuinely be...

Nope. She would not entertain such foolish thoughts either.

There had only ever been one time when she'd thought one of the males she had ensnared began to love her in earnest. For months she'd feared releasing him from her spell. When she finally did, thinking her happy ending had come, he'd looked upon her with such disgust, such hatred.

Had he not been chivalrous, to this day Jessie thought he might have hit her for what she'd done to him. When he walked away, she had been devastated.

She was not going to make the mistake of assuming Draco was interested in her beyond what her spell required him to be.

Of course, Patrick and Carlton were showing hardly as much interest, and James showed none at all.

The two leaders of their people were bound to have more of a resistance to her whims, and James could be the sort of male who had more tolerance than was normal.

Draco was most likely weak-minded. They were bespelled much easier than anyone else tended to be.

The thought brought her no comfort.

A soft knock sounded at the door.

Jessie paused. "Who is it?"

A soft, feminine voice sounded from the other side of the thick, wooden door.

"Miss? I am here with your new clothes."

She hadn't ordered any, but Jessie announced she was free to let herself in anyway.

The heavy door opened, held open by one of the nameless dragon warriors sent to watch over her by Carlton, and in stepped a woman so tiny Jessie didn't know how it was possible she didn't fade away.

She was only a touch shorter than Jessie herself was, but the horns sprouting from her forehead and curling out like a ram's horns proved she was of dragon descent.

She also had a small bundle of clothing in her arms.

Jessie watched her. Even the smallest of packages

could be deadly. If this woman attacked, Jessie could hardly command her to stop.

Someone had attempted that on her once.

She hadn't enjoyed the experience.

The girl lifted the bundle of clothes a little higher, as though gesturing to them before setting them on the bed.

"What are those for? I didn't order any clothes."

The girl tensed. The door remained open. The two warriors watched Jessie and the little servant girl with raised brows, as though they were more concerned for the servant girl than anything.

Or they could be waiting for their little assassin to strike.

"I was told to bring these to you. They said you would want a change of clothes."

Jessie didn't see what was wrong with her own clothes, but the dress this girl wore looked to be something Jessie had seen servants wearing in the fifties. A black dress that went to the knees with a white apron. The clothing on the tiny bed was also black, the shoes a plain brown. They looked like work shoes, which did not give her a good idea of what Carlton thought of her.

"Where did these garments come from?"

"Oh, well...I brought them from the laundry room. They are freshly cleaned and pressed, miss."

That was not what Jessie had asked. She reached for one of the black dresses and...yeah, this was definitely the same servant's gown the girl in front of her wore, only it lacked the white apron.

She tried to decipher the message, what it could mean aside from a lack of civility on the part of her new hosts.

"Do you find my clothing now to be insulting?"

The girl tensed. "What?"

"Is what I am wearing now a problem?"

"Oh! Well, no. I find it to be very pretty." The girl blushed a little as she eyed Jessie up and down, taking in her attire and her shoes.

One of the warriors had to speak up. "You draw too much attention to yourself with that. There is no gala or ball happening around here, so you might as well dress in something more fitting."

She narrowed her eyes at the warrior. "I do not draw attention to myself with my clothing."

He sneered back. "Yes, you do. You know you do, that's why you wear that when you cast your wicked spells."

The other warrior reached across the space of the door and punched his friend in the arm. There was a growling sound coming from him. Jessie couldn't even see the man from his position, but she knew what he was communicating. He was likely glaring at his friend, commanding him to shut the hell up.

Right. This was going to have to be something she spoke with Patrick and Carlton about.

"Of course I would not expect men to be able to control themselves when one is dressed as well as I am. Tell me, girl. Do you think I draw attention to myself with my dress?"

Another blush. This was a shy one, wasn't she?

"Well, I think it's lovely, but...no one else looks the way you do."

Jessie's heart sank. "Really? I expected some support from a fellow woman."

"And you have it," said the girl quickly. "But, there are a lot of people here angry with you. If you continue to dress like that, they will spot you much quicker."

"And what does that matter to me?"

"You walk around like a princess," said the warrior,

clearly ignoring the warnings from his friend. "You piss people off when you act so pompous."

"Pompous?" She couldn't believe the filth she heard from their mouths.

Though the girl had already betrayed her, Jessie turned to her anyway. "Do you think I am pompous?"

The girl cringed. "I...well..."

"Sarah, come out of there. You owe her no explanations."

The girl looked towards the two guards; the relief on her face was not something Jessie had thought she would see.

Without a glance back, she rushed back to the door, as if that was where safety really was.

Jessie watched her go, stunned that such a small thing could feel safer around two males over one woman.

With a backwards glare, the warrior slammed the door shut.

There was no sound of a lock sliding into place, but that didn't matter. There didn't need to be. Jessie may not be entirely alone; even if no one watched her, she was certain they could hear her.

But she felt alone.

Because she was.

And for the first time in a long time, that feeling of isolation, of the weight of others despising her, crushed her.

She turned to the clothing left behind for her. Jessie lifted the plain dress.

It was clean. She had to give it that. There were no places that were in patches, but it would not fit her correctly, and she was absolutely not wearing those shoes.

Beneath the black dress was a pair of threadbare teal capri pants and a crop top, most likely meant for sleepwear, along with a toothbrush, fresh in its packet, and a tube of toothpaste.

No shampoos, conditioners, face creams, body oils, or perfumes.

The fact that these were her offerings was insulting. Jessie had been in vast homes, castles that could put this little village carved into the mountain to shame, where she had been welcomed and treated like a queen.

It may be an insult...but she would not let it break her.

They wanted her to blend in? Fine, she would, but she would do it her way.

Jessie put on the dress, but she was going to make a few minor touch-ups to it.

And she was not wearing those awful shoes.

When she was through, she would prove that, even dressed as a peasant, she could woo her new alpha males.

Their defenses were up? So be it. She hoped they were ready to have them taken down.

19

PATRICK

"ARE you sure this is such a great idea?"

Patrick didn't like it. His first instinct was to turn away from the thought entirely and not allow any of the men here to convince him of something so foolish, something that could hurt Jessie in the long term.

Draco seemed the most convinced, and the fact that he had James on his side proved he was able to make his case well enough.

Patrick still was not so sure.

Carlton seemed more interested.

"She wants to play games with us? Why should we not do the same back to her?"

"But it won't entirely be a game," Draco said quickly, turning back to Patrick. "She wants our loyalty. If we have hers, this will go much better. She will be willing to trust your command, and she won't simply get in the way when you both are having the sort of argument only an idiot could make."

Carlton glared at his second in command from behind him.

Patrick thought it was interesting the way the two of them seemed to come up with different ideas on how to best handle this situation using the same plan.

Draco seemed more interested in Jessie's best interests, which was hardly shocking, considering the way he mooned over her. Carlton, however, seemed more interested in taking back control over his life.

If the pull of loyalty he felt towards Jessie, and the lust that Patrick felt was anything to go by, then Carlton was only half serious.

He looked back down at James, knowing his friend inside and out. "Do you really believe this is the right course of action?"

James inhaled deeply through his nose. "I think we need to make her trust us. I don't want her to stand by while the two of you are fighting like that."

"She could have been doing that for any number of reasons," Draco said, always quick to defend her.

"She could have," Patrick agreed. "But I for one am grateful she chose to keep out of it."

James seemed scandalized to hear such a thing. "You both could have killed each other! And made our pack fight to the death with a clan of dragons on their territory."

"Afraid of being thrown off a cliff, little wolf?" Draco asked, and his smile annoyed even Patrick.

James growled. "Do not call me that."

Draco shrugged. "Whatever you say."

"You and I are the same height."

"But you are not quite as magnificent as I am. You cannot fly, and you're scared of losing to us, soooo....yeah, I'm all right with calling you out."

Now James looked as though he was the one who would fly into a rage. Patrick grabbed his friend's shoulder, and he looked at Carlton. "Would you?"

"Yes." Carlton brought his hand back before swinging it harshly forward, slapping Draco on the back of the head.

The other man jolted forward a bit, clearly thrown off by the strike he hadn't seen coming. He slowly turned back to look at his clan leader, eyes wide, betrayed.

Carlton shrugged. "He wasn't the only one you were annoying."

"Wonderful. Now that you're not pissed off, you can both pretend like you're the voices of reason when you nearly killed each other an hour ago?"

"Yes," Carlton said simply, which only seemed to annoy his second even more. If the man was not a dragon, Patrick might have liked him. His leadership style had a casual air about it, and yet the way Draco held his tongue suggested a great respect for his commander. Patrick only hoped he had managed to run his own pack in a similar fashion.

He was never telling that to Carlton, however.

Carlton looked to Patrick, now ignoring his friend. "I think it would be a good way for us to gain some of our own self-control back. You should think about it."

"I think that if we fuck around with a powerful succubus, or ghoul, or whatever the fuck she is too much, and she finds out about it, having to kill her former master will be the least of our worries."

"It's not that simple, we're not doing this maliciously," Draco said. "This is just to warm us up to her. You're all so cold. I can't do all the work by myself."

Patrick raised a brow at him. "What?"

Draco rolled his eyes. "Not that I'm faking anything. I meant everything I said to her. She is a beautiful lady, and I want to give her the freedom she craves."

"And maybe stick around to pick up the pieces when you're done with her former lover." Patrick was not asking a question.

"If she will have me. I happen to be a gentleman."

Patrick doubted that, but he was getting mixed messages here. "Are you telling me that you want us to seduce this woman so she will be more lenient with the commands she gives to us?" He looked at James. "Not so worried Carlton and I will kill each other if she is not there to command us, are you?"

James would not look at him. Patrick was still pissed off with the man, for being a traitorous bastard and demanding Jessie abuse her power over him simply because he and Carlton had been having a disagreement.

That was not in the least what he was interested in dealing with.

And James knew it.

"No, don't think about that," Draco said. He clearly was enjoying this idea a little too much, and he wanted to run with it. "This is not about hurting her. You are simply giving into the spell. You already feel this. The lust for her, the need to protect her. That's why you're struggling with the idea so much. You don't want us to hurt her."

"Because her spell forces that out of me. The same with you, in case you forgot."

Draco shook his head, a smile on his face that Patrick would have loved to punch off his mouth.

"I recognize true love when I see it, so don't you worry about me."

Patrick was taken aback by that. "What?"

"The dragon thinks he's mated to the woman," James deadpanned.

This time Patrick thought he'd definitely misheard something. "What?"

Carlton rolled his eyes, as though asking what could be done?

Draco smiled triumphantly at them, as though he was defiant in the feelings that had been revealed to them, daring any of them to question his love for the woman.

Patrick thought he was more likely to get his heart ripped out, if he was being sincere, but he honestly didn't care where the man directed his damned feelings. They were not Patrick's business, and he had no interest in learning more about the matters of his heart.

This situation with the four of them was already fucked up enough.

"I don't want to do anything that could make her harm my people. We know nothing about her, how violent she is willing to get, what revenge she will take on my pack or your clan if we fail, let alone what she might do if she discovers we're not entirely sincere."

"It's a spell designed to force loyalty and encourage lust," Carlton deadpanned. "Of course we're not sincere. If she does not realize that from the start, she can only be a fool."

That was the truth, and Patrick hated that it had been Carlton to point it out.

"So, will you agree?" Carlton asked. "This can only be helpful for all of us."

"If she wants to fuck, none of us here will have much of a say in it anyway, which I'm sure Draco will be more than pleased with."

Draco stuck his hands over his heart. "My queen can tie me down and have her wicked way with me, and I will be her humble servant throughout the entire process."

Patrick shook his head. "God, I hope your alpha slaps you again."

"On it," Carlton said, winding his hand back, but Draco

was quick to duck out of the way before the other man could take his swing.

The man pointed at his leader and laughed. "Ha ha, not quite so fast there now, are you?"

"He doesn't need to be." James made the wind up this time, and because Draco didn't see it coming, James got the privilege of striking Draco on the back of the head.

Draco turned, teeth and claws at the ready before Carlton reached out and grabbed him by the back of the neck, yanking him away.

"Stop that. James, thank you."

James nodded. "You're welcome."

Patrick rolled his eyes. This was going nowhere. He wanted to get this over with, and it seemed he wasn't going to get out of this without being strong-armed.

They were determined, and every objection he'd had to their ridiculous plans was met with the sort of explanations and cushioning that would have made the three men around him excellent salesmen.

"All right. I agree."

James looked at him. "You do?"

Patrick clenched his teeth. He didn't want to do this. He wanted to stay loyal, honest. He wanted to serve her.

He wanted to save her.

"It's like you said." Patrick mentally repeated the phrase in his mind over and over again. "If she wants our bodies, it's not like there's much I can do about it to stop her anyway. Might as well give in and give her what she really wants when she comes to take it."

"But just make sure you do it with a smile," Draco said, smiling widely himself as he pointed at Patrick.

Patrick didn't understand it. "If you honestly believe she is your mate then why the hell would you want me to do this? Why would you want to share her with anyone?

Spell or no spell?" Patrick had never been mated before, but he was willing to bet that he wouldn't want to share the woman he'd mated with for anyone.

Draco frowned at him. "What are you talking about?"

Patrick couldn't believe it. "Did you really not think about this before agreeing with this stupid idea? If you honestly think you're mated to the woman, why would you ever bother with sharing her with someone else? Let alone three other males?"

Draco stared at him, his brows still furrowed, as though he hadn't thought of it at all and didn't quite know what to say now that the subject had been brought up.

Patrick was ready to yell at the man for being such an idiot when a heavy knock sounded at the door.

The four of them spoke in unison.

"Not now!"

A guard called out to them from the other side. "Miss Jessica is here to see you."

The lot of them froze. Patrick had never felt such a chill run through his blood before.

Had she heard them? What would he do if she had?

His entire pack, his best friend, were all at her whims and mercy. If she knew they were plotting against her...

"Let her in," Carlton called, composing himself before anyone else seemed to.

The door opened. Jessica stepped inside, wearing...not what she had on when he'd first seen her in the woods.

The little black number with one strap across her shoulder was gone. This was something plainer, but with her scarlet scarf wrapped around her waist and tied off in a bow at her side, while still wearing the same heels he'd met her in, she was as stunning as ever.

Her slim legs, which he hadn't been able to see so well

in her other dress due to its length, shone like the stars they were.

Patrick cleared his throat, willing his body to stop being so tense as blood began to flow. "I thought you said you were sending her plain clothes to wear?"

"I did," Carlton replied, narrowing his eyes at Jessie's impish smile. "I sent you something common."

"And I am wearing it."

Patrick barely stopped himself from smiling.

She was wearing it all right.

Somehow, she'd managed to make herself appear just as beautiful and glamorous as if she was wearing the same getup she'd worn when he met her.

It was the heels. Had to be. Patrick could recall one of the women of his pack wearing jeans, a simple white T-shirt, hair in a loose ponytail and sunglasses resting on top of her head, the picture of casual, so he didn't understand why she'd bothered with the black pumps.

"Shoes make the outfit," she'd replied in a way he didn't entirely understand, but still had to agree with.

Because he could see the proof first hand. She had looked as though she'd barely rolled out of bed, slapped on her clothes before applying some lipstick and sticking her feet in those heels, and yet somehow, she managed to look ready to meet the president.

Jessie looked ready to meet the queen of England.

And Patrick cursed Carlton for his sloppy thinking, because now all Patrick wanted to do was get her out of those clothes to see how the rest of her body looked. He had a general picture in his head, but now it was time to see if the fantasy matched the reality.

And it helped not at all when Jessie made a flirty little twirl. The dress fanned out, exposing more of her legs, showing just a touch of her thighs.

Enough to tease.

Unfortunately, it looked as though the dress itself wasn't designed to go up any higher no matter how much twirling she happened to be doing. Otherwise, Patrick was positive she would have been twirling the night away, giving them a real show.

"Do you like it? If I'd had more time, I could have added more to it."

"You tore the sleeves off," Carlton said accusingly.

"What is she wearing?" James asked, clearing his throat as his voice croaked just a touch.

"That's supposed to be one of the dresses the cleaners wear," Draco said, his voice laced with accusation.

"Right," Jessie said. "That nice girl you sent to me said you wanted me to blend in a little more, but there was no way I was going to wear this as it was. So I shortened the sleeves—gives my arms some breathing room, and I really couldn't stretch like that, and with my scarf tied to the side, I think it adds a touch of color to the piece."

"Where are the shoes she gave you?" Carlton sighed.

"I was never going to wear those."

"You can't run in high heels," Patrick said, knowing where this was going.

Jessie shrugged, as casual as though she was entirely in command of the situation. "I have no intention of running, and it's not sexy wearing shoes like that. It encourages slouching."

Was that true? Her shoes did make her legs look... tight. What was it about high heels that made a woman's ass and legs look so good he wanted to reach out and touch them?

And why the hell couldn't he control himself? He was a fucking alpha. He knew how to put the needs of his pack over his dick; he'd done it before. Spell or no spell, this should have been easy.

Yet his wolf pulled him to this woman. It howled at the sight of her.

Because she was as worthy of worship as any full moon.

"You're not here to look sexy," Carlton said, showing a better level of control, and anger, at her design choices. "You're here for our protection. I don't want you to stick out like a wounded calf among lions."

"Bit dramatic," Jessie deadpanned.

"It's not dramatic; it's the truth. I don't know what happens to Draco, my clan, or myself if you die while I'm still bound to you. So I won't have anything happening to you until we have that man's head."

She smiled at him, and Patrick found himself so infuriatingly jealous that he wanted to go over to Carlton and punch the bastard in the throat.

"You do care."

Patrick wouldn't have thought so, and yet the soft accusation made the man actually blush?

Patrick couldn't believe it—he blinked a few times just to make sure—but sure enough, there it was. The man was blushing. The flush rising up his neck was plain to see, even if his expression remained neutral.

Draco stepped forward. "We do care, sweetheart. We want to help you."

"That's good," Jessie replied. "Because, while you were all up here talking about seducing me, I thought I would come and make it just a little easier for you all."

Patrick was dick-punched with those words. Not just him, either. It was as though the air had been sucked out of the entire room, and as Jessie approached him, there was little Patrick could do but stand there, waiting for this demon-like creature to exact her revenge.

"This was our decision, and the pack had nothing to do with it," Patrick stated as she stood before him, staring up at him with that deceptively sweet smile. "Or his clan." Seemed only fair to point that out, too. Just in case she happened to be plotting something unfortunate for the dragons who lived here as well.

The look on her face suggested that wasn't exactly what she had in mind as she put her arms up and around Patrick's neck.

Aside from when he'd drank her blood and was put under her curse, this was the first time she'd touched him. Her skin was soft, warm, and inviting. He was suddenly much more aware of the floral scent of her, and with how close she was, her bottom lip seemed so much fuller. It looked naturally red.

He wanted to bite it.

"Don't worry. I think it's a great idea," she said, and he could do nothing as she pulled his face down and kissed him on the mouth.

JAMES

HE COULDN'T BELIEVE IT. She was just…kissing him.

And James was stuck, right here, watching her, so unbelievably jealous of her, and of him. He didn't know what to do with himself.

The other two men in the room were silent as they watched the show. It was slow kissing, quiet, kind of sweet. Patrick wasn't grabbing at her ass, and she wasn't exactly throwing her leg around the back of his knees, clutching at him like she wanted to do him in front of everyone.

It seemed more a gentle, promising sort of kiss.

And James wanted to tear her away from Patrick. He wanted to put his mouth against hers because he wanted to know what Patrick tasted like. It would be the closest he would ever get to kissing the other man, but he also wanted to know what *she* tasted like.

He wanted to know what Patrick and Jessie together tasted like, what they felt like against his mouth and on his body.

And that was so fucked up he didn't know what to do with it, and yet, he couldn't turn away from them either.

Couldn't stop blood from rushing down to his cock.

Draco openly groaned, making no effort to contain himself, the whining prick.

"Uh, okay. I really thought you would want to kiss me first, but I guess I'm going to have to wait, aren't I?"

"You'll get your turn," James snapped.

And he had no doubt the dragon would.

She might not entirely be a demon, a ghoul, a succubus or whatever, but she was partly those things.

They all wanted her, and she'd known they were planning on going against her wishes. She'd known they were plotting behind her back.

So of course she had to prove who was really in charge around here.

Jessie pulled her mouth back from Patrick's slowly. A pretty flush had formed across her cheeks as she smiled at him.

Patrick's lips seemed a little darker now than they had been a moment before, and James was so fucking jealous his stomach knotted.

The way he looked at her...the way she looked at him...

Too much. It was too much to handle.

Except then Jessie half turned in Patrick's arms. She looked right at him, reaching out her hand. "Don't just stand there like a third wheel. Get over here."

He tensed. "What?"

"Come on," she said, then looked at the others in the room, and if he wasn't mistaken, there was an aura of shyness around her. "I've never done four at the same time before, gentlemen. You're all going to have to be a bit gentle with me."

Draco groaned again. James looked right at Patrick, catching his eye.

She wasn't just going to take them one at a time. She was really...

"Well, come on now." Jessie motioned for him to come closer, and this time, he couldn't refuse.

Now he was the one feeling shy. He wanted her, but he wanted Patrick, too. To stand this close to the both of them together excited him, made the hairs on his body stand on end and his skin vibrate with anticipation.

"I'd like to ease into it, if you wouldn't mind. I'll start with the two of you. Carlton and Draco can stand back for a bit until I'm nice and comfortable. How does that sound?"

James swallowed hard, looking between her and Patrick, and something passed between him and his alpha, a sort of knowledge of where this would end up when they were done.

It was Patrick who answered. "That sounds fine to me."

JESSIE

FOR THE FIRST TIME IN...SHE didn't even know how long, Jessie felt a sense of nervous, sexual anticipation.

There was nothing fearful in it. Not like her first time seducing a man for Valbrand. She'd known she was beautiful then, and it was simply a matter of putting the artistry of her looks and grace into practice in the bedroom.

To steal a man's soul, and make him happy to have it gone for her, required a delicate touch at some times, and a firm hand at others.

This was different. Patrick pressed his lips to her throat, and as though his mouth was made of fire, liquid heat cascaded down her throat and shoulder, across her abdomen, and to her sex.

She opened her mouth, a silent sigh escaping her.

But he was not done yet. Strong hands gripped her by her waist, and that same heat imprinted on her skin through her dress.

How...was he doing that?

James watched. His pupils dilated. She could make out

the sound of his heart thudding heavily against his ribcage, as though it was trying to pound its way out. Through the heat that overwhelmed her, Jessie smiled at him, knowing this was everything he could ever want. She could be cruel and let him watch for a little while longer. But that didn't seem right.

Not for the moment that was being created between the five of them.

Despite the fact that this was being set up to be the best orgy of the year, there was a pleasant vibe in the air that she didn't want to break.

A fragile mood that warmed her.

Safety.

Not simply because she could command these men, but in the short time she'd known them, she'd come to discover that these males had honor.

Genuine honor. They didn't simply preach it; they lived by it.

She could release them from their bonds, and they would not dare harm a hair on her head.

That was a nice feeling. That was something that made it easier when James came to her.

He seemed so innocent. She knew he wasn't. It was this particular scenario that was new to him.

And he wanted Patrick as well as her.

"Have you ever had a threesome before?" she asked, knowing the answer before he spoke.

He didn't answer so much as he glared at her, his cheeks coloring.

"I didn't think so."

"Don't tease him," Patrick said, his voice a firm rumble against her skin.

She sighed, closing her eyes. "I am not teasing him. Just checking." She reached for James, taking him by the back of his head and pulling him forward. He went with ease, and it was sweet the way his eyes fell shut before their mouths met.

Yes, he was definitely the boy next door type. One of her favorite types.

Right behind the protector, which every male in here more certainly was.

She pressed her tongue forward, parting his lips, then gasped her shock when James threaded his fingers through her hair, gripping tight as he turned her head at just the right angle to take control.

And did he ever take control.

It was so unexpected that for a good two seconds, Jessie found herself simply standing there, a shocked noise escaping her as his tongue pushed deep into her mouth.

And…she couldn't lie to herself. It was nice. A weak-kneed sort of nice. The kind of nice that made her have to hold onto his shoulders just to keep herself upright.

Not that she was going to let him know that. Jessie locked her knees, and she made sure to keep the pressure on his shoulders to a minimum. So long as he didn't feel too much of her weight holding tightly to his body, it should be enough to prevent him, and any of the other men in the room, from knowing how much this got to her.

That wasn't right. This should not be getting to her like this. She needed to take back her control over the situation and remind him of who was really boss around here.

And yet, she could not.

It was as though his mouth, his hands, the firm press of his strong chest, all worked together to create a neat little blanket of warmth and protection around her.

How could she not be lulled into a false sense of security by something like that?

Pulling her mouth back, Jessie was finally able to get a look at James's face again. The ever so slight separation between their bodies also allowed her body temperature to simmer down to something a tad more manageable.

Though she was still burning up, and James looked at her as though she was something to eat.

Jessie withdrew herself a little.

She wasn't used to that. To people looking at her like that. At least not after the kissing and heavy petting had already begun. Before the clothes came off, and even a little bit during the seduction, sure, Jessie would allow her prey to feel as though they were still the ones in control.

This was not the same as any of that. This felt more as though she'd fallen under his spell, without even knowing he'd cast one to begin with.

James' eyes fell to half-mast. Jessie could make out the heavy thudding of his beating heart.

He had her exactly where he wanted her, exactly where he could hurt her, and yet his hands remained gentle with her.

Oh, right. Her spell. He couldn't hurt her even if he wanted to. He didn't have any choice in that.

So why did it look as though he'd forgotten about her spell as much as she had?

"That was…"

Jessie shook herself out of that warm, fluffy blanket she'd found herself curling up in. She brought herself back to the real world before she could let herself lose sight of what was really important around here.

Not wanting Patrick to feel as though he was the third wheel here, she reached out for him, too.

He wasn't exactly far away, and when her hand

touched his enormous forearm, the heat in his body shot through her as though powered by a missile.

He stepped into their circle. She didn't have to pull him. He was already drawn to her, to them, like a magnet.

"Want to taste?"

Jessie brought her hands up, cupping his cheeks. He was all hard angles and edges. The rough texture of his face stubble against her hand excited her, and when she brought him down to kiss her...

It felt a little as though he was kissing both her and James, which was even better.

James groaned, watching them. She felt the heat of his body radiating from him as he was forced to look on as the man he loved kissed the woman he was in lust with.

Since he was so clearly enjoying the sight of her mouth in Patrick's seconds after she had been kissing James, why not see how much farther she could take this?

The instant Patrick groaned, the sound a gentle vibration against her mouth, Jessie let her tongue slide across the crease of his mouth before she pulled back.

His wasn't the only groan she heard as she turned her attention back to James.

"God, I wish I was you right about now," Draco said, watching Patrick with a clear look of jealousy in his half-lidded eyes. His lips were parted just slightly, a dusting of pink across his cheeks and nose.

And she knew James was thinking the exact same thing.

Only inverted.

He was jealous of Jessie.

Of her mouth.

"Want to know what he tastes like?"

If it embarrassed him for her to say that in front of Patrick, or the dragons in the room, he didn't show it.

In fact, James leaned into her, eager to taste her, to get any hint of Patrick off her mouth as he tilted her head back and made her feel like a woman for the first time in years.

Not simply something meant to be fucked, or a distrustful demon.

But a woman worthy of worship.

And she was into it. Jessie didn't think she would be. She couldn't believe that James, of all people, was making this heat surge through her.

She'd had him pegged as the shy one.

But he commanded her mouth, licked her tongue, and made her body sizzle like a true expert in the field.

She had to pull back from him, if only because he was showing a little too much talent in this regard, and she needed to catch her breath.

Not that she was ever going to let him know that.

"You are talented, but let's take this somewhere more comfortable."

She took James by his hand, reached for Patrick's, and led both of them towards the bed.

They came with her easily. Though they were hardly lambs to the slaughter.

Despite her efforts, the seduction she put forth into the world around them, they continued to exude a certain control she could not overcome.

All the while, Draco watched them with a fixated expression. Carlton crossed his arms, looking as though this whole thing was something of a bother, but Jessie knew better in that respect as well. He was just trying to be a big and tough alpha. He'd get his turn.

Jessie sat on the bed. She pulled James with her first and was pleased when he looked only at her; when he came to her as though Patrick was not even there.

She grabbed his shoulders, pulling him on top of her, but he stopped quickly.

"Wait."

She froze. "What? What's the matter?"

"Well…" He looked back at Draco and Carlton.

Ah, yes, there was the shy aspect about him that she knew and loved.

Carlton smiled in a way that showed off one of his fangs.

"Feeling a little shy now, pup?"

James growled at him.

Draco shrugged, grinning. "Hey, if you want me to step in until you're ready to be a man, I'm totally all right with filling in until you get your shit together."

"Gentlemen." Jessie rubbed James' neck and shoulders. "No fighting over me. This is meant to be a bonding moment." With a small touch to his cheek, she pulled James' attention back to her. One look was usually all it took to convince the men, and even the few women, she'd seduced to see things her way, but he still seemed unsure.

It was Patrick who saved the day when he put his hand to the back of James' neck.

James snapped his attention to the other man, and even Jessie was impressed with the eagerness in Patrick's eyes.

"You and I are going to show those lizards how it's done."

"Hey! Who are you calling a lizard, you furball?"

Everyone ignored Draco.

James' pupils dilated. Jessie would have to be blind not to see it.

The strength of which Patrick held James under his own spell was impressive. Perhaps even stronger than any spell Jessie could cast, and he wasn't even intending on doing it.

She was jealous of him because James' affection for Patrick was at least real.

Great, now she was finding herself struggling not to hesitate.

Patrick's powerful hands took her face, he turned her attention back to him, and she was all he could see.

"Don't get cold feet on us now."

He kissed her, and, ah, there it was. That sweet heat and tingling lust she'd almost lost with her pesky second thoughts.

Patrick let his tongue slip into her mouth. He tasted her sweetly before pulling back, reaching for James, and pushing them together so James could, once again, taste Patrick on her mouth.

And he was determined to take as much of the other man's flavor as she could give.

Jessie was stunned that she could hardly keep up. That hadn't happened in well over a century. Where a man could leave her as breathless as James and Patrick were both doing to her right now. No matter. It had been some time since she'd had sex. Her body was just in need of the release. There was nothing special about the situation that required any of her attention.

Holding onto James' shoulder, sighing as he pushed her to lie back on the bed, Jessie could say she was sufficiently buzzed on pleasure now as he lifted her skirts and settled between her legs.

JAMES

THERE WAS something so utterly erotic about kissing this woman and tasting the man he really wanted on her mouth.

Both of them. Together. Watching Patrick kiss her, seeing his tongue tasting her lips, and then to have this demon woman reach for him, pull him close, and wrap herself up around him...

He was entirely under her spell, and so long as James got to kiss her like this, he didn't care.

She could suck the soul right out of him, and he would give it to her.

He would give everything to her and not make a single complaint.

As long as she let him taste her.

Jessie lifted her knees, her thighs squeezing James' waist, encouraging him to push against her, his cock throbbing against his pants and her panties. He felt her heat there, sensed the throbbing of her heart, and knew she wasn't faking her reactions.

He'd expected that of her. Why wouldn't a succubus

creature fake pleasure when she was in the middle of taking what she wanted from her victim?

But no. It was all over her.

"You're liking this," he said.

She blinked. Her pretty eyes dilated. James hadn't noticed how long her lashes were before now. He liked that, in the men and women he was with.

"Why wouldn't I enjoy it?"

Shit. He didn't think it would be the best idea in the world to answer that.

Luckily, Draco opened his big mouth again, and it ended up saving the day for him.

"Not that I don't enjoy a little bit of erotic dirty talk, but if you're going to grill her about this, I'm telling you, I wouldn't mind taking your place."

James tried not to roll his eyes. He really did, but he couldn't help it. "If you would shut the fuck up, that would be great. You're a little too distracting over there."

Draco's offense was obvious in his voice. "What?"

Carlton growled, and James glanced to the side at the other two men in the room just as the other dragon slapped his hand over Draco's mouth, stopping him from saying whatever stupid thing he'd been about to say.

"He will stay silent, or we will walk out of here and give them their privacy. Won't we, Draco?"

It was clearly a threat, and while part of James wanted them to get the hell out of here so he could enjoy Jessie, just him and Patrick and her, another part of him, the part that was being manipulated by the spell, wanted to keep them here.

For several reasons. One, because Jessie didn't entirely belong to him, and she wanted them here, but also, he wanted them to see that he was going to be the first person to take her. Even before Patrick.

And they were all going to have sit back and watch.

But not Patrick. James was more than happy to share his first time with a beautiful, morally dubious seductress with Patrick.

It could almost be a bonding moment between the three of them.

And keeping the dragons out of that, even for a few more hours, seemed petty and fun.

Draco glared at him from beneath Carlton's hand, but that was too damned bad for him. James didn't so much as look at the other man in case he was to take the smile on his face as a challenge.

Not that James wanted to piss off Jessie too much either.

No man wanted to irritate a woman moments before getting laid.

Well, not unless that happened to be their thing, but James didn't know her well enough to make that risk.

"Since you were told about this dress, I'm pretty sure Carlton will forgive me for this."

"For what? Hey!"

She learned real quick what he was doing, and James was pretty sure she heard the ripping sound of her dress before she saw his claws come out.

James couldn't help but take a little pleasure in tearing the dress down the middle of her breasts.

Of course they popped out perfectly. Everything about her seemed to be perfect. He couldn't figure out why, other than that was how she was designed.

To be the perfect soldier of seduction for her former master.

He banished the thought, putting more of his focus on her breasts as he freed them, all the while enjoying the jealous stares he could feel on his back as he tasted Jessie's nipple.

Her fingernails scratched through his hair and against his scalp. Her gasp was the fuel he needed to keep going as she thrust her chest forward, as if that would put her pink bud deeper into his mouth.

That was fine. So long as she kept scratching at his scalp, he would do whatever she wanted him to do.

Patrick groaned. "God, James. You should see what you both look like right now."

James didn't so much as let himself look at the other man. He kept his entire focus on Jessie. If he distracted himself from her body, he knew she wouldn't forgive him, and she might throw him off in favor of one of the dragons to spite him.

And since he would rather slice off his own pinky finger than let Draco at her first, he kept to his task.

And honestly, she tasted good. Better than any other woman he'd ever had.

With a soft groan, he brought his mouth to her other nipple, licking and teasing it, waiting for his body to remind him that he shouldn't want this so much, that he should not be putting so much of his focus on giving her any sort of pleasure. He was supposed to be playing a part here.

This was meant to be work, not pleasure.

But he was weak, and her taste intoxicated him. Patrick's eyes on them made him even drunker on that pleasure, and before he knew it, James found himself thrusting against her sex, her panties wet.

He could smell her. His own musk, Patrick's skin, and the other males in the room all came together into a heady mix that made him need to be inside her all the more.

Patrick's voice, encouraging him on, was enough to make James tremble.

Jessie's soft groans of pleasure as he stripped her out of the rest of her clothes, cutting away some material and slowly sliding the rest off her shoulders and down her legs, just added to the sensation.

"Inside me. Hurry." Her raspy breathing against the heat of his shoulder, the scrape of her teeth against the shell of his ear, spoken softly as it was, might as well have been a command given by a queen.

James wouldn't dare disobey.

Yes, he could see why she was a succubus. And a talented one at that. She was good. Good enough that he not only didn't care, but he was starting to forget. As he spread her thighs open, settling himself between them and pressing the head of his cock against her sex, James started to think of her almost as though she was a real woman.

Thrusting forward, spurred on by an animalistic desire to fuck, to mate, it was easy to understand why his body would make the mistake of assuming this was a human woman.

She sure as hell felt like the real thing around his shaft.

Draco groaned from where he sat. James didn't look at him, but he kind of hoped the dragon shifter was touching himself.

Jessie opened her eyes finally after having them squeezed shut. When she looked at him, there was something innocent about her, and James felt a swell of protective instinct well up within him.

Playfulness, too.

"Gotta give the lizard a good show," he said.

Jessie blinked at him, the deeper shade of pink flashing over her cheeks and nose.

God, why did she have to be so fucking beautiful? Especially when she smiled back at him and gripped at his hair again.

"A good show," she agreed. "And make sure to share with your friend over there."

Even as James shallowly thrust into of her, he couldn't help the rush of embarrassment when she said that.

Not that it was enough to make him stop thrusting into her, but he couldn't believe that he actually managed to forget about Patrick.

This was definitely a spell. Otherwise that *never* would've happened.

Patrick was as good and patient about this sort of thing as James would have thought he would be. He sat on the bed, reclining mostly, watching the pair of them fucking each other in front of him, inches away, with his eyes half-lidded and dark with lust.

Their eyes met, and James was pretty sure he didn't see any of that lust diminish as Patrick stared back at him.

Distracted, James briefly stopped thrusting into Jessie.

It was almost as if some of that lust was meant for him...

"Don't stop," Jessie begged, her grip on his hair becoming painful. But in a good way. "Don't stop." She began thrusting her pelvis back against his, desperate for some of that friction, even if he wasn't moving.

But her sweet, begging voice, the grip on his hair, and the way she sucked back against him was enough to snap him out of his distracted thoughts.

Because now there is something a little more interesting happening.

Keeping his gaze locked on with Patrick's, James fucked into her, giving her exactly what she needed, what she *begged* him for.

Release.

He felt it when it hit her, the clench of her wet sex around his cock, her pussy so hot and slick that the sounds of her moaning beneath him, the way she dragged her fingernails down his back, made it impossible for him to hold off that surge of pleasure that threw him over the edge against his will.

Better still was when Patrick leaned between them, his mouth capturing Jessie's in a passionate kiss as she squirmed and moaned beneath James.

James groaned, the grip of release finally letting him go, leaving him weak and heaving for breath.

He watched with pleasure as Patrick closed his eyes, enjoying Jessie's mouth in the throes of her pleasure.

He was so lulled by the sight he didn't have the chance to feel any sense of jealousy over it, just a peaceful air that this was right.

Patrick wasn't his, but Jessie was theirs, and that was something they could share.

So, as those thoughts fluttered lazily through his head, James had no chance to bring up any sort of defense when, out of the blue, Patrick pulled away from Jessie's mouth, grabbed James by the back of his head, and kissed him full on the mouth, too.

James tensed. He held perfectly still, did not move as Patrick worked his mouth open and licked inside his mouth, and it was...

Holy shit.

Patrick pulled back quickly, looking massively pleased with himself when he smiled like that.

Draco whistled, and when James looked down, Jessie seemed oddly pleased with herself, as though she had been the mastermind behind this entire scenario.

23

PATRICK

PATRICK WASN'T sure where it came from that he did such a thing as kiss his best friend while he was still inside the woman Patrick wanted to fuck, but in that moment, it seemed right, so why not do it?

And he had to admit, it was amusing the way James stared at him. Wide-eyed and deer in the crosshairs during hunting season.

"What...what was that for?"

Jessie continued to stroke the back of James' neck and shoulders. The pleased expression on her face made Patrick want her all the more.

But watching her touch James, knowing she would soon be touching him like that, that she was his as much as she was James', excited him like nothing else.

"Patrick, why did you do that?"

He shrugged. "Why not?"

"He's just trying to make you relax," Jessie said. "Worked, didn't it?"

She wouldn't stop smiling. She knew what she'd done. Patrick had picked up on what James did not. He was the one most suspicious of her, and so she'd allowed him inside her first, allowed her guard down for James so he could fuck her, kiss her, and even love her.

Within the bounds of the spell they were all under, but it was clearly a tactic that had worked.

And James had been none the wiser about her scheme. Patrick was even willing to believe that his need to kiss both of them had been part of her plan.

But to want Patrick to kiss his best friend would require this demon woman to not have a heart made entirely out of stone.

Perhaps there was something here he wasn't seeing.

Draco saw it. Carlton? Hard to tell, but if this was the direction of Jessie's plans, Patrick could allow himself to believe that she wasn't all bad.

For now. This could be part of her plan as well.

The mark of a true manipulator would be her ability to keep her prey from knowing what she was really doing.

For that, he would still keep his guard up. If only a little.

James turned away from Patrick, still looking dazed, his face redder than it had been when he'd orgasmed.

Jessie laughed. "Don't get shy on us now."

"I'm not," James said, and Patrick was charmed by the pouty tone of his voice.

Draco groaned. "I just hate both of you right now. You've got a goddess in your bed, and neither of you will shut up. Only one of you has had your fun, and it's like you're both purposely taking your time to torment me."

"All good things come to those who wait, my darling," Jessie said, looking toward Draco, adjusting her grip around James and winking.

Draco really did look as though he was about to implode. He was the one who claimed to be naturally mated to her, after all. If that was the case, he must be desperate to make his claim.

Carlton seemed to be holding himself together well. Which meant he had a better poker face than Patrick would have thought possible, and that he had to hurry up.

Two horny dragons might pose a problem, and it was either a miracle or the product of the spell that they weren't all killing each other for their chance to get at Jessie.

Patrick grabbed James' shoulder, kissed him there, and then his throat, feeling the hitch in the other man's breath and the jumping of his heart as Patrick leaned in close to his ear.

"Keep watch for me, James. I don't want these dragons to try anything."

Draco growled. From the corner of Patrick's eye, he could see the man's scales and a few of his horns appearing over his flesh, but Patrick ignored it.

James was quick to do as he was told. He pulled back from Jessie. She didn't so much as move to cover herself. She smiled up at him, perfect breasts moving in time with her breathing. A painted fingernail slid across the side of her mouth, almost as though she was thinking about something as she looked at him, waiting.

The only thing she did do was press her knees together, but even that made her allure that much more powerful.

Patrick leaned in as James sat back.

Jessie tilted her head to the side as Patrick's hand slid between her thighs, finding her wet sex.

"Mmm, I thought the point of bringing both of you into bed with me was for a little togetherness bonding. Are you all really going to take your turns with me one at a time like this?"

"I have no problem stepping in if you want," Draco said.

If a man could ever sound like a kicked puppy, then it was Draco who pulled that sound off better than anyone Patrick had ever heard.

And he wasn't the canine in the room.

Jessie didn't take her eyes from Patrick, and when she glanced down at James, Draco, and Carlton, she nodded. "I see. You want someone to keep watch in case the big bad dragons try to do something you don't want them to, is that it?"

"The only reason we're not killing each other right now is because of your spells," Carlton replied. "He would be a fool to lower his guard around us."

Draco looked very much as though he wanted to say something to that, but he chose to keep his mouth shut, which was probably for the best.

Likely, he didn't want to appear anymore desperate now than he already was.

Jessie, on the other hand, seemed entirely unconvinced by the dangers of two enemy species sharing not only their space, but a woman, and between four of them made it worse.

She was entirely unmoved by this. She rolled her eyes, and Patrick had never seen a more dramatic eye roll in his entire life. "Men. I swear you can do nothing right when measuring your dicks."

"I'm not measuring anything but the time it's taking me to get at you," Draco said.

Jessie nodded sagely. "Good to know."

"Wait, are you going to measure us?" James asked.

It was not the sort of question he would have expected to hear from his friend. Patrick looked at him, and James rubbed at the back of his neck, pretending there was something just above the bed that was much more interesting for him to be looking at.

"I might be," Jessie said, shrugging. "I still have yet to pick my favorite among you."

Draco choked back a shocked noise, his eyes flaring wide. Patrick couldn't tell if he was more horrified or stunned.

James's mouth pressed into a firm line. He refused to look at her, color rising up his chest, neck, and into his face.

Patrick was certain he didn't imagine the small clenching of Carlton's jaw, and he had to admit that he didn't feel so great about the comment either.

Jessie laughed. "I really am making the lot of you jealous, aren't I?"

"No!" said James and Draco at the same time.

Jessie sighed. "I was worried something like this might happen. All right. All of you in bed with me, right now."

James tensed. "Wait. What?"

"It's going to take more than this before we're all besties, isn't it?" she asked as if the answer was meant to be honest. "Come on. There's more than enough room for all of us in here."

"Finally," Draco sighed, jumping to his feet.

James tensed. "You can't expect us to share a bed with dragons."

"You're more than free to get out of my spot there, pup," Draco said, shrugging out of his shirt and kicking his pants off.

Patrick eyed the man's body as he put his knee onto the bed and crawled towards Jessie.

A swell of protective jealousy came over Patrick, but he would be dead before he admitted it was there.

169

Draco waited no time, crawling over Jessie's naked body, his eyes locked onto hers.

James growled a little at the man as he got into Patrick's space, but Patrick could handle himself.

He put his hand out, stopping Draco before he could entirely take over.

More of Draco's scales appeared, scattering across his body, and where Patrick's hand was on the man's shoulder, he felt the point of one of his spikes coming through.

"Not a good idea to get between a man and his mate, my friend." Draco's smile couldn't hide the threat that was very clearly in his words.

Patrick smiled back at him, not about to be put off by the snark of a low-level dragon. "It would be even more unwise for you to attempt to side step an alpha, friend."

Draco growled at him, but before Carlton could call off his lackey, it was Jessie who once again decided to bring peace between them.

Even though she was the main reason for their bickering.

She sat up, her hair falling around her breasts, and she sighed dramatically. "All right, I suppose I will have to let you both have me at the same time. Carlton, I really hope you don't mind waiting a little while longer, unless you want to sit with James for a moment."

Carlton stood. "I'm sure James and I can amuse ourselves while the three of you put on a show."

James tensed. "What?"

Patrick was curious about that, as well.

"I didn't take you for the type who swung both ways."

"Does it matter?"

Shit.

"Provided James has no objections, not at all."

"I've got none," James said, and the fact that he

sounded as though he was trying to overcome a challenge didn't make Patrick feel any better about what they'd gotten themselves into.

Patrick would have asked him if he was sure, had they been alone, but James was a grown man. He could make his own decisions, and if Patrick attempted to coddle him in front of two dragons, James might take it as a slight against his nature as a warrior.

Though Patrick couldn't stop the protective feeling from coming over him as Carlton came to sit on the bed.

He took James by his jaw, turned his head back, and leaned in.

James accepted the kiss from the dragon warrior. He did not tense, and his gaze remained determined, but Patrick did not imagine the sudden jump in his heartbeat.

Even Jessie was mesmerized by them.

"Well then, it seems I'm not quite as good as I thought."

James yanked his mouth away from Carlton's. "I wasn't suggesting that."

She shook her head, chuckling. "Never mind, sweetheart. I was not talking about sex. You were more than fine in that respect."

Patrick grabbed her by the wrists, yanking her closer, leaning over top of her and ignoring the low growl from Draco. "You're about to find out how much better it gets."

"Promises, promises."

Even so, her smile melted away when he leaned in and pressed his lips to hers.

She moaned, her fingers pushing through his hair, scratching at his scalp, pulling his hair.

He let his hand trail down her belly to her pelvis, around the curve of her soft thigh and to her pussy. Pushing his fingers inside, Patrick swallowed down her sweet little moans. They invigorated him, made him

MANDY ROSKO

desperate for more of her. He pushed his fingers deeper, felt the clench of her sex around them, and he couldn't wait to be inside her.

He'd had all the patience in the world letting James do as he wished to start off with, but now that he was getting the chance to taste her for himself, he realized just how screwed he really was.

He wouldn't be able to think right if he didn't make his claim and put his scent inside her.

As he kissed Jessie, finger fucking her and enjoying the little motions of her hips as they thrust against him, Patrick felt Draco behind him, saw the way his hands stroked up and down Jessie's thighs.

Feeling a little bad for the man who was acting as though he was dying of thirst in a hot desert, Patrick felt generous enough to let him in on this a little more than he originally intended.

If this was what it felt like for him now that he had a taste, it probably meant that Draco, who wanted Jessie regardless of any spells she cast, had been showing a lot more restraint than Patrick had thought.

"Sit up." Patrick grabbed Jessie by her shoulders, forcing her to sit up before she could do as he asked of her.

He settled her on his lap, loving the way her legs wrapped around him. As if she was made to be there, her pussy wet against his cock, teasing him as he gently thrust forward against her folds without penetrating her.

"You getting in on this or what?"

He looked to Draco, who seemed shocked to have been spoken to at all.

"Uh..."

Jessie rolled her eyes and reached back for him. "Don't you start getting shy, too. You're the one who's supposed to be my mate here. Get over here and please me."

Patrick shivered. Fuck, why was it sexy when she got so bossy?

But Draco scrambled into position. His entire body seemed to be buzzing with anticipation. His scales formed in patches all across his body, as though he was some sort of warped Dalmatian.

Otherwise, he seemed in perfect control when he wrapped his arms around her middle and kissed the side of her throat.

"Baby, you're not going to regret this."

Jessie swallowed. She smiled, though it seemed a little too bright. A little too forced.

"I love it when men learn how to share. Now let's give our friends over there a show."

Patrick couldn't agree more, though when he looked at James, he saw the other man getting into Carlton's kisses.

He wasn't sure why, but that jealousy came back to him. Not simply because of James either. The fact that either male would be enjoying themselves without him seemed...

No, he couldn't think about it like that. Because it wasn't like that. All four of them were getting in on this. This was about all of them. No one was going to be left behind, because in that moment, Patrick realized something.

It wasn't just James he was concerned about. That protective instinct he had for his best friend was also reaching out for Carlton as well.

He wasn't sure if that was part of her spell or not, but there was definitely something happening here, something connecting the four of them to this demonic woman.

That thought was only solidified when he and Draco thrust into her, their cocks coming together, her sex so tight with both of their dicks inside her.

Nothing was ever going to be the same when she was through with them. As he fucked into Jessie at the same time as Draco, James, and Carlton next to them on the bed, kissing and touching each other, Patrick realized without a doubt that was the case.

24

DRACO

SHE WAS PERFECT. She was his. Draco was annoyed when Patrick tried to take over. He'd wanted to throw the other man off his mate, but he couldn't.

Because the spell prevented him, for one thing, but on the other hand, he wasn't sure he would have wanted to take the pecker head out when he was on top of Jessie.

What if he hurt her by doing something like that?

No. He absolutely would never allow that to happen, and if this was how his woman wanted things done, if she wanted to have the wolves inside her first, even if she wanted to leave Draco for last and step all over his heart, he would let her do it with a smile on his face because he existed for her.

His smile would be fake, of course, hiding away the shattering of his heart and the blackness in his soul such a thing would create, but he would still do it.

He groaned, kissing and sucking on her throat, his hands fumbling to cup her breasts from his place behind her as he fucked into her.

He'd never had another man's dick touching his, but

he'd never double penetrated a woman before either. Not using the same entrance, anyway. He'd had threesomes before. With two women, and once with a one woman and another guy, so it wasn't as though he'd never had this much testosterone during playtime, but…

Well, actually, he hadn't. There were three other men here, and two of them were getting hot and heavy with each other right next to him while he was inside his mate.

Draco had never known that about Carlton, that he swung for the other team as well, but so long as he was happy doing what he was doing and Draco got his chance to be with Jessie, finally, then he would cheer on his best friend and leader until the cows came home.

Jessie reached her hand back for him, cupping his face, but she did not lean in for the kiss he thought she wanted.

"Slow down, sweetheart," she said.

Draco tensed. "What?"

She smiled at him, and he only just now realized that her lips looked naturally that red.

"Good things take time to enjoy. Take your time. You've got as much of me as you want."

Draco wasn't entirely sure if he believed that, but he supposed he didn't have much of a choice in that matter. If she wanted him to take his time, then he would. A woman needed more tender attention. Even a ghoulish succubus, it seemed.

So he closed down. Draco hated that Patrick, the damned mutt, was already going at an easy pace.

His face was flushed with glowing color, but otherwise, he'd managed to stay in control over himself. If he was going to prove himself to be a worthy mate, then he'd better do the same thing.

Patrick grinned at him. "Matching my pace?"

"Shut up," Draco said, and indeed, he was matching the other man's pace, but only because it made sense.

When he thrust forward, Draco pulled back, and when Patrick pulled back, he thrust forward, keeping in perfect rhythm with the other man so Jessie would, at all times, feel herself being well loved and stretched between the both of them.

"God, that's so good," he moaned, taking her nipples between his fingers and tweaking them, enjoying her soft sighs.

The only times it became difficult for him to match Patrick's rhythm were when Jessie tried to fuck against the both of them. She'd asked Draco to take his time, but she seemed to be having some difficulty with following her own rules.

He liked that. She'd tried acting as though she was the one in control, but she wasn't. She wanted this just as much as he did.

Cupping her breasts, Draco let his teeth scrape down the side of her throat.

"You're into this, aren't you?"

Patrick looked at him, his brows furrowed. Jessie had much the same expression when she looked back at him. "Of...of course I do."

"But you really like this. You don't want to admit it to us. You want to come off as all confident and in control, but..." He thrust forward harder, pushing his cock deeper, ignoring the rhythm he and Patrick had built.

Jessie tensed, then shivered, exposing her throat as she threw her head back, leaving her perfectly open for Draco's mouth.

"You're as out of control by this as we are, aren't you?"

Puffing for breath, her perfect breasts heaving, pink

nipples brushing against Patrick's chest, she glared back at him. "I...do not need anything from anyone."

Such bullshit and he saw right through it. And it was great that he could finally see through it.

It made him feel protective of her.

More so than he already had been, knowing she just wanted to get away from that abusive little twerp warlock.

"You want to feel out of control. You like that we do this to you," Draco said, looking at his partner in crime. "I bet even the doggo over there can tell."

Patrick made a rumbling noise in the back of his throat. Draco was going to take that as a form of agreement.

James and Carlton said nothing on the matter because they were too busy dry humping each other to notice.

"When was the last time any man made you feel this alive?"

"Men make me feel alive all the time. You're nothing special."

"Ouch. That hurts. Might hurt more if you actually meant it."

"Draco," Patrick said, a warning in his voice.

Draco didn't care. He was onto something here, and he wasn't about to let it go.

"You're a succubus. You seduce men and steal their souls as a career, but I'll bet everything I own right now..." Draco let his hand slide down to her sex, his fingers playing around with her folds, even touching Patrick's cock as the man thrust into her, barely slowing down. "That this is really getting you off. You're not faking this, are you?"

He knew the answer as her wet cunt clenched around his and Patrick's cocks.

He was right. He fucking knew it.

And he loved it. He loved not only being right because he was a petty motherfucker and not ashamed to admit it in the least, but it meant there was something here.

She wasn't cold. She wasn't a monster. She might be a demon, but she was a warm-blooded woman, and Draco was going to give her everything she needed and more.

"I think you're right," Patrick said, canting his hips, pulling Jessie's attention back onto him. His hand slid across her collarbone, to the back of her neck before his thumb stroked her lips.

Draco loved that. She almost looked helpless and not entirely in control.

Which was how she'd been desperately trying to come off as from the moment they met her.

"Do you want us to save you?"

She yanked her face away from his hand, glaring at him. "No! I don't need—Oooo Oooh!"

Draco thought it was funny, the way her voice went low and high like that as he and Patrick reminded her of her position between them.

"You came to us, sweetheart," Draco said, kissing her throat, teasing the soft shell of her ear with his mouth.

Even Carlton and James, who were still stroking, kissing, and rubbing up against each other couldn't help but reach out for her, their hands sliding along her calf and thigh.

"You make us hot for you, but I'm willing to bet you're feeling this same desperate lust that we are."

She wouldn't stop denying it as she panted for breath, her cheeks and neck flushed with heat and color. "I...I don't need...anyone."

"You're mostly right, baby," Draco said, pushing her further to her own edge, for a moment his own orgasm forgotten about as he worked to bring her to her own pleasure. "You don't want to need anyone, and you do a fine job on your own, but you do need people. You need me. You need *us*."

He almost didn't let that last little bit slip. Because he didn't want to admit that she needed more than just him. That she needed the other three men in the room to protect her and kill the man who had destroyed her life.

And if Draco loved her, he wouldn't get in the way of that. Spell or no spell.

Jessie groaned, pressing her forehead down onto Patrick's shoulder, as though accepting defeat.

Draco stopped moving. So did Patrick.

She wasn't crying, but her body language, the way she clenched her eyes shut, suggested she was close to something of that nature, and even Carlton and James quickly separated from each other, getting up and surrounding her.

James on one side and Carlton on the other.

Carlton pushed her hair out of the way and kissed her shoulder. "With the exception of Draco, none of us here would have chosen you, or this situation, but I'll be damned if I sit by and let you be torn apart by that filthy warlock. I will protect you for as long as you ask me to."

"Me too," James said, nodding, his hands on her arm, as though he needed to touch her.

"I think it goes without saying that I'm throwing my hat into the ring here, too."

"Because of the spell," Jessie said. "I'm...I'm the worst person in the world. I'm no better than Valbrand."

"No, baby," Draco said. He kissed the cute little mole growing at the back of her neck. "You don't get to speak about my mate like that. I'm here for you. No matter what. These guys, too. Even though two of them are a couple of filthy mutts."

They didn't growl at him for the comment. At least it meant they had some sense of humor and could tell that he was mostly joking.

"We've got you. You can let go with us."

Jessie clenched her teeth, and in that moment, Draco really worried she was about to cry.

Not that it had ever happened before, but Draco figured he would not like it when a woman cried while his dick was inside her.

Might ruin the mood.

But she didn't cry. She didn't sniffle. Jessie sucked back a hard breath, looking back at Draco, pulling his mouth forward for a hard kiss.

Draco groaned, sinking against her mouth. He knew what she was doing, trying to take control again, but that was all right. If she needed to feel as though she was in charge to feel safe, then he would let her do whatever she wanted to.

Patrick started moving again. Not to be outdone, Draco canted his hips as well, groaning against her mouth, and the pleasure started to build again.

She pulled her mouth from his, looked at Carlton, whom she had yet to give as much love to, wrapped her arm around his neck, and kissed him hard on the mouth.

Carlton was not the sort of male to let her take the command she wanted, and he didn't. He tilted her head to the side and kissed her with the aggressive certainty of a male who knew what belonged to him.

Watching Jessie moan, then give into his dominance, was beautiful, and when Carlton finished with her, he let his thumb slide over her top lip. The Cupid's bow. Such a fitting name. Someone had shot them all with something other than lust.

Draco had worried the other men would hold their

grudges against her for however long it took them to deal with this Valbrand prick, but the way they were acting now, like they genuinely wanted to protect her...it made Draco more confident in them. Even the wolves.

So long as they were here to protect her, to keep her safe and prevent her from going back to that asshole, Draco would forgive their initial distrust.

Like she'd done with Draco, Jessie pulled away from Carlton 's mouth with a heady gasp. Her lips, already so bright in color, seemed to turn a shade of deeper red as she reached for James, kissing him on the mouth.

James closed his eyes, tilting his head just a little, but Jessie didn't attempt to dominate him as Draco and Patrick fucked harder, and faster, into her.

She seemed to be waiting to see if he would take command, just as he'd done before.

James did not disappoint Jessie or Draco, and as the wolf shifter slipped his tongue into her mouth with a groan, Draco could no longer keep himself from entirely losing control.

He fucked hard and fast into the woman he loved. He groaned and growled, his claws coming forward when he didn't mean for that to happen, scales appearing in random patches across his body.

His dick swelled, and Jessie moaned, breaking off her kiss with James with a heavy sigh. She looked at Patrick, then back at Draco before she smiled slowly through the building sheen of sweat across her porcelain skin. She didn't say anything, but between him and Patrick, she knew who was responsible.

Throwing her head back, Jessie seemed to lose all control. She panted for breath she could not seem to catch.

"Oh God, oh...I'm close," she moaned. "I'm gonna...I'm right there..."

Draco wished he could say something profound to her, something romantic or even sexy to push her over that edge, but because he was so close to that ending himself, there was nothing he could do except fuck into her harder, faster, giving into his own baser desires over hers even though that was the absolute last thing he wanted to do.

Thankfully, it didn't seem to matter. As Patrick and Draco fucked into her, as James kissed her throat and stroked her arm, Carlton threaded his fingers together with hers, his mouth sucking on her collarbone and chest as he stroked his cock, all of these things seemed to come together and bring about the desired end.

Jessie clenched tight around their pricks. She had to use her free hand to cover her mouth, holding back the noises she wanted to make.

James wasn't having that, and he grabbed her wrist, pulling her hand back, forcing her to release those sounds out into the world, and fuck, that was hot.

Draco's entire body clenched and spasmed. The heat built just at his lower belly and released like a wild animal hyped up for the charge. He growled. He bit down on her shoulder even when he didn't mean to, but thankfully, he was able to stop himself from breaking the skin.

Again, Jessie didn't seem to notice or care. She thrashed through the crash of her own orgasm, canting her hips, fucking down on the two men inside her until her strength seemed to suddenly vanish.

Draco, Patrick, Carlton, and James held her up between them as they finished.

Carlton came with a groan, spilling onto Jessie's leg, putting his scent on her as Draco and Patrick spilled inside. James was still hard, but he still seemed satisfied. Possibly because he'd already orgasmed, and now he was able to watch Jessie as she recovered?

Draco didn't know, and while his buzzing brain struggled to recover from the best workout a body could receive, he realized he didn't care.

A turning point just happened, and as Jessie snuggled between them, her features soft and innocent, Draco was going to enjoy the moment for as long as he could.

Until Carlton had to ruin it.

"Is she sleeping?"

Draco struggled not to growl at his friend. "I'm trying to sleep, too."

"Too bad," Carlton replied, keeping his voice low so as to not wake their sleeping princess.

"We've got to start our plan of attack if we're going to kill this guy."

"Can't it wait?" James asked, and Draco decided he liked the guy. At least he knew the importance of rest.

"No," Carlton said, growling. "In case none of you noticed, there's a fire burning over there."

"What?" Draco turned to the fireplace. A bright, healthy fire crackled inside.

"Who lit that?" Draco looked at James, suddenly not liking the man so much anymore.

He hadn't lit it, and he was pretty sure Patrick hadn't either. Carlton wouldn't be that stupid, so that left only one other person.

James tensed, face twisting with anger, but before he could start shit, his alpha nudged his shoulder and put a finger to his mouth, pointing at Jessie.

A clear sign to shut the fuck up.

"It wasn't me," James hissed, still looking at Draco as though he was the asshole here.

"It wasn't any of us," Carlton said. "It was dead in there when I started kissing you."

"So then…"Draco didn't even want to think about it.

Patrick had no problem stating the obvious while James jumped out of bed and killed the fire with a sand bucket they kept nearby for their fires.

"We had a little spy."

Draco was going to kill that motherfucker. He hoped Valbrand had a good show because he was *never* going to give Jessie back to him.

25

CARLTON

THEY LEFT Jessie sleeping soundly on the bed. Carlton worried she would wake when all limbs and appendages were properly separated from each other, but it seemed even a ghoulish succubus could be drained of all her energy with one high-powered fuck.

She slept like the dead.

Carlton didn't want to think too deeply about what that might possibly mean about her, so he put it out of his mind and focused on the task at hand.

That perverted warlock had been spying on them. He doubted Jessie knew.

She didn't seem like the type who would be comfortable sleeping after fucking, much less sleeping after fucking while the male she hated more than anything spied on them.

So he, Draco, James, and Patrick worked to figure out what their next step would be.

"He's building a report on us," Patrick said. "He's trying to figure out what makes us tick. He wants to know who's most affected by Jessie's spell, and how loyal we will be to her."

"But we didn't give anything away that would let him know anything about us, did we?" James asked, frowning, as though he was trying to recall every move he'd made, every sweet whisper he'd spoken into Jessie's ear.

Draco seemed the most concerned. He stood in their circle, arms crossed, but the wide-eyed look on his face suggested there was so much more happening there.

Carlton knew his friend. He was pissed. He was hiding his terror. Doing his best to contain his rage, likely because he didn't want to wake Jessie.

A quick glance back showed her still sleeping, hair splayed out behind her as she snuggled the pillow they'd put near her after tucking her in. As though she thought she was snuggling any one of them in her sleep.

"We don't know what specifically he got of us other than we're serious." Carlton rubbed his jaw. "He knows her spell has its hold on us and we're not fighting it anymore. That's all he needs to know."

"So how do we draw him out?" Draco growled. "I want to kill that sack of shit right now. He was watching me and Jessie together. I don't want him breathing for that."

"I know."

Draco wasn't done. "I'm going to skin him alive and wear his face like a fucking battle mask for the rest of my life."

"We'll get this done, but Jessie said he wouldn't be coming for her until he was ready."

Jessie had promised to release them from her spell if Valbrand took his sweet time to claim her, but Carlton didn't think that would be happening. He'd gotten the feeling, and he didn't think he was alone, that Jessie wanted to release them from her spell, that she didn't enjoy having the four of them as her little servants, regardless of the attitude she put on about it.

She hadn't. Carlton was willing to bet that had more to do with fear than anything else. The fear that her warriors would abandon her the instant she released them from the spell that held them, that she would be forced to face Valbrand on her own as punishment for what she'd done.

She wouldn't. Carlton trusted that Draco was never going to leave her side, but Carlton hadn't been lying when he'd promised to serve her. He didn't think the wolves were lying either. They wanted to be Jessie's sword. They wanted to free her. The spell only made them obey her, made them feel lust for her. She had no say over whether or not they offered their services or made genuine promises.

Carlton suspected she *wanted* to trust them, but years of servitude, of promises and lies, were likely the reason why they were all still bound to Jessie by her spell.

That was fine. Carlton was going to free her.

And after…

He didn't know.

Draco claimed to be her mate. Her true mate. He'd actually volunteered for this, but Carlton…

If she was not his mate, and another male was laying a claim to her, then what right did he have to dwell on feelings that may not truly exist?

None.

When this was done, he would be free of Jessie, but he would also free her of himself. There was nothing else to think about. He was in lust with her, and any feelings he thought might be kindling were only a product of that lust spell, her control over him, creating his need to serve her, and, he had to be honest about this, her sheer beauty.

She did not belong to him. He glanced back at her. She

really was a sleeping beauty, but she did not belong to him, and she never would.

She was Draco's, so he might as well get that through his head right now.

That way, when it was time to release himself of her, it wouldn't pain him.

For that reason, he was glad he hadn't penetrated her in bed a moment ago.

Fingers snapped in front of his face, yanking him out of the daze he'd fallen into.

"What?" he asked, playing it off as though nothing of note had happened.

Draco raised both brows at him. "I was asking what you thought we should do to lure the prick out? If you were already thinking of some way we could do that, then please, let us in on it."

Fuck. The pecker had to be this way, did he? Carlton knew of a way, but he also knew Draco would shoot the idea down in an instant. "We use Jessie as bait. Valbrand wants her so bad? We use her to bring him out."

"No fucking way." Draco crossed his arms, shaking his head.

"It's the only way. This is a guy that can live for centuries. He can hang over her head, over all of our heads, for decades before he comes for us."

"You're out of your fucking mind if you think I'm going to let you do that." Draco frowned, showing off a little teeth now. Yeah, he wasn't a fan of this idea.

James rubbed the back of his neck. "Your alpha has a point, though. What if this really is the only way to make this work?"

"No!"

"Shhh!" Patrick smacked Draco upside the head.

Everyone had a look to see if their queen was disturbed by the outburst.

No. She didn't so much as stir, her face as peaceful as ever, chest and shoulders rising and falling as she dreamed.

"This might be the only way," Carlton said, noting the steam that literally ghosted from the man's ears. He was heating up and getting ready to explode with his rage. That wasn't a good sign. "Draco, I know you don't want to do this, but you need to be reasonable. We either sit around and twiddle our thumbs, waiting for an attack to come that might take years, or we end this as soon as possible."

"You would risk her life? Are you kidding me? I know you hate her, but Jesus Christ, Carlton!"

Carlton had to suck back his pride at the insult. He was the commander of his clan. He was used to giving orders, even to Draco, but this was different. The fact that Draco believed himself to be genuinely mated to Jessie meant more delicacy was needed. That was the only reason he didn't grab his friend and throw him down on the ground before putting his boot on the man's neck.

"Draco, do you want a life with this woman or don't you?"

"Of course I do." Draco's eyes burned a bright golden color. Flames sparked inside his nostrils.

Yes, he was definitely holding himself back with this. Carlton didn't like that.

"Do you want children with her?"

Children that would never be Carlton's.

Draco furrowed his brow. "Of course I do. I want to keep her for the rest of my life."

"Then stop being a child and see reason. Do you really think you can protect her every second of every day? Even with the four of us working together? It's impossible. She will bear your hatchlings. You will father one or more dragon chicks with her and be comfortable knowing that at any moment they can be taken from you?"

"I could protect her," he said, though the way Draco clenched his hands into fists, the way he ducked his head just slightly, was proof enough that he was starting to come to terms with a few unhappy realities.

"No, you couldn't," Patrick replied, though not with any sort of glee in his voice. He sounded just as dejected by the idea as Carlton felt about it. "Our guards will fall. We'll become comfortable. We will forget, even if it's just for a moment, and a creature like this is one that cannot be taken lightly."

Patrick's words put a drain on the air around them. Everything seemed darker, more hopeless and desperate than it had a moment ago. As though someone had walked in and told the lot of them their pets were all dead.

Carlton gripped Draco's shoulder. "From the sounds of this guy, he will hunt her down until he's either dead, or she is back with him, or she is dead. Only one of those is an acceptable option, and if you are comfortable with the chance of her death if you lower your guard even once, then we'll do it your way."

"All of our guards were lowered when we were in bed together." Draco narrowed his eyes at Carlton. "You were hardly paying attention to the fire that started up on its own when you were necking with James."

James' cheeks brightened with a heavy blush. God, that guy was easily embarrassed for a warrior.

Carlton barely blinked, feeling little to nothing at the dig. "Yes, James and I are both in lust with your mate, as is proper with the control she has over us. The fact that she could have taken our souls while you and Patrick were inside her, when James fucked her, is proof enough that she is worthy of protection."

Draco eyed him suspiciously. "Is that why you didn't penetrate her?"

"I don't fuck women when they are unconscious, no." Draco glared at him, but he dropped the accusation, which was good, because it had come a little too close to home for him. "That, and I would rather she lived through all of this than died because any of us is too proud to do what needs to be done."

Draco's eyes burned. He grit his teeth, sparks emerging from between them as he tried to keep himself in check.

"You can fight us on this all you want, but this needs to be done. We can't be sitting around all the time with our thumbs up our asses waiting for something to happen."

"So you'd risk her life?"

"We don't have anything else to put on the table."

Draco still looked like he wanted to rip Carlton's head off, and he couldn't believe he had to deal with this right now in his best friend.

"Any other time I could make you see reason. Stop letting this control you and *think*."

"She is *not* controlling me."

"That's not what he said, idiot," James said, crossing his arms as if Carlton needed the help.

Draco snapped his fangs at the wolf, and he might have gotten James' throat, too if his alpha hadn't stepped in the way, grabbed Draco by the forehead, and pushed him back. That only seemed to piss him off even more as his scales appeared, covering almost the entirety of his body as he lunged for James again.

This time, Carlton had to step in, grabbing his friend by the horns that sprouted on his forehead as he surged forward. He yanked Draco back, putting pressure in his neck, but Draco was a warrior, he would handle it.

The man threw a spiny fist at Carlton's face, however, which Carlton absolutely did not appreciate, even as he managed to grab it in his hand. The spikes still hurt. They broke Carlton's skin. He held back a hiss as he stared hard into those glowing golden eyes. "Stop this, right now. I will not ask you again."

Draco growled, so Carlton figured he'd given the man warning enough. He grabbed his friend around the waist, lifting him off his feet, spinning him around and slamming him hard onto the ground.

Draco's eyes bulged, his mouth opening in a heavy cough as the air likely fled his lungs.

Then he wouldn't stop gagging. "Going to relax?"

"Holy shit," James said. The man's eyes were wide as if he couldn't believe that Carlton had just done that to a friend.

Whatever, Carlton didn't care, he had better shit to deal with, and he was pretty sure that behavior like this wasn't all that uncommon in a wolf pack either.

"Are you going to relax?"

Draco growled at him. He clenched his teeth so hard Carlton worried he might pop them, but eventually, the man heaved a sigh, and Carlton could feel the aggression simmering out of him.

" Just get off me already."

Bossy little bastard. Any other time Carlton would've smacked him for that, maybe even made him eat some of the grass outside in front of the rest of his dragons just to make sure he really knew who was boss, but this was a special circumstance.

With a light growl of his own, Carlton released to the man and stepped back. Draco rushed to his feet, but he didn't look to be in the mood for another attempt at a fight. He crossed his arms, and Carlton could tell he was embarrassed. He would die before admitting it, but it was there.

"We'll work this out."

Draco shook his head. "I don't care how this gets worked out. You want to use her as bait."

"I don't want to do anything other than get back in bed with her and stake my own claim. This is as much for you as it is for her at this point. Any feelings I have are not real." He could've sworn that he felt a knife sliding slowly between his ribs. Inch by inch, cutting flesh, stinging like the bite of a bullet ant.

He ignored it.

"You're serious about her being your mate?"

Draco rolled his eyes. "Do you want me to take a lie detector test about it or what?" The fire started to come back into his eyes. "Yes, she is mine and mine alone. I'm just sharing her with the three of you for now because you will need her, because of her spell." The more he spoke about it, the more irritated it seemed to make him. He also looked as though he was lying about something. "I need all of you around now to protect her. Not to poke her on a hook like some worm for fishing."

"Absolutely none of us are doing that, nor do we want to do that." Carlton was starting to get seriously pissed off about this. He wasn't used to having to repeat himself again and again and again. He was used to his dragons taking his orders, following his command, and realizing that he was the one who knew what was best for the situation at hand.

All this handholding shit was really starting to get on his nerves.

"It's not your decision to make anyway," Carlton said. "It's hers."

Draco frowned, and then he seemed to realize what was going on as he snapped his attention towards the bed.

Carlton had vaguely been aware that she was waking up after he put his foot on Draco's throat. It was the tiniest little sound in the world, but he caught it, even when putting his idiot friend in his place.

The sound of Jessie's heart beating not quite so softly anymore.

She'd sat up sometime during their argument, and was now watching them with interest. The covers were pulled loosely over her knees, just barely hiding her breasts. She had her arms leisurely wrapped around her legs, chin resting on her knees as she observed the four men in front of her.

Carlton didn't even care how long she had been listening in on them, or what she thought of the display. "What do you think?"

Jessie nodded. "I hate the idea."

Draco threw his hands into the air. "There! You see?"

"We should do it anyway," Jesse said.

For a brief second, Draco sounded as though he was choking on his own rage.

Carlton didn't like it. Part of him had even hoped she would turn the idea down. But he had to respect that she knew this was the proper way. Still, he couldn't help but ask, "Are you sure this is what you want? If we start this, there's no stopping until the job's done."

She shrugged, but it wasn't the uncaring thing he was used to seeing out of her. She looked as though she was trying to mask something painful. "You're all big boys. If this is what it takes to kill him, then so be it. You all just better make sure you protect me from anything he tries to do. You don't get to slack off on being warriors just because you took me to bed."

"That's not how this works at all," Patrick said.

Carlton finished for him, knowing exactly what he was going to say. "We'd work harder to protect you because we *did* take you to bed."

She might not entirely realize it, but spell or no spell, the four of them were wrapped around her little fingers.

26

JESSIE

IF THE ONLY way to get these idiots to stop biting was to go along with their little plan, then so be it.

Not that she had immediately thought it was the greatest thing she'd ever heard, but the more Carlton and Patrick spoke about it, the more focus they spent on her and her safety, as well as the plan of attack, the more Jessie started to come around to their idea of thinking.

She wanted this done and over with.

Draco, on the other hand, was still trying to talk her out of it.

"You don't have to do this. We can think of something else. We haven't even tried looking for another way."

The fear in his voice, for her, sounded a little too genuine for her comfort. Jessie struggled to continue looking at him when the warrior insisted on behaving like a kicked puppy.

"I want this over with as soon as possible. Your leader is right, and so are your new friends. Valbrand can wait for years. For decades. Even with your lifespans, the amount of time he has over all of you is infinite in comparison."

"We can flush him out," Draco insisted. *"I'll* flush him out."

Draco sat beside her, took her by the hand, and with all the sincerity he had in his body, told her they could find another way with his eyes alone.

She had never seen a man so utterly devoted to her safety. Not even the males she had used her influence on in previous years.

She didn't know what to think about that. It made her...uncomfortable.

He looked as though he meant it. This paranoid terror over her well-being didn't seem staged, and she could sniff out an actor faking sympathy and concern anywhere.

Draco seemed to take her silence as a reason to continue to attempt to persuade her.

"Give me some time. We'll work on this. We'll get that little bitch to come out in the open and make him eat shit in front of you if that's what you want. I promise you that."

Jessie pressed her lips together. She gripped Draco's hand a little tighter without meaning to.

All men wanted something. All of them wanted either her body when she put them under her spell, or her power when they discovered what she was. Maybe one or two believed themselves to be genuinely in love with her, but it was nothing that had ever been able to overpower her spells or Valbrand's evil.

A man about to lose his soul tended to throw away a whole lot in an attempt to keep it. Even the woman he, supposedly, loved more than his own life.

Jessie pulled her hand away from Draco's. "You're sweet, but it's better that you don't make something of this that it's not." She didn't look directly at him, but from the corner of her eye, Jessie was certain she wasn't mistaking the gutted expression on his face.

Whatever. He would get over it. Every male who had managed to escape her grasp, and there weren't many, always did.

Forgetful, flaky, constantly on the search for their next piece of tail.

He would find another damsel in distress to protect when she was out of the picture. It was as simple as that.

Draco stood, and he seemed to stand once more with the males he needed to stand with.

Likely thinking what an ungrateful bitch she was.

She didn't care. Didn't bother her at all. Why would it when she had bigger fish to fry?

Crossing her arms, she put her focus on Carlton and Patrick.

"What do you have in mind to lure him out? If it involves tying me to a stake and getting the matches out, then you can forget it."

James' brows lifted almost all the way into his hairline. "Christ, that's pretty…specific. Who did that to you?"

Asshole.

"I just want to make sure I have a way out in case your great big plan to use me as bait goes to shit."

She hadn't been in their presence for long, but already she'd started to feel a little too cozy with these people. That was not a good thing. She needed to get her shit together and remember who was actually in charge here.

Her.

These guys were her employees. Her underlings. Not even friends with benefits. Just some guys she'd fucked to boost their morale for what they needed to do for her.

"We won't be tying you to train tracks if that's what

you're worried about," Patrick said. "If your former master is really an expert on the demonic magic you use, then it would do us no good anyway. He wouldn't believe for one second we would betray you."

Jessie groaned, angry with herself for not having seen that coming.

She ran her fingers through her hair. He was absolutely right.

"Goddammit."

Her freedom, which had seemed so close before, was now so cruelly ripped away from her. *God*, how many more decades was she going to have to wait before she was free of him? Jessie had allowed herself to believe that she was so close to the finish line that she could almost take a breath.

That she could almost relax.

She glanced up at the four men in front of her, all of whom seemed a little too sincere in their need to help her. Maybe she'd even allowed herself to believe that, when all was said and done, perhaps there was something that could be...

No. It was best to not let her mind wander to such areas. Why was she even allowing herself to think like that? She barely knew these men other than that they were all capable warriors who were willing to kill to get the job done.

A couple of hours of playing house and male bonding time seem to make her forget about her mission. Made her think they could actually get along together after all of this was over when they'd made it perfectly clear that the second they were free from her spell, they'd be at each other's throats again.

"There is one way we could make this work," Patrick said.

Jessie loosely wrapped her arms around her legs, unable to help herself as years of habit made her want to show off the curve of her waist and the swell of her breasts as the blanket slip lower down her body.

At the last second, she adjusted the sheets around her just a little more to cover up, not wanting to make it too obvious that she was still giving in to baser instincts.

"Whatever you have in mind, I'm open to hearing it."

Patrick shook his head. The bastard actually smiled a little, resting a hand on his hip. "After you hear this? I doubt you'll be so jolly about it."

Jessie frowned, suspicious now. "Why?"

Patrick stuffed both hands into his pockets. "Because in order to make your old master believe we would betray you, you're going to have to release us from this spell you've got us under."

She blinked at him. Waited for the words that came out of his mouth to mean something else. Didn't happen. Nope. She hadn't misheard that. "Are you out of your fucking mind?" The fact that he looked serious made it all the more troubling. "You want to take away the only protection I have? Is that it?"

"See? I told her you would be pissed."

Jessie pulled the sheets around her body and came to a quick stand. She needed to be on her feet for this one. "I am pissed. Pissed that you think I'm that stupid."

The best part about this whole thing was that Draco had suddenly gone very quiet. The man who couldn't shut up a minute ago about how much she wanted to keep her safe, about how he was willing to do anything to make sure that she was free from Valbrand, was suddenly trying to look at anything and everything but her.

"You can't tell me you think this is a good idea? Two seconds ago you were telling me that you wanted to keep me safe. You were saying that you're my natural mate, and I'm still not sure I believe that, but you know what it means if I undo my spell."

"I know."

"They won't just abandon me; they will tear me to pieces. I'll literally be thrown to the wolves. Two of these men right here are *wolves*. Do you remember that?"

"I do." He looked her right in the eyes, that determination coming over him again. "I won't abandon you."

The sharpness in his words made her chest constrict. A painful sensation she was not used to. The worst part about it was that Draco wouldn't stop looking at her like that. As if he was challenging her to believe him.

"I won't abandon you. You can think what you want about these guys right here, I can't stop you, but I won't leave you. No matter what happens."

Why was there suddenly so much less air in this room? "Why?"

Draco frowned, confused. "Do you really need to ask?"

She did, and she was constantly annoyed that she needed to point this out to him. "Because I cast a spell on you. You want me because of the spell."

The growl that came from Draco, so animal and ferocious, made her take a step back.

Carlton looked at his friend with an expression Jessie couldn't place. "Draco, relax."

"No, I won't fucking relax. After everything I...I fucking volunteered for this! I practically begged you to let me stay with you. I didn't care if you cast some dumb spell then and I don't care now. It doesn't matter! It doesn't mean a damn thing. You hear me?"

Again with that pain and constricting in her chest.

He could be lying. It could be the spell that made him believe these things. Her spells forced the men she influenced to be in lust with her, to do as she commanded, but it did not create loyalty. They could say whatever they wanted.

They could lie.

They could tell the truth...

It was stupid. It was beyond reckless, but even if he was lying, even if this was an elaborate trap, would it really be the worst thing in the world if she let herself pretend it was real? If only to see where this went?

Those who took the biggest risks reaped the largest rewards.

Or crashed and burned.

Biting her bottom lip, Jessie came to a realization.

If Draco betrayed her, if any of these men betrayed her, she was going to be crushed.

"All right."

Draco blinked. "All right?"

Jessie stood straighter, pushing her shoulders back. She wasn't about to make herself look small and weak as she gave up her own leverage here.

"I'll free you. All of you. Don't make me regret it."

All four men grinned, all four of them showed off the whites of their fangs.

She was already starting to regret this just a little, even before she removed her spell from them, freeing them of their lust for her. The only leverage she had over these men, these warriors she needed to defend her, she let it go.

PATRICK

PATRICK FELT it the instant her influence over him was gone. He sensed it in the sudden change in his body. The heat within him was not quite so drastic and uncontrollable anymore. He could look at this woman who had manipulated and trapped him with something other than a desire to fuck and a twitch in his cock.

In fact, as he looked at her, her hair still beautifully messy from being fucked by him, by James, and by Draco and Carlton, all he could think of was how much he wanted to fucking destroy her.

She clearly took note of the rage in his eyes. So did Draco. He was the first to step between her and Patrick, his claws coming out, scales forming across his neck, face, and shoulders, ready to form a protective layer around his body for a fight.

"Don't even think about it."

Patrick inhaled a sharp breath. He glanced at James, who rubbed his mouth and shook his head. The guy seemed to be going through a mini-crisis of his own. Then he looked at Patrick before quickly glancing away again. He bit his lips together, a hard flush of color climbing up his neck and face.

Right. He was embarrassed. Was he thinking about when Patrick kissed him or the things he'd done with Jessie and Carlton?

Patrick imagined any man would have a lot to feel embarrassed about if he woke up and realized he'd behaved in a way he normally wouldn't.

And the person responsible was standing right here.

"You said you wouldn't betray me," Jessie said.

The way she held the sheet around her chest, fists clenching the fabric that kept her dignity...was she purposely trying to look so small and helpless? Or was that also part of her manipulation?

"Draco promised you that. James and I gave you no promises."

Draco's eyes lit up like they were on fire. "You mother-fucker. You stupid cocksucking sack of sh—"

"Draco, *enough.*"

Carlton's command was what cut through Draco's rage before he could finish that sentence.

Not that it mattered. He seemed to get out everything he wanted with just that.

Patrick looked to Carlton. As far as he was concerned, Carlton was Draco's leader, and Patrick was on his territory.

"We made her no promises, and neither did you. If you want to throw your hat in the ring for her, be my guest, but I would like your guarantee that James and my pack will be allowed to get off your mountain without incident."

Carlton eyed him. He looked at Draco, still standing in front of Jessie. The woman stepped up behind the other dragon. She reached her hand out, gently touching his forearm.

Perhaps she was shocked Draco was actually sticking by her. That at least one of them would be defending her.

Did she honestly release all of them without knowing for certain she would have one warrior still on her side?

That seemed...rather stupid for her to do.

She had seemed so confident in her ability to entrap any male, to make them do as she wished, and now there she stood, looking at Draco's arm as though she couldn't believe he existed at all.

Patrick pushed down the sympathy that rushed him. He had responsibilities to attend to, and she was not one of them.

"You have my word. Take your men and go," Carlton replied.

Draco looked about ready to explode again as he spun around on Carlton. "You've got to be fucking kidding me. You're just going to let them go?"

"I can't exactly keep them here," Carlton deadpanned.

Patrick liked him. The man took no shit from his subordinates. It made Patrick respect him a little more.

"As for the matter of the land," Carlton said. "We'll work something out when this is said and done. I don't feel like backing Draco in some fight against an evil wizard just to come back and face off with you over who owns what. I trust you won't stab me in the back if we were to shake on a deal right now?"

"Carlton, Jesus Christ—"

Carlton snapped a clawed finger in Draco's face. "You can shut your mouth right about now because I have zero interest in hearing anything from you."

Still furious, Draco's body trembled as though he was holding back an active volcanic eruption.

He managed to hold himself back, blowing out a heavy sigh as though he was releasing all that steam. "Whatever," he said, crossing his arms.

The dragons were not so different from the wolves, it seemed. Draco still responded to his commander in the way Patrick's wolves responded to him whenever he made a decision they didn't like and he told them to suck it up.

Not that it meant Patrick would enjoy getting into discussions with a dragon about who owned what in the land they quarreled over.

But at least this was something. Maybe he could even work it out in his favor, get a majority of the land and leave Carlton and his dragon clan with enough to stop bitching at him about. If they could grow their own produce, then there was no need for the dragons to go to war with Patrick over land they clearly did not own.

"What do you say?" Carlton held his hand out.

Patrick eyed it, then took it. "We will discuss it at a later time, amicably," he added.

Carlton smirked, as though he knew Patrick would try to get the better end of the deal.

"All right, get out of here, the both of you. I'll give Tristan a text, tell him not to bother you too much when you all fall off the mountain."

That was right. There was a climb back down.

Shit. They'd only been here a few hours. The pack wasn't going to like this.

"We need them to help us," Draco said, sounding very much as though he was speaking through clenched teeth. Breathing, eating, and shitting fire right about now, he was.

"Come on, James," Patrick grabbed his friend by the shoulder, turning and walking out of the room while Draco argued with Carlton.

"Wait, are the dragons going to just let us walk out of here?" James said, glancing back.

"We'll find out, won't we?"

James unlocked the door to what had been their private little love nest, and as it closed behind them, he couldn't help but feel as though he was leaving something important behind.

A few somethings.

28

CARLTON

Draco was losing his mind, and Jessie, for an all-powerful succubus, looked a little too small and helpless behind him. It could be an act, but it worked because Carlton never wanted to see a woman in such a fearful state.

He kind of hoped she was faking it just so he would have the knowledge he was not instilling this kind of fear in her. Even if she might deserve it.

"I can't believe you're doing this. We need them."

"I thought we didn't need wolves? Isn't that your belief?"

"Fuck you. I'm not in the mood for this. Wolves and dragons hunting down this piece of shit is the best course of action. He'll never suspect we're working together."

"After seeing us all in bed together, necking and fucking, that's exactly what he would expect." Even as he looked at Jessie, even as he pitied her situation, he couldn't help but be furious at her.

She had used him. She was likely still using Draco, but he was allowing it because he was mated to her.

Considering he was still standing at her side, there was no longer any doubt in Carlton's mind that was the case.

"I need to text Tristan, let him know to not give the wolves any grief when they try getting down the mountain."

Knowing Tristan, he might want to throw rocks at the wolves as they went just for the fun of it. If Carlton was going to get that agreement on the land he and Patrick had been fighting over, he would resist that urge.

"I can't believe you're just going to let them leave."

"I'm not about to keep them prisoner here," Carlton said, shooting off his text to Tristan.

"It's not keeping them prisoner! It's asking them to do the right fucking thing."

Carlton glanced back at his friend. Jessie looked up at him, but Draco was too focused on Carlton to notice. It was the look in her eyes, the other shock that anyone could ever stand up for her like this.

"Did you really think he was lying to you about the mating thing?"

Jessie jumped. Carlton didn't think he would ever see her as stunned as this. Jessie was the image of the confident, powerful, and dangerous demon princess. He wondered, was this what she had looked like when she was learning what her new powers were? When Valbrand was bringing her into this world of deception and seduction?

She tried to bring back the image of a haughty, snobby queen, someone who was in absolute control over the situation at hand, but she didn't quite pull it off. It looked a little too forced. Maybe she needed to go back to acting class.

"I knew he was telling the truth the entire time. You don't have to worry about me. Those wolves were right, none of you made any promises to me, so I don't expect anything out of any of you."

"Then why do you look so disappointed by this whole thing?"

She tensed, though the way she refused to look at him was proof enough that he was right. For Draco's sake, he wasn't going to rub that in her face too much.

"The point is that you thought they would stick around," Draco said. "I promised you up and down that I would stay, and I meant it, and those fucking traitorous wolves said nothing. They knew you would think my promise applied to them, too."

"What makes you think you could make promises on their behalf? Or mine?" Carlton was most interested in that.

Draco said nothing, just a clenching of his teeth and fists.

"I can't believe I need to explain this to you. Are you not one of my warriors? A goddamned adult?"

"I get it," he snapped.

Carlton wasn't entirely sure that he did, but there was nothing he could do about it.

What was done was done, and now he had to clean up after Draco's shit.

Carlton glanced at Jessie. She looked stuck somewhere between an embarrassed pout and the intense desire to vanish into the floor. Being the commander of his clan meant he was often in charge of cleaning up other people's shit, so he supposed this was no different.

"I will help you. You're an idiot, but you're still part of my clan."

Draco's shoulders sagged. Had he really been that worried?

"Thanks, Carlton, I promise you're not going to regret this."

"I'm already regretting it, so that's out the fucking window, isn't it?"

He glanced at Jessie once more. She smiled at him softly. Maybe it was her way of saying thank you since he wasn't sure if she knew how to say it.

Either way, the vulnerability was something that didn't fit her.

He didn't want that. Not for her. She might deserve it, but...

Maybe he would finish that thought at a later time. There were other things to worry about right now.

29

JAMES

"ARE we seriously just walking away here?"

They weren't exactly halfway down the mountain, but it was no longer quite so terrifying to move, and he was at a point where, if he were to fall, James was pretty sure it wouldn't kill him.

At least the moon allowed them to see decently enough, but climbing down any mountain, even on a clear night sky, wasn't the sort of activity James took pleasure in.

Or any of the other wolves in their pack, all of whom were bitching about being forced to climb up the mountain, and then back down again in the same day.

James expected an extra helping of that bitch fest from Roger, but no. Much as the guy grumbled about being hungry and tired and never rock climbing ever again, he seemed happy enough to get off the mountain and away from the dragons.

As well as to be away from, "that filthy bride of Satan,"

Not his best insult, but the man did say he was tired, after all.

"Patrick?" James asked, sliding down a particularly tricky rock before catching up to his alpha. He grabbed Patrick's shoulder, just to pull back when the man shrugged him off with a growl.

Then James got mad. "All right. Okay, I see how it is."

"No, you don't."

James crossed his arms. "Right. That lust spell is off you, and now you're pissed off that you fucked her."

And kissed him, but James wasn't talking about that. He was never mentioning that ever again for as long as he lived.

"I'm not pissed off that I fucked her. She's a succubus, or a ghoul, whatever the fuck she is. We didn't even entirely go over that, but it's basically her purpose, so I don't exactly care that I stuck my dick inside her. She's used to that."

James growled under his breath. Those sounded a little too much like fighting words, but they weren't. He knew they weren't. His alpha was just pissed off that they'd been forced to waste this much time at all, and now they were heading home.

As if nothing had ever happened.

"Don't talk about her like that. It's not becoming of you," he added, knowing it made zero sense for him to defend Jessie at all.

"What are you assholes talking about?" Roger asked, an actual spring in his step as he stepped up to both men. He threw an arm over James's shoulder, but again, Patrick stepped out of the way before he could get chummy with him.

"All right, cool. Want to be the lone wolf right about now? I can deal with that."

"What are you doing?" James asked.

"I'm being your cheerleader, which is more than you guys deserve considering you're the ones dragging down morale with the rest of the pack."

"We're not dragging down anything. We're just tired, and we want to go home."

"Right, makes sense. So do we all, and we're all thrilled we get to do that without the demon bitch whispering into your ears."

Patrick growled again.

James looked at the man's hands, and he could see the claws coming out.

James' spider senses kicked off. He was pretty sure Patrick wasn't pissed off because he'd had sex with Jessie. Maybe a little annoyed and embarrassed that he'd kissed James in the heat of the moment, but now...

James was positive the majority of his alpha's annoyance stemmed from the fact that they were leaving.

James stopped. Roger was forced to stop with him. The man nearly tripped and fell onto the hard rock, but he caught himself.

"What the hell, man?"

James ignored him. Patrick turned back to have a look. He raised a brow at him.

"What are you really so pissed about?"

Patrick glanced behind him. The others weren't so far behind. They wouldn't exactly be able to have a private conversation like this.

Patrick knew it, too.

"If you want to sit around the damn campfire, holding hands and singing Kumbaya, going over our thoughts and feelings, then you can do that shit without me because I don't need it."

He started walking again. Roger watched Patrick go,

eyes wide, mouth pursed. James wasn't done, though. He followed his alpha.

"You were never exactly against the idea of us holding hands and singing songs before now. You miss that woman already, and you think you can take that shit out on us?"

"Enough, James."

But James was fucking pissed. He suddenly didn't care if the others heard him or Patrick.

"If you want to go back and take her away from the dragons, just say the word, and I'll help you do it, but don't you dare act like a lovesick puppy over her."

"I fucked her once, and you think I'm in love with her?"

"Who knows? Maybe you are."

It wasn't exactly as if that was uncommon for shifters. Sniffing out their mates and all that.

And that made James stop again. Roger, again not expecting that, slammed into James' back from having walked too close.

"Fuck! God dammit, James!"

James ignored him.

"Are you mated with her?"

"No! Don't be an idiot!"

Patrick wouldn't stop walking. He kept his fists clenched and his spine stiff, and right then, James knew he was lying.

Maybe he never realized it. Or he'd been lying to himself about it because Draco was the one who had insisted right off the bat that he was mated to Jessie, that he was the one who wanted to be her savior, but was it possible...?

"Patrick...are you mated to her?"

"I'm not! Stop asking!" Patrick glanced back, flashing

his red eyes and white fangs.

James' heart clenched, a painful squeezing he only seemed to get when talking about his alpha. Only now it was worse because this was being confirmed. Even if Patrick didn't want to see it.

"Patrick, stop being a cunt. You're mated to her."

Patrick stopped. He looked back at James, those intensely red eyes looking as though they were getting ready to bore a hole in the middle of his forehead.

"You shut your fucking mouth."

"All right, guys, settle down, we're not off the mountain yet," Roger said, and James wished he could listen to the man since he was the only reasonable one here. He really did wish he could do that for him.

James squared his shoulders anyway. "You're mated to her, and now you're pissed off that you have to leave."

Patrick turned, walking towards him.

"You wanted to stay," James said, even as Patrick pulled his fist back and launched it forward.

He didn't step out of the way.

Not because he was a sucker for punishment, though. No, that wasn't it, and when James' back slammed painfully into the rock wall of the mountain, he grunted, but he kept to his feet.

"For fuck's sakes, Patrick," Roger moaned, throwing his head back, but he stepped out of the way, giving his alpha space.

He knew how this tended to work. James was challenging his alpha. He needed to be put in his place for that.

James didn't care. He didn't cower either. He wiped the back of his hand over his mouth. A little blood came back on it, which he'd expected from the sting, but otherwise, he was all right, and he was *not* going to submit.

"You're a fucking coward."

Patrick's red eyes flashed. "You want to say that shit to me again?"

"Yeah, I do, and that was a free hit. I don't give a shit if you're my alpha. You want to fight me then fight me, but we're hashing this shit out right now."

And he didn't care that the other wolves in their pack closed in on them, gathering around, some on rock higher above, some closer to their level, but all of them paying very close attention to what was happening.

At first, James thought maybe he'd shocked Patrick into giving in, into admitting that he wanted that woman without the help of some manipulative spell.

Then he growled, and as swift as the damned wind, he flew forward, clawed hand wrapping around James' throat, slamming his head back into the rock.

Okay, yeah, he wasn't going to lie. That sucked.

"You do not get to talk to me like that, you little shit. Not in front of them!"

He'd never been so prideful about what the rest of the pack heard before. There were some things they couldn't know in the moment, at least if he wanted to keep the respect of the pack.

But Patrick had always been different. James had seen the way other alphas behaved among their wolves. He'd lived it, even. Patrick wasn't like them. He didn't treat the wolves beneath him like they were his subordinates. Everyone was a friend, and every sacrifice the pack made for the good of their lives as a whole was respected and thanked.

It wasn't just expected because they had to obey.

Which was why James refused to submit right now. His alpha needed him, even if he didn't want to admit it.

"Submit."

"No."

Patrick growled, his fingers squeezing harder, and fuck, it started to feel as though his claws were sinking into James' skin.

Even Roger couldn't stand it anymore. "Patrick, that's enough." He put his hand on Patrick's shoulder, this time not allowing himself to be shrugged off. "Look at what you're doing? For that woman? She didn't care about you. Don't let her manipulate you like this. She's still doing it. Come on. You would never have acted like this before."

James was grateful for the help, even if he knew the source of Patrick's rage was just a little different.

"Patrick, he's not going to submit. He's turning blue."

Okay, James really wished he hadn't heard that, because now, knowing he was changing colors freaked him out a little.

Patrick exhaled a hard breath. His eyes stayed red, but he did let go of James' throat, and thank God he did because James really needed to take in a breath.

And he'd been close to submitting just so he could.

Otherwise, it felt amazing to be able to breathe again. He bent over, sucking back huge gulps of air before he realized the entire pack watched his every move.

And Patrick stepped away from him, a hand on his waist, head down, as though deep in thought.

Rubbing his throat, James didn't hesitate. He stepped up behind his alpha. He didn't touch the man. That wouldn't be welcome right now, especially not from him, but he could still be there. Do something. Say anything that would make this better.

"If you want her so bad, then don't leave."

Patrick wouldn't stop growling. His entire body vibrated. "It's not real. It's that fucking spell. She used me, she wanted to use the pack, and she used *you*."

"And if this isn't a spell? You can feel the difference. I know I can."

"Then it's an after effect of what she did. It will pass on its own."

James glanced around at the other wolves, all of whom still watched the show. Not that there was anything else they could watch since James, Patrick, and Roger were in their way, preventing anyone else from getting down the mountain.

And higher up the mountain, he could hear the dragons stirring, their cackling roars filling the air. A few took flight, but James was confident they weren't coming down for a fight. No, they were flying somewhere else.

Where was Carlton sending them? Off to look for a place where they could lure in Valbrand? Or did they already have an idea of where he was?

James sighed. He was going to regret this, but...

"Patrick, we need to go back."

Roger snapped his attention to James. *"What?"*

James didn't look at him, or any of the other wolves. This was Patrick's decision. "We need to go back. You don't want to leave. You're not finished with her, and...I don't want to go back either. I want to find the male who imprisoned her and turned her into what she is, and I want to see with my own eyes when we kill him. I need to know, and you still want to protect her. I don't care if you say it means nothing. We need to do this."

More dragons took flight. More flew away from the mountain, which meant time was running out.

Patrick looked up, watching as the dragons flew off the mountain and towards the distant moon, one by one. They were getting ready for something big.

And James wanted to be in on whatever plans they had.

"Patrick, we have to go."

"You can't be serious," Roger said. "The bitch released you. Patrick is suffering the side effects, and you want to take him back to her?"

"My alpha wants her. It's as simple as that."

And it was. Patrick would never want James the way James wanted him, and hell, even James felt an itch to go back to her.

It wasn't exactly gentleman-like behavior to leave a woman in need when there was an evil wizard out to make her into a sex slave anyway, so he had that excuse going for him.

"Patrick, tell me you're not listening to this," Roger begged. "We're more than halfway down the mountain. Everyone is tired. Come on. We want to go home."

But Patrick was clearly thinking about it. He wasn't done. James felt it.

There was too much left to be done. Too much that had been left unsaid. Too many questions that needed answers.

And, if James was honest with himself, Jessie wasn't the worst person in the world. She just wanted to be safe. He could forgive her for what she'd done to him.

At least, with her help, James had been able to feel what it would be like to have Patrick kiss him, at least once.

If for no other reason, he owed her for that.

Patrick looked up at his men standing around him. "You all know why we went up there. A succubus cast her spell on James and me. She released us. I'll go back up, just to talk about what happened with her former master, and maybe offer my services. Anyone who wants to leave here and go home, I will ask no questions, and no one will be reprimanded. I'm going back up to find out what's being done before all those dragons leave."

Even as he spoke, more took flight.

Christ, Carlton and Draco worked quickly.

Roger crossed his arms, clearly pissed off. He didn't want to be there. He wanted to go.

But he didn't. Neither did anyone else.

30

JESSIE

THESE BOYS sure did work quickly.

Jessie had flown before; it wasn't hard to find a demon with wings that she could bum a ride from, but there was something a bit different about being on the back of the dragon.

Dragons were Earth's original demons. Nature's most beautiful animal. Better than horses. More noble and majestic than whales. Humans adored and feared them, but everyone wanted to be them.

Still, even with the wind flowing through her hair, her hands gripping tightly to Draco's horns, Jessie had to admit that it would've been way more awesome if she had not only her little army of dragons, but a pack of wolves snarling and snapping at their heels while they went to chase down her former master.

So to speak. Obviously, wolves couldn't fly, but that wasn't the point. It still made for an interesting visualization.

Draco hummed with pleasure beneath her, as though he was still inside her. Jessie smelled his musk. He seemed to get a sexual satisfaction all of its own out of having her ride him like this.

If there was something to be salvaged after this was said and done, she might just allow him the honor of letting her ride him again in the future.

But not because she thought it was fantastic or anything. No, this would be strictly for his benefit.

"Just say the word when you're ready to land, sweetheart. We'll get everything set up as soon as you're sure."

Jessie patted the scales on top of his head and between his horns before she could stop herself. She clenched her hand into a fist, hoping he didn't notice, and gripped his horns tightly once more as though she was riding a bike. "We just need a clearing. Then we need a fire."

They needed something to make it look as though she was fighting with them. The fact that the pack had abandoned her would make it all the more realistic.

Though it stung deeper than a dozen needles to think that Patrick and James were gone, even though it shouldn't, but at least she could use it to her advantage. Jessie had learned a long time ago to use whatever was available to her. This was no different. At least the betrayal, as small as it was, could be turned into something much better. It could be a bitch and a half trying to find the plus side to his shitty situation. But then there were the times when it was easier to do than others. When the solution came without a struggle.

Patrick and James were gone. But in their leaving her, they would unknowingly play right into her brand new plan.

Valbrand was the sort of stupid idiot who would believe she had no other plot to hatch. Or, at the very least, he would think that she had exhausted all of her other options.

Playing dumb and helpless in front of him had gotten her quite a few things she had wanted over the years. Not her freedom. And not her total control over him. But it had been enough to keep him docile, and enough to give Jessie a certain limited freedom that had brought her here now.

But it would be nice to have the wolves with her.

She'd thought that she was just getting through to James in particular. It was a shame, really. She'd liked those wolves.

Carlton angled his wings and flew up beside her and Draco. He seemed distracted. Jessie didn't like that. Just because she could use the fact that the wolves had left her didn't mean she would be safe if the dragons decided to drop her off.

"Having second thoughts?"

Those big, golden eyes barely spared her a glance. "Why? Are you worried?"

Jessie made a show of turning her nose up and away from him. "Hardly. I know you'll help, if not for me then at least for your friend."

Draco made an injured noise beneath her. "Come on, baby, that sounds so cold."

Jessie's heart constricted. She'd been called worse things in the world, but it was a reminder that she was as connected to Draco as he was connected to her.

She patted his scales again, this time not pulling her hand away or hiding the fact that she'd done it. "Sorry."

He purred beneath her hand like a giant kitten. That tender warmth that kindled inside of her flared to life.

She had to yank her hand back because of it.

If Draco noticed, he didn't mention it. "Nothing to be sorry about, sweetheart. We'll take care of this bastard, and then you can go back to being your best self as soon as possible."

She wasn't so sure she was buying that. "You're telling me you don't care if I'm mean all the time? What if one day you get sick of the way I act? Most people don't think it's cute to have somebody biting at them all the time."

Draco positively rumbled beneath her legs. If the buzzing of his body against her thighs wasn't enough to let her know how carefree he was, then the dragon-sized chuckle was.

"I'm a dragon, baby. And I don't know if you noticed it, but you made me the happiest man alive when you decided to stop fighting me on the whole mating thing. I can handle whatever you decide to throw at me."

"Don't tempt her. She just might decide to do it."

Draco left again, and while the humming of his body beneath her should have made the whole thing seem a little more cheerful, Jessie wasn't so sure that Carlton was playing around.

He looked at her with a worried expression on his scaly face. Maybe he knew what she was thinking. Jesse wasn't so sure she wouldn't go for it. Part of her desperately wanted to test Draco's love for her. He said he could handle anything? Why not see how far she could take that? How long she could poke and prod him before he finally gave in and proved her right.

But that was a sick and twisted game all on its own. A game that, if she decided to play it, both her and Draco would come out on the losing end.

She'd already lost to the wolves. Jessie didn't even want to think about why that hurt so much. Keeping Draco with her, and by extension, Carlton as well seemed of the utmost importance.

"Let's just do this, please. I want to get this over with."

"You and me both, baby."

Jessie sighed. She didn't like this. Her hands started to sweat as she held tightly to Draco's horns. The only person in the world who willingly offered his loyalty to her. No manipulations, no spells, nothing on her part to influence him.

Nothing except for his biological need to fuck and reproduce.

But it was still adorable that he was here at all.

She should be grateful she got this much, and all she could think about was...

"Just make sure to keep a distance from Valbrand. He'll try to sneak up on you, and he can throw projectiles even from a distance."

Another rumbling purr vibrated between her thighs. "Are you worried about me, sweetheart?" Draco angled his long neck to look back at her. It was a bit of a difficult position, considering she was still holding onto his horns and needed them to keep her balance.

"Just keep your eyes on the sky, please."

Jessie worked to control the sudden heat in her cheeks. Thankfully, the cool breeze of the twilight air helped her with that.

Draco flashed a toothy smile at her.

She absolutely did not think it was cute.

Beside her, Carlton still seemed distracted. He somehow managed to keep a balanced flight while he stared down at the earth below.

Jessie tried to look down and see what had him so occupied, but even she couldn't stomach the heights they flew at. She had to turn away and stare ahead. "What are you looking at?"

Carlton hardly missed a beat, turning his attention

back to her. "I'm making sure there's nothing unpleasant following us."

That made sense. So why was she left with this uneasy feeling? Because she was finally going to confront her master?

Jessie had always thought that she would show a little bit more composure than this. It was humiliating, actually. If Valbrand ever figured out that she was getting the heebie-jeebies from the thought of facing off against him, then, regardless of whether or not she killed him, she'd never live it down.

"Right. Let's just get this over with." The sooner they did, the better.

DRACO SENSED the unease of his woman.

He could smell it on her. He could hear it in her voice.

It was unacceptable. His beautiful and dangerous succubus, his ghoulish hellcat, confident and cocky as all hell, practically trembled on top of him as he rode off with her to face her own personal demons.

He didn't like that.

It was enough to make him wonder just what exactly Valbrand had been doing to her all these years.

Draco hadn't known her for long, but in the few hours they'd had, it was more than enough for him to know that she would be too proud to ever tell him the specifics.

Whatever they were, whether she decided to share them with him or not, Draco decided right then and there that it would be his mission to make this a puny little dweeb pay for whatever terrible things he had done to her.

Or the terrible things he had forced her to do.

She clearly didn't believe that he was mated to her. He could sense that, too. It would take an idiot not to notice it. No doubt she was also making big plans on how she would get him to dump her. She seemed as though she would want to test him in some form or another at some point.

So, his first act of proof of his love would be to defend his woman's honor, defeat the weasely little prick that turned her life into a nightmare, and then take her home for some more sweet love-making.

One-on-one, preferably.

Not that the sharing hadn't been hot, but that didn't mean he wouldn't enjoy giving a little one-on-one attention to his mate.

The fact that Carlton was hiding the fact that the wolves were following them was interesting. Draco didn't understand it, but his fearless leader usually had a reason for these things, so Draco kept his mouth shut and let Jessie lead the way.

It was kind of fun flying high while the wolves struggled to follow them down below, so he was enjoying that.

JAMES

HOW FUCKING FAR OUT WERE they planning on flying?

James didn't often lose his breath when running, but these dragons sure were giving him a run for his money.

The fact that they were able to keep up at all either meant that the dragons knew they were following and were taking their time, or James and everybody else was just that fast.

He knew how fast dragons could fly. Even if they were just going at sprightly sort of pace, there was no way James, Patrick, Roger, or anybody else in the pack, should've been able to keep up like this. Which meant the fuckers knew they were being followed.

He would've been irritated if he wasn't so desperately out of breath already, but he forced himself on.

Roger, on the other hand, wouldn't stop growling and bitching. He didn't have to use words for it to be obvious that he was pissed off about this entire thing. Occasionally, he would sprint forward, running alongside Patrick and James just to throw nasty glances at them and snap his teeth, letting them know exactly how he felt about having to do this.

Tough shit for him.

Patrick had offered every single one of them the chance to back out. The fact that they were all running after a bunch of dragons was their own choice.

They ran for over two hours before the dragon showed any sign of slowing down.

Thank God.

James had started to get winded a little over an hour ago. His lungs had started to burn twenty minutes ago. Now that the dragons circled, as though they were looking for a place to land, James figured he would keel over if they didn't stop for a break.

He practically did. James found a spot and some tall grass, and he let himself flop onto his belly. Even the cool earth against his heated skin wasn't enough to chase away the heat.

His heart pounded. His legs, paws, ears, body, and tail all trembled. Now that the adrenaline rush was done and over with, he didn't think he'd be able to get himself back up to chase after the dragons if they decided not to land.

Please, God, let them decide to land.

Patrick came to stand beside him. James wished he wouldn't. He loved the man, but he could feel Patrick's heat radiating off of him. James wanted no part of that right now

"Time to get up, soldier."

James growled a little, unable to stop himself from warning the other man away from his rest. But, of course, the alpha had to get what he wanted. That was sort of the point of being an alpha. Patrick reached out and grabbed onto both of James' ears, yanking him back up to his paws and leading him away from where the dragons looked as though they were getting ready to land.

It hurt, being let around like that, and it wasn't exactly flattering to have the rest of the pack see, but he was so exhausted that he was willing to put up with it. Though James did manage to get his act together when he noticed that the rest of the pack was already recovering, most everyone shifting back into their human shapes.

Roger still looked annoyed, as though somebody had told him he had to work on his Saturday off. It was irritating to know that James couldn't outlast the other man, but at least he could take comfort in knowing that he wasn't as much of a bitch about this.

Patrick dropped James suddenly, growling a little under his breath at the show of weakness.

"That's enough. I get the point; you're tired. We're all tired. But we know why we came here."

Yeah, James did know why they'd come here, and part of it had been his own idea. He wanted to be here. He couldn't give her up. Even after her influence over him had faded to nothing.

He almost laughed at that. Faded to nothing? Yeah, not really.

"Do we at least have a plan for what we're going to do here?" Roger scratched his hands through his hair. James couldn't tell if it was an angry tick, or if he was simply scratching all the dust, dirt, and twigs out of his hair after a long run. "We practically went all the way up the mountain twice just to have to chase those dragons down when lover boys decided to take off before we could see them again. Do we even know what they're doing?"

"We know they're going to confront her former master." Patrick scratched at his chin. "The details are another matter."

Roger rolled his eyes. "Well, that's really encouraging."

James let the shift take over. He could still communicate with the rest of his pack while in wolf form, but there was something about being upright on two legs, having opposable thumbs, and an easily understood voice that made it the more preferable option for communication.

"I don't want to risk getting in their way if they've got a plan going. In fact, I'm willing to bet that they're going to use Jessie as some sort of bait to lure him out."

Patrick frowned at that.

"Let me see if I can't sneak in a little closer to their landing pad. If I'm already there while they get settled, then I will be less suspicious, and it will be easier for me to sneak in."

He would much rather just walk up to the dragons and tell them that a mistake had been made, that he and Patrick were here to help. Regardless of what Jessie might've done to them, forcing their hands, forcing them to obey her like mindless slaves, she was still worth saving.

Besides, it wasn't as if he and Patrick couldn't admit that they hadn't enjoyed themselves.

Patrick didn't seem all that convinced at first. He eyeballed James as though trying to determine how sad he was for a mission like this.

James rolled his eyes. "You've got to be kidding me. Just let me do this without you looking at me like that, all right?"

"I just want to make sure that you go in prepared."

Whatever. James knew better. Patrick did watch out for him from time to time, but the man never showed this kind of hesitation. Not in front of James, nor in front of the rest of the pack. It made James look weak. No fucking way was he letting that stand.

"I'm going. I'll come back soon with news on what they're doing."

"Make sure you avoid any fires they light. I don't want you being seen by the dragons, or by whatever the fuck that Valbrand guy's going to use on them."

James nodded, then shifted back into his wolf shape and scurried off. He didn't want to use too much of his energy, so he put his focus on staying out of the way of any places the dragons looked to be preparing for a landing. Every time they did, they dropped like the cartoon anvils on sneaky coyotes. Since coyotes and wolves were still part of the canine family, James was very aware of the reference, that he was the coyote in this situation, and how much he didn't want to get crushed under the weight of a scaly, oversized lizard.

He worked to stay closer to the larger trees when the dragons began landing on the shrubs, crushing the plants under their massive weight.

And he could feel the rumble of the earth under his paws. Definitely not in the same way he felt it whenever a rabbit scurried by. No, this was kind of fucking scary.

He might love that woman, in his own sick and twisted way, but James was starting to regret volunteering for this plan.

God, please don't let them crush me.

It really would be the most embarrassing way to die.

Draco would just fucking *loooooove* that.

Luckily, he was able to find a place to hide his furry ass until all of the dragons had landed. It was almost as if a small earthquake had taken place, and James had started to worry that maybe they would even start crushing the trees beneath them. Unlikely, but that didn't mean he shouldn't think about it.

Jessie slid off of the back of one of the dragons. James

was still so new to this that he didn't realize it was Draco she had been riding until the dragon shifted into his man's shape.

Jealousy rushed through his body. The lucky fucker could have Jessie riding on him. Actually riding him, as though he was a battle horse of some sort. He would never be able to have Jessie riding on his back like that. He shook the thought from his head. Why did it matter?

He twitched his ears. All the dragons changed with the exception of maybe two or three of them. James doubted there were any more standing around that he couldn't see, not unless Carlton had decided to leave any of them behind to act as a lookout.

Jessie stayed close to Draco's side, and James definitely noticed it when she reached for his hand and he took hers, lacing their fingers together.

That was definitely very telling.

Jesus. Maybe there really had been more to her aside from her spells and the weird influence she held over him, Patrick, and Carlton. Maybe it hadn't been bullshit when Draco had insisted they were mated.

It kind of made him feel guilty, actually. To know that there was something real here, or potentially real, and he'd just walked out on her. He had his reasons. So did Patrick. Patrick, more so than James. James had to remind himself of that again and again. He shouldn't feel guilty for walking away.

Could Patrick see this? He had to be able to see it, right? Just because James decided to get a little closer didn't mean that anyone else in the pack wasn't paying attention.

He still had to focus in order to hear what was being said. The dragons were whispering amongst each other, even though it was getting dark and cold out. There was no fire for them to be spied on, and they kept their tones hushed as though worried there was somebody watching them after all.

James exhaled hard. Right. He should've seen this coming. They were most likely trying to keep things quiet in case Jessie's former master was listening in on them, but James was no fool.

The dragons might just as well know that they had been followed. They might be trying to keep their voices down in order to keep the betraying wolves from listening in on them. If that was the case, it added a whole new level of complication to this, and he didn't like that either.

Why the hell did dragons have to be so secretive? If they weren't so stubborn, so big, and so annoying, they might just be more of a pleasure to hang out with.

The fact that Jessie was mated to one of those damn dragons was just the icing on the shit cake.

He needed to get closer. They were lighting the fires. They clearly had a plan.

Glancing back, James could see that his pack was still watching him, still silently rooting him on. What was Patrick thinking right about now?

No matter. James had a job to do.

Luckily, he was good at staying silent and low to the ground. It was one of the talents that he took pride in, his ability to swing from place to place unnoticed, sometimes more like a cat than a wolf.

The closer he got, the more he could make out specific details of what Draco was telling her. He held onto just her hands, patting them, but it looked a little more as though he was comforting himself as much as he was her.

"We can do something else." Draco actually looked kind of nervous, as though he was sticking his own balls on the chopping block here. This was definitely a man who thought he had a lot to lose.

"If you're not ready, say the word, and I'll think of something else. This can wait another couple of days when we get together a different plan."

Jessie, who when James had met her had seemed like the pinnacle of confidence, a woman who could be knocked down by nothing, the embodiment of strength, resilience, and annoying stubbornness, shifted from foot to foot.

Her spine didn't look quite so straight anymore, she didn't have that stick up the ass sort of air about her, and the way she didn't quite meet Draco's eyes said more than any words could.

Holy shit. She was just as nervous as he was.

"I want to get this over with. I want…I want him out of my life. You could be tricking me all you want, fine, but if you're serious about helping me—"

"I am, and it's not a trick."

"Even so, if you were tricking me, and you wanted to help me with this, if you got rid of him for me, for real and for good, you could turn around and say this was all just a big joke, that we weren't mated, and I swear I think I would still love you for it."

Hearing her tell the dragon that she would love him if he helped her get rid of the man who would ruin her life brought a sting to James' heart.

And jealousy. Fuck, but did that ever make him insanely jealous.

As did the way Draco touched her cheek.

It was also intimate. The body language of two lovers who knew they were about to go through a trial.

James wanted to be the want to touch her. He wanted Patrick to be the one to touch her. It just seemed so wrong that only one male was with her right now when she had three more ready and waiting to serve.

Perhaps she'd sunk her claws a little deeper than James had thought.

James was too focused on them. He couldn't look away from their joined hands, and when Draco started walking in the other direction with her, James struggled to keep himself from following them.

He barely succeeded. James slunk into another set of bushes before he could stop himself, though he didn't think he been spotted.

The fires were getting bigger. He didn't know much about how these things worked, but he was willing to bet that the larger the fire, the more Valbrand would be able to see. It wasn't as though it made sense that a man could see so well through a pinhole, after all.

But James didn't hear the sounds of his friends softly trying to warn him. Nothing as obvious as whistling or bird noises, but there were other ways to do it. Crunching down on dry leaves, or snapping twigs was an excellent way to get his attention while ensuring that the people he was trying to hide from didn't notice he was there.

Not until he felt the heated breath of something very big directly above him.

James rolled his eyes, irritated with himself for letting this happen as he slowly glanced up into the golden beach ball-sized eyes of the dragon in charge of this whole thing.

32

JESSIE

SOMETHING WAS SERIOUSLY WRONG HERE. She felt it in the way the hair at the back of her neck stood up. Goosebumps formed all over her arms and legs.

Was she really that nervous about what was about to happen?

It might make her feel a little better if Draco didn't look as out of sorts as she was, but she supposed that was to be expected. After what she had done, the only reason he would have any backup at all was because he had twisted Carlton's arm.

She stopped walking, pulling against his hand when he kept trying to go on.

Draco looked at her, confusion in his eyes. "Are you all right?"

Jessie wet her lips and struggled against the dryness in her mouth. "I'm going to say this, and I will say it only once."

Draco released her hand. He turned so his body was fully facing hers, and he crossed his arms, which made them look even more massive over his already huge chest.

But he was still giving her his full attention. "I'm listening, but if you think for one second you're going to talk me out of sticking it out with you, then you're out of your mind."

Well, he was right about that. She was out of her mind for even thinking that this might be real, but every second that went by, her hopes grew, and they grew. Like weeds, or bamboo shoots.

"I want to believe this so badly, but here's what I'm going to say. Even if you're serious, you do not have to do this."

Draco jerked back from her as if she had punched him. "What do you mean? Of course I have to do this. You're my woman. This motherfucker hurt you."

"You don't even know the details."

"I know the man forced you into becoming whatever you are right now. I know you didn't want to be this; that's more than enough for me. If he wants you back, he's going to get a fight before he gets you. He'll have to go over my dead body."

Such a cliché thing to say, but it made her wince nonetheless.

Of course he had to pick up on that right away. "Does it make you uncomfortable? Me talking about dying, even if I'm just joking about it?"

"You don't know that it's a joke. That's the thing; he's powerful. He might be taking his sweet time getting over here now, but he can still be a pain in the ass when he wants to be. He can still get a jump on people."

"He won't get the jump on me. It's easy for me to joke about dying because I know that little shithead won't be able to touch me when I get moving."

"Your confidence is nice and everything, but I want you to be serious for two seconds. If I could force you, your leader, and a couple of alpha wolves into following me around when they clearly didn't want to, then what do you think Valbrand can do? He's an idiot and a massive dork, but that doesn't mean he doesn't have a lot up his sleeve."

Jessie wanted to reach out for him, to touch him again, but she didn't. This was all so new. The idea that somebody might actually want her for her, and not because she was manipulating them by using her magic, or her tits, was kind of a scary thing. If Draco didn't make her feel like such a damn maiden then maybe it wouldn't be so bad. But he did, and it was weird that she liked it. The idea that someone genuinely wanted to take care of her after so many years of being used up, of working for Valbrand, it was...pleasing.

And frightening.

"Are you worried this isn't going to work?"

"Yes."

It was a mistake to admit to weakness. Weakness allowed others to find the cracks within her and exploit them.

"We'll get this done." Draco was too damned confident for his own good. "Carlton might have a stick up his ass all the time, but he's a surprisingly good actor, and honestly? I think he likes you enough to want to help you with this."

"I doubt that." She did not mean to say that out loud.

Draco smiled at her. It was irritating.

"Will you stop looking so Goddamn confident? This is serious."

He put his hand behind her neck and pulled her close, kissing her, then pulling back before she had the chance to really figure out what was going on. And he was still smiling at her. "I think you're hot when you're mad."

"Right. Of course you do."

"I haven't exactly kept it a secret, and I mean it. Part of me wants to keep you all to myself, but another part of me doesn't mind it if I'm sharing you with my best friend."

Jessie was so not used to blushing that it felt strange every time she did it. "How do you know I'd want to be shared?"

Draco's smile looked oddly soft in that moment, as though there was something he wanted to say but couldn't.

A noise in the distance caught his attention. Jessie didn't hear it, but she didn't have shifter ears either.

"I think it's time we got back. The fires are getting bigger."

She could see their glow in the distance. He was right. It was time to go.

She really hoped this worked.

33

DRACO

The plan was simple enough. Draco was going to stick to being the knight in shining armor. He would stay by Jessie's side as Carlton pretended to betray them. There would be a fight. Fire would be blown; they might even take out a lot of these trees if they weren't careful. Luckily, Draco smelled rain. They were going to need it if these fires got out of hand.

And they might.

The fun part was how the show had already gotten started.

Draco dragged Jessie away so that when they came back, the fires already had a chance to burn, giving Carlton and the others the chance they needed to rile themselves up, just in case that little pecker head was already watching them.

And the wolves were off in the distance somewhere. Doing God only knew what.

Since those fleabags weren't already fighting with Draco's friends, that had to mean Carlton had found them, talked sense into them, and now they were going to be here when shit went down.

It was a shame to keep it from Jessie, but the touch of realism to everything was nice.

And it did feel good to launch his fist into the face of one of his oldest friends.

Carlton fell back a step, stumbled, and Draco was pretty sure it wasn't because the other man was faking it.

Carlton even had the decency to look a little pissed off as he wiped the back of his hand across his bleeding mouth, spitting more blood. Maybe Draco did feel a little guilty about that, but it was only what Carlton deserved, considering he wanted Jessie, too, and since Draco would be required to share his mate, he was owed one punch each to these fuckers by default.

He didn't say that, of course. He and Carlton fell into an interesting improv, fires blazing around them, highlighting the sweat on their bodies and the angry crowd that gathered around. They jeered and cheered as though this was a real fight they were getting worked up for. As though they were honestly rooting for their leader to smash Draco's head in.

Meanwhile, Tristan and one of the other guys had grabbed Jessie's arms the instant they came back into the group, as though springing some sort of trap.

She was their little fake hostage, but she did look kind of worried for him.

Don't make it seem too real or anything, guys.

His inner wild child couldn't take it if Jessie was sincerely worried for his well-being.

"All right, you little prick. *Now* I'm mad!"

Draco couldn't help himself. "You weren't mad before?"

Getting his fearless leader's panties in a bunch would definitely add to the realism he was going for here.

Which was the excuse Draco comforted himself with after Carlton roared, charged him like a linebacker, and knocked the damned wind out of him.

Wait, no, the wind wasn't knocked out of him until the bastard lifted him clear off his feet and threw him down on the ground.

And then landed on top of him. Then it got a little too real. It was all for show, but the punches were real. Painfully real. Draco started to fight back. And then he started to get mad.

The entire point of this was to draw out the real baddie, but the things Carlton said, fake as they were, pissed Draco off as much as they probably pissed off Carlton.

But he was still saying them.

"You brought her on us!" Carlton slammed his fist into Draco's nose. "You put that filthy plague on us!"

Another strike and Draco started to realize how delicate his face was.

"She's my mate, you fuck!"

"Fuck your worthless mate!"

Draco flailed at him. He went Beast Mode on the guy because, holy shit, he might not be meaning the things he was saying, but he sure as hell knew how to push Draco's buttons and make him fight as though it was life or death. He had to make it look as though it was, so why not go all out? He brought his claws out, scales forming over his skin without even thinking about it in a protective layer against Carlton's claws.

Not that it worked so well. Dragons could break through each other's armor with enough effort. He didn't want to break through Carlton's scales, and he was pretty sure Carlton was trying not to hurt him too badly either, but then Draco felt the sting of something sharp through his scales.

Holyshit. Was he actually using his claws?

When he'd said he was going to make this look real, he hadn't been picking around. Even in a fake fight, Draco felt the damage. They were all flesh wounds, nothing deep. And the more they fought, the more Draco remembered how outmatched he was. If Carlton really wanted to fight him, really wanted to hurt him, he could, as was evident by the way he couldn't seem to get out from under the other man.

Carlton was a beast, even in what was essentially a wrestling match, put on just for the views. Valbrand had better be fucking watching this. Otherwise Draco would be getting bloody for no reason.

He needed to get Carlton off him. If Valbrand wasn't watching him, then Jessie was, and for sure the wolves were around here somewhere, and he wasn't about to have his woman, or those mutts, thinking that he could be pushed around like this.

Pushing his wings out from his back, he created the momentum he needed to launch himself forward, throwing Carlton off him, and it was *sooooo* satisfying watching that asshole hurtling towards one of the trees, cracking his back against the base of one of the thicker oaks as Draco got to his feet.

Of course, the crowd booed him for that. They were supposed to be on Carlton's side and everything, but that didn't mean it didn't feel good.

Glancing to the side and catching Jessie's eye...yeah, the pride on her face was evident. She glowed with it. She was likely worried for Carlton, too, but he could handle that. Just so long as he got to show her what a protector he could be.

Draco threaded his fingers together and pushed out, cracking all ten of his knuckles. "Stay down, asshole." He really wished Carlton would. Instead, his own wings burst from his back so quickly that Draco could hear the ripping of his flesh, and smell the blood as his skin fought to knit back together.

Holy shit, that was insane, and Draco nearly turned and ran for it when the other man charged him again.

He planted his feet instead.

Carlton grabbed him by his throat. Fuck, his hands were big. His fingers seemed to go almost all the way around his throat.

Jessie yelled at them. "Stop that! Carlton! Let me go, you idiot!"

Of course, Tristan couldn't do as she commanded. She had no way to feed him her blood. That was the only way they could make this somewhat believable.

But Draco could see her thrashing around in Tristan's grasp, desperately trying to yank her arms away. Tristan and the other males holding her overpowered her easily. Jessie reached down and bit her arm. Blood pooled from the wound, and he could tell what she was trying to do.

No.

"Carlton, stop!"

This was getting too real. Jessie was freaking out. It wasn't worth it. They had to stop before this went too far.

"Carlton! Get the fuck off me!"

He wouldn't. He attacked Draco as though he was one of the wolves, as though he was the enemy.

Too real. It was too real. Draco fought to defend himself. He struggled to get out from under the man's grasp, but he still held tightly to Draco's throat, still punched him in the stomach again and again.

The fucker seemed to know how to keep Draco down. He couldn't take in a breath. He couldn't breathe!

Draco grabbed at his throat. Carlton pulled back from him, but he couldn't breathe. His lungs wouldn't open, and he made little hiccupping sounds. Since he didn't trust Carlton not to turn into a complete dickhead and kick him while he was down, Draco rolled away from him. His throat was finally working to take in tiny sips of air whenever he could.

"Draco!"

Tristan must have released Jessie because he could see her feet rushing towards him.

And then jump over him.

Not exactly the welcome he'd expected from the object of his adoration, but he'd work with it. Especially when he heard the crack of her hand over Carlton's face.

"What's the matter with you?"

Finally, the light of his life fell to her knees next to him. Draco was at least able to take in small enough breaths to ensure he wouldn't pass out, and it felt pretty damned good to have her hands on him like this.

She stroked his face, wincing at his nose.

It couldn't be that fucked up. He was still breathing through it. Even if it did sound more like whistling than breathing.

Then her beautiful face twisted into a snarl that she aimed back at Carlton. "You fucking asshole! Did you have to do that?"

Draco grabbed her hand, squeezing even when she tried to pull away.

She could be mad all she wanted, but there was no way

he was going to accept taking a beating like this for no reason.

He'd let himself get bloody, and his poor lungs and spleen were going to need some TLC, and he didn't even know how he was supposed to give them that sort of care.

"Jessie…"

She yanked her hand away, shoving hard on Carlton's chest. He fell back a step. Draco suspected it was more because he was choosing to back off rather than by her own strength.

She wouldn't stop shrieking at him. "You stupid dickhead! That's too much!"

The many fires lit around them, already crackling with life, erupted, as though dragons were flying out of them.

The fires had been lit as far away from any trees and shrubbery as space would allow for, but even Draco could see the way his friends backed away, the way the flowers and shrubs blackened and died. The way the bark of the oak and pine wilted and burned.

He could smell it, but nothing caught fire, especially the pine trees, which was the most shocking since they had all the peat on them.

The fires had their impact, but there was no fucking way it was natural that nothing else burned. Valbrand was clearly making that happen, and the piece of shit had the most punchable look on his face when he stepped out of the flames.

34

PATRICK

THE HAIRS on his back and neck stood on end when the male Jessie feared the most stepped out of the fire.

His hands were folded gently together in front of him. A serene yet patronizing smile was on his face as he stepped towards his former student, forgiveness, and mercy in his expression. As if the little pissant thought he was Jesus Christ or something.

James bit him on the ear hard.

That was good. The flare of hot pain was enough to snap him out of it.

James didn't have to say anything for him to get the hint.

Stop being a fucking idiot and get your head back in the game!

Right. He growled low in his throat at James, but then he put his focus back where it belonged.

Jessie stood frozen. She was already pale, but the blood positively drained from her as Valbrand approached. Her hands clenched into fists, and he could see the inner struggle.

She wanted to run.

She wanted to hold her ground.

Both options terrified her.

She'd made fun of Valbrand enough, called him a number of names, but seeing her so fearful, like a kitten standing in the way of a lawnmower, did something to his stomach.

James growled at him again. Something small and barely there, but Patrick needed it to get his focus when Valbrand reached his hand out and touched her cheek.

Draco roared. Sloppily launching himself to his feet, he tried to sucker punch Valbrand in the back of the head, but...

The warlock moved quickly. Patrick blinked, and their positions seemed to change. Valbrand was about to get decked out one second, and the next, he held Jessie's shoulders, putting her in the way of that fist that Draco could barely stop. Patrick's heart squeezed at the sight, and it didn't start beating normally again until he realized Draco had stopped himself in time.

Patrick moved quickly. He couldn't stop himself, even though he heard the light whimper of James behind him, his second-in-command loyalty following him as always. Sometimes Patrick needed that. He needed his best friend to tell him when he was going too far with something, or when he wasn't thinking right.

This was one of those times. It didn't matter. Patrick needed to see. He needed to get closer.

Draco slowly pulled his hand away from Jessie's nose. He hadn't hit her; otherwise, the damage would've been evident. It didn't seem to matter, though. The pale horror on his face was almost equal to that of Jessie's.

Valbrand, that little sack of shit, looked positively pleased with himself. The way he stroked Jessie's chin made Patrick want to rip out each of his fingers one at a time.

"Nearly had a little accident, did we?"

Draco growled at him. "You will take your disgusting fucking hands off of her right now, or I'll cut your hand off and feed your fingers do you like little sausages."

Valbrand shook his head, his nose twisting in light disgust. "Honestly. So crass."

"Why?" Draco rolled his wrists, cracking them. "Does it piss you off?"

"Only in your lack of imagination. It's difficult to say anything to me that I haven't heard already before. I would've expected you to have a little bit more creativity, especially if you're the one my darling Jessica wants to choose."

He tried stroking her chin again in that creepy way that gave Patrick the vibe of a distant, too clingy relative.

Jessie must've decided that she had enough. She snapped out of whatever spell of fear Valbrand had on her, slapping his hand away and stepping back towards Draco. "Don't touch me. You never get to touch me ever again." She smiled a little, the adrenaline of the situation clearly getting to her.

Because she knew this was it. Whether he took her back or not, this would be happening.

Valbrand crossed his arms, that strange robe fluttering in the barely-there wind. His whole body seemed to glow as he stood in all that firelight. "You think you have some leverage over me now, do you?"

Jesse frowned, jerking back at those words, as though they were the last thing in the world she thought she'd hear.

"What are you talking about?"

Meanwhile, the Harry Potter wannabe kept smiling at

her, as if he had some big secret over her head. "Do you really think I didn't know the wolves were watching this? That I wouldn't know what you were doing?"

As if to accent his words, the son of a bitch dared to turn his head and look right at Patrick.

Fucker smiled, too.

35

JESSIE

SHE DIDN'T BELIEVE IT. Jessie glanced back, searching for whatever it was Valbrand was looking at, but she wouldn't believe it until she saw it. And then she did. The first wolf stepped out from the shrubbery and trees, a twig stuck in its fur between its ears in a cute and scraggly way.

James.

Patrick stepped out next. She'd only seen him a couple of times before in his wolf shape, but it was enough for her to be able to tell this was definitely him.

Roger came next, at least she thought it was Roger based on the snarl on his muzzle. The way his whiskers trembled as he sniffed and growled at literally everyone and everything meant that it was probably a very good chance it was indeed him. More wolves stepped out, maybe it was even Patrick's entire pack.

Jessie's heart flew. Could she really be this lucky? Was it possible that they had to bend to her after all?

She didn't even care about the trick. If this was just something they had done in order to make her believe the ruse they wanted to play on Valbrand, then so be it. She was just happy to see them all. Even Roger.

But Valbrand, the asshole, did a slow clap. As if he was getting one over on the wolves and the dragons for their trouble. "Very nice. Honestly, I'm kind of impressed. I would've been more impressed if you'd actually managed to stay out of the way and surprise me, but, you know what they say, you can't have everything."

Roger growled again, his ears folding back.

Draco seemed the most annoyed out of everybody as he pushed himself to his feet, ignoring Carlton's outstretched hand. He wiped his mouth with the back of his hand and spat. "You're telling me that I took a beating like that from my best friend for nothing? For fuck's sake."

"Yes, so very sad for you, but you should've made sure your little plan would work before you bothered with the theatrics."

Jessie really wanted to smack him.

She wasn't the only one, but it was Draco who mouthed off.

"Maybe you shouldn't be talking shit to me about theatrics there, *Duncan*."

Valbrand's eyes flew wide. Jessie saw the murder in them before Draco did. Or maybe he did see how much she was pissing off the other man. That was sort of the point, after all.

No longer looking quite so entertained with himself, Valbrand spoke in a low, hissing sort of tone. "What did you just say to me?"

This wasn't good. "Draco, you should stop."

He didn't heed her warning. "What? That's your name, isn't it? *Duncan Dingburry*?"

One of the dragons snorted, likely somebody who hadn't heard the name spoken out loud before. The others did a somewhat better job of holding back there snickers and snorts. But it wasn't by much.

And Valbrand noticed it. He whipped his gaze around to Jessie once more. "You *told* them. I said that to you in confidence. You fucking bitch. How could you?"

She couldn't believe him. "How could I? Fuck you! How could *you*? You did this to me! You took my life."

"I gave you power. Extended life. Everybody loves you, and they want to be you, and you keep punishing me for that."

It was unbelievable how he sounded as though he believed it. She supposed she shouldn't be shocked. He was a little out of his mind, so why would it be out of the realm of possibility to believe that he would do the mental gymnastics to convince himself he'd done her a favor?

And she was angry. So furious that it fucking boiled her blood and bubbled her skin. Decades, centuries of holding this shit in, pretending to be his friend and his little plaything came out right in the open.

"My daddy was sick. I fucking asked you to save him. I begged you to save him. I thought you were a Goddamn angel!"

"I did save him." He blinked his eyes at her, as though he really couldn't understand the problem. "I explained to you what would happen. I said he wouldn't be right."

"*Bullshit*. You told me there were side effects. And, fine, maybe I should've asked a few more questions about what they would've been, but you didn't tell me that he'd be a rotting, walking *corpse*. You didn't tell me he would never get better!" She stabbed her manicured finger in his general direction. Her voice cracked on the last words. For a split second, she forgot that she was being watched by a pack of wolves and a clan of dragons. She barely noticed that they were hanging onto her every word as though they were watching an intense drama on TV.

She didn't care either. Fuck them and fuck the man standing in front of her. She would be embarrassed later. She would be ashamed later. Right now, she wanted to stick her perfect little pointed fingernails right into his BDI's and watch that strip down his face as he screamed.

She didn't always have to be the succubus. Sometimes, she could be a ghoul. Might as well act like it from time to time.

Valbrand, however, looked at her as though he was bored. As though the drama on TV he was watching didn't quite interest him the same way it did the wolves and dragons.

It was because he'd seen this TV show before. Carlton, James, Patrick, Draco, and their respective men were all basically watching the final season of *Game of Thrones*. They hung on to every detail. Meanwhile, Valbrand had already spoiled everything for himself by reading the script online. He basically knew how this ended. He wasn't the least bit impressed.

"Everyone always thinks that the rules do not apply to them. I told her you—"

"Shut up! Shut up!"

She didn't want to hear it. Because he was right. Jessie had been young, but she was old enough to know better than to take something that was too good to be true. She was old enough to know, to at least suspect, that the man in front of her offering up such miracles really wasn't an angel. She'd felt it in his offer. And in his smile. Something sinister. Something not quite right.

And her daddy had told her that nothing in life came for free.

It was just a shame that she needed to learn that lesson through the flesh of her father.

"You're the asshole who thinks he's Gandalf the White or something, but you're just a snake oil salesman taking advantage of people. Not even in stupid, petty ways. You destroy people's lives."

"You were hardly complaining when you were in my bed," Duncan shouted back. He pointed at her, facing the wolves and dragons who still watched the show in front of them with fixed interest. "How many of you want this whore now? Now that you all know I had her riding on my cock and liking it?"

"The only pussy you get is the kind that pretends to like it, *Duncan*," Jessie said, shaking from the sting of his words. "So don't go bragging about how amazing you are in bed."

His eyes actually changed color. As though he was the wolf here, the dragon who could eat her alive with a single gulp.

He could, but she had her backup, now.

"Watch your mouth and know your place. The village whore likes to think she has power over her clients, but she is still a whore. You are only as powerful as you are because I made you."

"So take it back! I don't want it anymore!" She didn't want to bleed black. She didn't want to crave sex from men or women at all hours of the day, and she didn't want to walk around feeling as though she'd used Patrick, James, Carlton, and especially Draco.

He watched just as carefully as everyone else. He pinched his nose, head partially back to stop the bleeding from his fight with Carlton. Normally, she could tell what men thought when they looked at her. Women were a little harder to read, but men were easy, part of her trade. The fact that she couldn't tell terrified her.

"I'm not a whore!" She sounded desperate. "I didn't want to do anything!" Weak and needy wasn't attractive, wasn't worth fighting for. "You believe me, right?"

So many men had walked away. Usually, after she'd let them go, thinking they might stay without the spell. Some during those few times when they'd broken through her spell with their own resolve and inner strength.

She'd thought wrong. They hadn't stayed. No one had.

Until now.

Maybe the four males she'd taken as her prisoners would have been able to break free of her influence with a couple of months to work on it. They were strong. Stronger than any of the males she had influenced. Of course, she hadn't told them this. They would have been able to walk away on their own with enough time and fight.

But she let them go. Now, she desperately wanted them to stay.

Draco's response seemed to take forever before it came.

Maybe time was just slowing down like that. As if she was stuck in a bubble of time and it wasn't working.

But then he smiled at her. The best smile she'd ever seen on a man who looked like he couldn't breathe through his bloody nose. "Of course I believe you, sweetheart."

She could breathe. Jessie could breathe again when he said those beautiful words, and she thought for a moment that everything might be all right.

"I believe you, too," James said, shocking her.

Patrick stepped forward, in his human shape, chest out and proud. "So do I."

Carlton slammed a fist against his chest. "And me."

The four of them looked at Duncan; they stepped forward as one. The wolves and dragons were still separate from each other, but they too lined up behind their leaders. Even Roger and Tristan and those two didn't even like her.

Jessie stepped back from Duncan. The look on his face was...interesting, to say the least. He sputtered a bit, probably unable to imagine the gall it took for them to line up like that. To get in his way.

Duncan recovered quickly. The perplexed expression on his face melted away to something more uninterested.

Yeah, everything just bored the fuck out of this guy. That's what he wanted people to think, anyway. Jessie could tell he was pissed. He just wasn't doing the best job in the world of hiding it.

"All right. You animals want to fight for my scraps? Come on then."

He did something Jessie had never seen him do in the near two hundred years she'd known him.

He turned into a dragon.

36

CARLTON

HE ALMOST STEPPED BACK. The sudden transformation had an effect on the air itself around them. The whoosh of hot air burned his face and hands, any part of his body that was still exposed.

He smelled burning hair.

A quick check proved it was not him, but then he had to get to Jessie, who stared up at the inflamed beast as though she had never seen anything like it.

Neither had he.

Carlton had never seen a demon like this before. It almost looked like a dragon, but dragons, despite the popular lore, were not actually made of fire.

Green fire. As though the thing were *Maleficent* from that old Disney movie.

He was no fairy tale fan. The dragons always died in those movies, but he still remembered watching it as a kid, impressed with how big the dragon got, how it towered over the prince before wussing out and dying with a single stab to the chest.

Duncan was just as big as that cartoon black and green

dragon. It towered over her. Taller than Carlton, Draco, and Tristan combined.

The only good news was that this new form had no wings.

A snake-like tongue flicked out at her. It was on fire, too. So were the eyes.

The thing was a fucking monster

He rushed forward, shifting into his full dragon shape, because fuck this halfway shit. He was going to need the entire form if he stood any chance.

Carlton leaped onto the dragon's firefly back, and then immediately regretted that such an action was needed when his scales and claws felt the burn. He opened his maw and bit down hard on Duncan's long neck, the fire burning his tongue, teeth, and nose. But fuck this guy because he was not letting go.

He wasn't alone for long. Carlton felt something heavy land next to him.

Draco. Back in his dragon shape, and even like that, his face was fucked up.

Carlton felt a touch guilty for doing that to him, but Draco had better things to worry about as he found one of Duncan's ears, right near a long, curved horn, and then bit down on it.

Duncan roared and thrashed. His tail whipped out. The cracks of multiple trees being felled like nothing were like heavy bangs of thunder.

Draco was the first to call away since he hadn't bitten anything with a lot of meat. When he was thrown from Duncan's body, he took the creature's ear with him.

Carlton let go on his own. He couldn't sit in the fire any longer. Even though it felt good to taste the blood of his enemy and hear his scream, there was only so much pleasure he could take from the act that would sustain him before he needed a break.

And with an inward apology to Jessie, he dropped off.

No. No. He should have hung on longer! But his paws and wings still burned. He needed water.

Duncan opened his mouth, that long, ribbon of a tongue curling out and tasting his pain as it leaned over him with those glowing green eyes.

Carlton growled at him, a warning to stay away. He couldn't seem to back up. His limbs refused to move.

A howl and a roar followed. The wolf pack charged as one, capturing Duncan's attention next.

The big monster blinked, not expecting the attack coming his way. He watched the wolves charge, as though unsure of their threat to him.

They couldn't jump on his back, but his feet weren't quite as on fire as the rest of him. Still hot, Carlton imagined, but fire burned up, and when the wolves darted forward two at a time to each paw, nipping and biting at his feet before backing away from the heat and letting others take over the attack, Duncan jumped, pulling his feet back. He whipped his tail out, spinning, flailing, and even trying to stomp on the wolves as they moved forward then back.

Forward then back.

"Carlton!"

He raised his head, struggling to his paws as Jessie came to him. She hesitated before touching him, her hand trembling, but her skin was cool. He leaned into her palm.

"Oh my God, you're hurt."

"I'll be fine."

"He burned you!"

"Don't tell me how much. Lie to me about my looks if you have to. I don't want Draco looking better than me.

The idiot will never shut up about it if he thinks he's more handsome."

She blinked at him, as though unable to tell if he was joking or not.

It occurred to him in that moment that Jessie's powers, all of her abilities, were based entirely on her ability to seduce men and bend them to her will. She could not shift into a dragon here. She had no magick to defend herself or fight with. In a battle of this sort, she was entirely helpless. So she needed her knights now more than ever.

The dragons rushed to help the wolves, and it was about fucking time, too. Carlton was going to have a damned word with Tristan about when it was time to take action and when he could stand back and watch what was going on.

But they were moving now. The dragons flew in, dipping low, talons outstretched and grabbing for anything they could take.

He didn't like thinking it about his own men, but it reminded him of vultures. Except they weren't fighting for scraps. They worked together to grab chunks of meat from wherever they could take it.

Scratching, biting, and diving at his face, feet, and back.

And that piece of shit was realizing his size didn't matter when he was up against at least fifty angry wolves and dragons.

Jessie's army.

He liked that. Carlton spread his wings.

"Don't go! You're hurt." Jessie grabbed the thin spot where his wings joined with his scaly back. He turned his long neck around to stare at her.

She didn't look like she was faking sympathy. She was as genuine as she had been when she confronted Duncan.

"Don't go," she said again.

Affection welled inside him for her. He couldn't believe she ever felt she needed to cast a spell on him.

And then he was ashamed she had needed to influence him in order to get his help. Especially after her outburst at Duncan.

He looped his burned wing around her shoulders as if he could shelter her from everything happening outside that space.

Her eyes widened. She had never looked more beautiful.

"Aren't you…worried I'll try to feed on you?"

"No." He brought his muzzle close, snuffling at her hair, taking in her scent. "You need to get out of here. This is for us to do."

"But I think I can—"

"No." He had to stop her right there.

Duncan whipped around again, his tail flying, slamming into one of the wolves and sending him flying over the fire. No telling if he was alive or dead; Carlton hadn't even seen who that was.

Didn't matter either because he needed to get his ass back in the game and fight.

"Get to a distance. Out of sight and away from anything he can throw at you. Away from the fire. Do you understand? You can't influence him, and I doubt you can drink his blood or eat his flesh like this."

Her bottom lip trembled.

He wanted to kiss her, but he didn't dare get out of his dragon form. It hurt enough with his scales protecting him from most of the heat damage.

"Go on now."

"I wish I…" She trailed off, stopping herself before she could let him know what it was she wished, but then she gave him his wish when she turned and started running.

His heart ached to see her go, but he wasn't well until she was out of sight. Now he didn't have to worry about Duncan grabbing a felled tree and throwing it at her. She might be a demonic creature made by the monster here, but that didn't mean he wanted to test how much she could handle before something killed her.

Carlton turned back to the monster.

He grabbed Tristan out of the air with his huge maw. Carlton watched that cock-sucking asshole slam Tristan down again and again until he stopped moving.

Carlton roared, strength returning to him as he charged the towering monster in front of him.

Duncan tossed Tristan away, lifeless and limp, as Carlton raged. He leaped in the air, wings and talons outstretched, but his target was the motherfucker's eyes.

DRACO

THE INSTANT DINGLEBERRY the Dipshit threw Tristan away like he was a sack of dead meat, Draco damn near lost his mind. He latched onto the top of one of the trees, eyeing where his friend landed.

Several dragons swooped into his location, grabbing onto him and carrying him away, out of the line of fire. Draco couldn't tell if he was dead or alive, but of the two wolves that had been kicked in the face and were out of commission.

But they weren't his friends. They weren't the men he'd fought and bled with for years. Seeing that happen to Tristan made him want to tear the fucker's eyes out of his skull and eat them like green, glowing grapes.

Carlton already had that same idea.

The dragon roared a battle cry, swooping down again and again on Duncan's eyes.

Despite having sat in the green fire for longer than Draco or anyone else, he swooped in and out with grace and speed, avoiding Duncan's claws as he swiped at Carlton like an annoyed cat chasing a fly.

Carlton was like an eagle chasing after a fish. He was much better at looking like he knew what he was doing than Duncan was. The guy might be huge, but even in this form, he flailed around with little skill, speed, or grace.

Draco didn't war cry. He didn't want to give himself away, no matter how cool and badass it would be to screech in revenge, but it was imperative the cunt couldn't hear him coming.

And he didn't.

Duncan swiped his claws back out at Carlton, missing him again, seemingly not bothered anymore by the dragons who scratched and whipped at his back.

Duncan noticed Draco coming too late, and he turned to look just as Draco reached out and sunk his claws into his right green eye.

38

JAMES

It was hot. So hot that he almost couldn't stand it beneath the belly of the beast. The fire didn't directly touch him, but it was still like standing so close to a furnace that his skin began to burn from prolonged exposure. The smell of burning fur didn't help so much, neither did the way Duncan Dickhead jumped around as he desperately tried to avoid the claws and teeth of the dragons swooping in from above, or the wolves who chased after his feet as though they were doing a shakedown for money.

Duncan roared suddenly.

Ear-shattering. The noise nearly threw James off, and when the belly of the beast pulled up as Duncan pushed to his hind legs, the sudden onslaught of cool air against his fur and flesh felt like ice in comparison.

He looked up and saw why.

Then he nearly puked.

Draco and Carlton were actively feeding on Duncan's eyes.

The warlock used his two huge paws to try and push them off his muzzle, but they held a tight grip.

A truck slammed into his side, sending him flying thirty feet away. He landed on cool dirt, hard rock, grass. Even his fur couldn't stop him from feeling the scratch, the brunt of the impact, but then he had the chill of air kissing his fur that didn't feel like it was on fire.

Patrick was there, growling in his face, looking furious, and James realized what the truck had been that hit him.

He could basically hear what his alpha wanted to yell at him.

Pay attention!

Right. The giant monster creature was still stomping around, screaming in pain as Draco and Carlton finally swooped off him, though Carlton landed sooner, one of his wings looking fucked up and shredded from the abuse Duncan had hit him with.

But Duncan still flailed, still pawed at his eyes.

They bled black, the same color as Jessie's blood.

James could smell it. He could always smell the blood of his prey, but this blood was rotting, filthy. He would have thought the blood would smell similar since Jessie's looked the same, and she had been turned into the thing she was by this man, but no.

This was the blood of a creature that had no soul.

He howled. He couldn't help it. He was an animal, and he charged for his bleeding prey. Even if he couldn't latch his teeth around the giant monster's neck and shake him like he did to squirrels who crossed his path, he would enjoy bringing him down that last little bit.

James flew. He charged as though he was the one with wings. He zoned in on the creature's massive feet, jaws open as though they were the most delicious things he'd ever seen in his life, and with the rest of his pack, and the dragons above, he took his pound of flesh.

39

PATRICK

James seemed to have his head in the game again. He'd been too distracted by the sight of the Godzilla dragon thrashing around, pawing at his eyes, that the little idiot nearly let himself get trampled by a stray paw.

Might not have killed him, but Patrick wasn't about to take that risk, not with some of his men being flung around like rag dolls, the dragons being ripped out of the air, and that fire spreading to the foliage and leaves of the taller trees.

He barely heard the clap of thunder in the distance. He thought it was Duncan still thrashing and kicking, the earth vibrating under his heavyweight. At one point, he started kicking his one foot in earnest, desperately attempting to throw Patrick, James, and any other wolf currently feeding on his feet off him.

Patrick thought he now knew what the rodents felt that he caught and shook for sport and food. He thought his neck was going to snap as Duncan kicked and flailed.

He didn't let go. He clamped his teeth down harder and held tightly.

The fires above him blazed. His fur burned. He grit his teeth even harder, but instead of giving him a better grip on the fleshy part of his scaled feet, it forced his teeth to bite down harder, which broke the skin even more.

Until he went flying, taking a chunk of Duncan's disgusting flesh with him. He nearly choked on the black blood that tried to sink down his throat, but he spat out the fleshy chunk and gagged until he was sure he swallowed none of that filth.

Jessie had managed to enslave him for a little while because he'd been forced to drink her blood. There was no fucking way he was risking that drinking any of his blood would have that same effect.

James was thrown from Duncan's feet as well, as were the other wolves, and the way the creature roared and shrieked, thrashing and dancing around like a child throwing a tantrum in the toy aisle, made it clear that it was no longer feasible to get close for the attack.

Even Patrick was starting to feel guilty for the poor bastard. His feet looked like they were suffering from syphilis.

He cringed again, though he took special note of his wolves, making sure they spat out any blood from their mouths before they could have the chance to swallow it down. The dragons did the same; they just did it from the tops of the trees.

They should have asked Jessie if there was a specific amount of blood that needed to be taken in before their minds could be taken over. He assumed there was a threshold that needed to be crossed for that sort of thing because he didn't feel the need to obey the bastard the same way he had the first time Jessie made him drink her blood.

And he didn't just drink one tiny little drop either.

Duncan continued to shrink in size. For the most part, he held onto his shape, but he wouldn't stop screaming, wouldn't stop holding onto his face, or even thrashing a hand out, fire, ice, steam, and sparks shooting from his fingers. As though he was terrified he would be attacked again at any moment.

Patrick didn't blame him for that. Everyone seemed to be waiting for the right time to strike. But everyone also looked at the warlock with a disgusted sort of pity.

He really was nothing special, was he?

He hadn't been born in this century, but the guy probably had his head stuffed in the equivalent of a toilet in his day plenty of times over. Was probably smacked around by his father and ignored by his mother, and that led him to become...whatever the fuck this was supposed to be.

His name was humorous to hear for the first time, but in that moment, he really did look like a Duncan Dingberry. With a name like that, even if he had the most perfect childhood imaginable, it was no wonder he'd turned into a psychopath.

But this psychopath had tricked Jessie and turned her into what she was now. He'd made her enslave men, drink their blood, eat flesh, and work for him. He'd turned her into something she clearly didn't want to be and raped her for years. He had to remind himself of those things. To force himself to feel no pity for the creature suffering in front of him.

This was the least of it.

Some of his wolves shifted back into their human shapes. A good number of the dragons dropped from the trees to be on the ground level, clearly trusting that the thing in front of them wasn't so much of a threat anymore.

"Guess it's hard to keep a spell like that together when you're being destroyed with pain."

Patrick hadn't realized James shifted back into his human shape.

He did the same, standing with him, and now that the alpha was on two legs, the rest of his pack felt it was appropriate to follow suit.

Patrick crossed his arms, watching as Duncan fell to the ground, rolling around in the flames that had started because of his own fire.

Light raindrops fell from the sky, but it wouldn't be enough to put out the flames for a little while. Duncan might even end up choking on the smoke before the fire could do more than lick at him.

"Should we kill him? Or should we just leave him like that?"

Patrick couldn't believe that was a choice they had to make.

But then something occurred to him. They didn't have to make that choice. This was someone else's call.

They all knew whose.

He, James, Carlton, and Draco turned. As though they had sensed her presence as one. Jessie stood right there, watching the scene, one of the fires that climbed the tree making her body glow. Like an angel about to deal merciful death. Or a demon ready to take pleasure watching a show of dying.

He couldn't tell. For the first time since he'd met her, she didn't exactly look human. Blue veins pulsed down her arms, across her shoulders, and down her legs. They climbed like reaching, skeletal hands into her face, cupping her cheeks. Thin pointed horns poked through the pores of her forehead and curled upward like a barbecue fork. Her eyes were black. There was nothing in them. Not even the whites that should have been there.

She finally looked like a ghoul.

40

DRACO

HE DIDN'T RECOGNIZE HER. He thought maybe this was something Duncan had done to her. A possession? Maybe part of his control over her, because there was no way in hell his Jessie could become…

This.

Carlton grabbed his shoulder, pulling him back when Jessie stepped forward. "Draco, get out of the way."

"What?"

She moved slowly, but not towards him.

"Come on," Patrick said, taking his other arm and gently easing him out of the way, allowing Jessie to pass.

She stepped into the fire. It licked at her skin, burned her clothes. At first, Draco thought maybe she didn't notice it. That this was like Daenerys Targaryen from *Game of Thrones* or something.

No. He could see it burned her skin. She wasn't immune to it, but she didn't seem to notice it either. And she continued to walk deeper into the flames.

"Jessie, hey! Jessie!"

"Don't."

Draco yanked his arm out of Carlton's grasp, but Patrick stepped in his way, both hands on his shoulders.

"You need to leave her alone."

"Get the fuck out of my way, you mutt!"

James stepped up beside his alpha, looking ready to start a fight if he needed to.

"Cut it out. She needs to do this."

"Her skin is peeling off, you stupid fuck!"

She knelt down next to Duncan, putting her hands right into the smaller fires that ate at the pine needles and dry twigs. Her clothes continued to burn, but she still didn't notice, even as she put both of her hands on Duncan's throat.

"Let her do this first," Patrick said.

"Then you can go and get her," Carlton finished.

He glared at the lot of them, but then stopped himself before he could cuss them out again.

It was the look on Carlton's face that stopped him.

Specifically, his eyes.

The poor bastard looked as hung up on the idea of Jessie's flesh burning and blackening as Draco felt. He was just more composed than Draco was. Because of course he was. The man was his leader. He could compartmentalize shit Draco couldn't even imagine.

Much as he didn't want to give them credit for it, Draco glanced at Patrick. He, too, had that look on his face. The sort of expression that said how much he didn't want to deal with this. How much he wanted to go over there, him and James together, and yank her out of that fire and hold her close. She might try to drink their blood and eat their flesh while they did it, but they wanted to.

"Let her do this," James said, never taking his eyes off her as she strangled the life out of Duncan Dingberry, the worm that had one too many fantasies about being the evil villain in a poor man's *Lord of the Rings* knockoff.

"She needs to do this."

Draco grit his teeth. Patrick and Carlton released him, apparently making the decision that he could figure out for himself what was the right thing to do or not.

They faced the scene, watching her. Everyone did. With a grim, sick fascination as a crying monster of a woman strangled the life out of her blind abuser.

Draco didn't move. He wanted to. His body itched for it, and he shook with the desperate need to run to her.

He didn't.

He waited until she finished. Until long after the pitiful creature on the burning ground stopped twitching. She held on for a while after that, the veins pulling back from her skin. As though fleeing something terrible.

Or something terrible fleeing from something good.

When she collapsed, he did his job.

41

JESSIE

The heat of the fire licked at her, but she didn't feel it, barely noticed it, and when she did, Jessie jumped up with a scream.

It was cold; her body was cold. Everything was cold.

Because she wasn't sitting in a fire. It wasn't dark, and there were no fires anywhere.

Except for the fireplace.

It crackled warmly, but she shivered at the sight of it.

Because *he* watched her. That's what that meant.

A quick glance at her hands showed each individual finger thickly bandaged. Even down to her wrists, and she felt the itch of those bandages wrapped around her legs and even part of her arms and throat.

Now that she noticed, *everything* itched.

But the fire still bothered her more than itchy bandages ever could. She could be eaten alive by fire ants and not be bothered by it to the same degree.

"Hello?"

Was that her voice? Jesus.

Once more, with feeling this time. "Hello? Is anyone there?"

Jessie grimaced, pushing herself to sit up against the small mountain of pillows behind her. She couldn't remember the last time her body hurt like this. Something was wrong with her. This wasn't natural. The tips of her hair even hurt, and there was no way that was supposed to happen.

What the hell did Duncan do to her?

But what did he do to Draco? Was James still alive? What about Patrick or Carlton? They would have fought until they couldn't anymore, and Carlton had been burned badly by the fire of...whatever the hell that monster had been.

Jessie pulled the blankets off her legs, pleased to see she was wearing something. Even if that something was a pair of boys shorts and a long T-shirt. Definitely not her clothes, and someone had dressed her. If they'd decided to partake in something they shouldn't have, she would eat their souls in front of them.

First, to find out what happened to her knights.

And to put out that Goddamned fire.

The wobble in her knees the instant she put her weight on them had her sitting her ass back down real quick.

"Okay."

She tried again, and felt a little like Ariel, learning to walk upright for the first time. It wasn't painful. There was no shooting of needles down her legs, but there was something fragile and scary about not being able to hold herself up under her own power.

And she was getting frustrated.

Jessie put her hands on her knees, willing herself to heal, or at least to have the energy to walk around while she figured out what was going on.

It was one of the more simple spells she could cast, meant to suck the energy out of the air around her. Being a ghoulish sort of creature meant she wasn't very good at it, but that was what made this spell perfect for little bumps and scrapes.

Except...nothing happened. Not just that there was no action, but literally, *nothing* was going on.

As though something was bottlenecking her.

Or full blown stopping her.

All right. She didn't like this anymore.

She tried again but didn't put so much time into it. If Duncan was fucking with her, then she needed to get out of here as fast as possible before it got to the point where she couldn't get out.

He might not be watching her right at this moment, but that fire was as good as a camera blinking at her. She needed to move before he saw her.

So she tried again, falling against the nightstand.

"Fuck."

She took a breath, testing her baby bird footing. All right, she could hold herself up on two legs so long as she had something else to grab onto.

Good to know.

She reached for the wall next, falling against it and sliding her way towards the door. Which wasn't exactly a treat either since it created a terrible friction against the bandages on her shoulder, and they still fucking hurt!

Jessie grit her teeth. What the hell did Duncan do to her?

Slowly, she got to the other side of the room. Not that she could briskly walk across the room like anyone else. No. She had to feel her way across as though she was trekking on undiscovered Martian land while blind.

Turning the doorknob, it was a shock when the door

swung open. So much of a shock that she didn't move, not trusting this wasn't some trick.

The door just opened? She wasn't locked in?

Maybe this meant she was supposed to stay here. This had to be a warning, something that required her to stay put for fear of the real threat out there.

Right?

She glanced out into the hall, shocked with the beige carpeting, the small ceiling, and wooden walls. It was clearly an old house, but not old in the same way Duncan would have liked. He liked antiques, and he adored old fashioned architecture, which was actually new architecture for him, but old for most other people on the planet.

This, however…was just an old house. Maybe built in the turn of the century, but not the sort of thing a wealthy, powerful male like Duncan would have wanted to grace with his presence. He would rather burn a place like this down, piss on the ashes, and then build something better on top before burning that down, too.

Just to show he could.

She slid outside, sticking to the walls and grimacing when the doorframe proved to be less forgiving to her wounds than a smooth wall.

Tacky flower painting on the wall, yellow lights, and a small window at the end of the hall…

Yeah, this wasn't Duncan's style, but it wasn't Carlton or Draco's home on the mountain either. She could smell it in the air. What she could smell suggested something closer to wet dog, and that made her smile.

Patrick and James brought her to their home. They were alive then.

That was so good she could cry.

Jessie let the weakness in her legs take over as she slid to the floor. She was so happy she actually did cry. They had to be alive, and if they were alive, there was a good chance Carlton and Draco had made it through, too. Now she just had to find out what happened to Duncan. How did the fight end?

The last thing she remembered was being told to run away. She'd hated that, but she had. She'd run away like a coward, but she couldn't bring herself to go very far when the four men she'd roped into helping her risked their lives for her.

She'd turned back. The sounds of Duncan's Tyrannosaurus screams pulled her towards him. Not just that, but the wolves and dragons who swarmed his enormous body like insects to some honey-covered human. Not the greatest way to die, but she'd wanted to make sure he was dead.

And then there was nothing.

"Hey, sweetheart."

Jessie snapped her head up.

Draco was right there, looking down at her, his hands on his knees, a gentle smile on his mouth.

James was right behind him. He pressed his lips together, as though holding something back. Something big.

"I'll get the others," he said, turning and marching out.

"The others? Wait!"

He stopped, glancing back.

"Patrick and Carlton are alive?"

"They are," Draco said, kneeling down, touching her shoulder, then her face, and then her hair, as though he couldn't help but put his hands on her. "Everyone's all right. Everything's perfect. James, go get them. They're gonna want to see this."

"What happened?"

"You've been out of it for a little over twenty-four hours," James said. "Duncan's dead."

Her heart swelled, and then it deflated, a weird and painful sensation she barely knew what to do with. "He's dead?"

But he'd been around for so long. She'd known him for so long. Of course, Jessie had wanted him dead, more than anything, but the idea that he was really gone...

And she was *free*.

She was *human*.

Now that her lack of powers suddenly made sense, she grabbed Draco's face, yanking him forward and crushing his mouth to hers, kissing him hard and deep before stopping with that and kissing him again and again. As much as she could. All over his face.

"Thank you." She was still crying, but he didn't complain. "Thank you. Who did it? Was it you?"

Draco shook his head. "No, baby."

"Then..." She looked at James. Carlton had been injured. Maybe he could have done it, but at this point, she was putting her money on him or Patrick.

James shook his head, however, destroying that idea. "Not me either."

Jessie swallowed. "Was it—"

"Jessie," Draco said, cutting her off. "It was you. You did it." He slid his thumb across her cheek. "You finished him off. We got that party started, but you snuffed him out good and dead."

She couldn't stop crying. "I did?"

"Yeah." He grabbed her hands, pulling her knuckles to his mouth before looking her right in the eyes. "Trust me."

She looked into his eyes. There was nothing there that would give her cause for concern. When Duncan had tried to come off as sincere as this, she'd sensed it. The too good to be true vibe. This was too good to be true, but she didn't get the sinister vibe.

Carlton and Patrick must have caught on that something was going on, because suddenly they were up the stairs, stopped at the other end of the hall, watching the scene unfold. And she smiled a wavering smile at them. She probably looked like swamp water served on ice, but they definitely seemed happy to see her. She didn't get anything evil or nefarious from them either.

She would deserve it if they did look at her like that, after what she'd done to them, but it wasn't there.

Jessie nodded, sniffing, rubbing her nose on the back of her hand. Definitely not seductive, but she didn't care. "I do. I trust you. I trust all of you."

42

JESSIE

THEY TOLD HER WHAT HAPPENED. She almost didn't believe it.

Really? She'd wrapped her hands around Duncan's neck and strangled him?

Just like that?

Not that she wasn't grateful that she finally had that stupid bastard out of her life, but it seemed kind of... cheap. There was something cheap about knowing that she didn't even have a memory of it. That seemed like the sort of memory she would want to hold onto. For God sake's, when she woke up, she thought he was still alive. She thought she was his prisoner.

Which was complete bullshit. In fact, it made her angry.

Jessie had wanted to relish his death. She had wanted the memory of it to nourish her for the rest of her life. Even the fact that she was, seemingly, now human again was soured just a little bit by the idea that she couldn't recall her revenge.

Draco was too patient with her. Of course he was.

He was her mate.

"Don't be so upset about it. Your memory might come back in a day or two. Maybe even sooner, and then you'll have all the fun of remembering his stupid bulging eyes as he took his last breaths."

Jessie smiled at him, appreciating the effort as she squeezed his hand. "Did his eyes bulge?"

Draco laughed a little at the question. "Like a bug being squished. You were amazing." He kissed her bandaged hands again. "The only thing I hate is that you were kneeling in that fire."

Jessie glanced at Carlton. All four men, and even a good number of the wolves and dragons who'd fought for her, had burn marks, but for Carlton, it was the worst. He was bandaged up almost as much as she was. They were like a walking pair of mummies.

She never did like costume parties, but this one she could handle.

"You all got it the worst." She almost didn't want to ask the next question, but it was inevitable that it had to come out. "How many of your men died?"

Now that everything was said and done, Jessie could let it hit her that what she had done had caused the deaths of some of their friends. She told herself that she didn't care about that sort of thing. She made herself believe that she didn't care. Why would she? She didn't know those people. They were supposed to be nothing to her.

And yet, she did care. Jessie tried to push those emotions away, that guilt, but it was there nonetheless, eating away at her. Because she was human? It was hard to tell. It had been so long since she had been human. How was she supposed to know what it was like to feel like one?

Draco sat next to her. He seemed to not want to let go

of her hand, his gaze never leaving hers. She had his full attention. Not because she was a succubus who had forced his hand either.

James was a little closer by. He leaned against the wall, arms crossed, watching the pair of them as they spoke, and occasionally offering his own input.

Carlton and Patrick, however, stood by the door, as though they were keeping guard of her. Or protecting her from what might be lurking outside. The pack. And the dragons. They were protecting her from them, not them from her. She could see that now.

Even stranger was how she knew she needed the protection.

Without her powers of manipulation to aid her, she really was a helpless little flower here, wasn't she?

"I think I should leave."

She might as well have sucked the air out of the room. In all honesty, Jessie had been expecting that reaction from the four men around her.

Draco sputtered. "Well, why? You're safe here. You do know that, right?"

"With the four of you around? Yeah, I know." She couldn't lie to herself about that.

"Why do you want to leave?" Carlton sounded stoic. Probably because Draco was his friend, and she was about to break his heart. Her own heart too, but she wasn't about to reveal that to them. No point in revealing how much she needed them. All of them.

The two wolves in the room or quiet. They watched her in a way that made her feel like a squirrel being watched by a dog right before it pounced. They were just waiting for her to reveal something. A little more patient than the dragons were. Barely. They were vibrating with energy. She could sense their need to want to jump in and ask their own questions, but they held back.

"Jessie?" Draco cleared his throat, composing himself. "I mean, if you need some space after what happened, then yeah. I get that. I think I'd want that too. But you are going to come back, right?"

Now she felt a little jumpy. "To be honest, I don't know. Are you sure you're still not under the effects of my influence?"

Draco growled. He released her hand and scratched at his chin. "You seriously want to ask me that again? For real?"

He didn't sound angry, but Jessie was still under the impression she needed to tread carefully. "You're clearly sincere, but…"

Draco stared at her, waiting for an answer. "But?"

She couldn't answer. She didn't know how to put into words what this was. This inner terror that Draco would look up one day and realize he made a mistake. She didn't think she would be able to handle it. She didn't want to.

"I want you to stay. And I want to stay with you. To be honest, though, I want to stay with all of you. You're my army. My brave knights, and you helped me kill Valbrand and turned me back into a human. I mean, I'm pretty sure I'm a human." She looks down at her hands, flexing her fingers, running her tongue over her teeth and finding no small fangs there. She tested out one more time her muscles and reflexes as she searched for the power she used to have. But she still felt cut off. There was nothing there, nothing for her to tap into at least.

She felt something closer to human.

Yesterday, she wasn't so high maintenance. Everything was getting to her. Everything was bothering her, making her paranoid and unsure. Her heart wouldn't stop pounding, and all she could think about was everything she could have done to make this happen for her faster.

Or without upending other people's'lives.

"You look human to me," Draco said, turning to the others. "Right, guys?"

James eyed her up and down. "You don't give off that blood-sucking vibe anymore, that's for sure."

"Maybe she should give us a command," Patrick said, rubbing his chin thoughtfully.

Carlton shook his head. "We'd have to drink her blood again for that to even work. Human or not, I'm not doing that again."

"That's fair. To be honest, I don't suddenly feel so good about cutting myself and making anyone drink my blood anyway." In fact, it made her stomach turn just thinking about it.

"Most healthy humans don't want to cut themselves, for blood drinking or otherwise, so the signs are good so far," Carlton replied.

"Should we be writing down her symptoms?" James asked. "I mean, if she's not sure, and she pretty much looks the same as she usually does…"

"She doesn't need it," Draco insisted. "Even if she's not entirely human, she's perfect."

Jessie shook her head. "But I'm not. There's something else I can't place here. Something selfish. None of you wanted me with the exception of Draco." She looked him right in the eye. She owed him that much. "I'm really sorry. I promise I'm not trying to do this to hurt you, and this isn't some sort of trick, but I just want to be near them. They helped me too. And, to be honest, I don't know what this thing is that I feel inside me now. Part of me is just terrified that I'm being overly sensitive now that I'm a human again. Because I don't know how to be human. I might just be over analyzing this, thinking that I want something when I don't, but I can't help but want it anyway."

Draco didn't look phased. "You don't have to worry about a damned thing. It's okay if you want to take your time to think about this. I just want to know if you're coming back."

"Draco, you might be freaking her out even more right now," James said.

"No." Jessie shook her head. "It's all right. I think I just…"

"It's a lot to take in," Patrick said. "Tell us what you want to do."

Her heart wouldn't stop pounding. She didn't want to get up and walk out of here, that was for sure, but it seemed wrong to stay. Yesterday, she wouldn't have thought so much about this. She might have barely cared, if at all. Now she was free. She felt guilty and disgusted, not just for what she had done to the four men here, but what she'd done since Duncan had changed her.

And now she had a choice. It was such a strange concept that she didn't know what to do with it.

"I think I don't know what to do. I think I should go and try to make amends for everything I've ever done, but I don't want to leave here either."

And she couldn't make that not sound selfish in her head.

Great. Now she was playing with them and confusing them.

It was quiet for a moment. The silence was crushing her.

Carlton spoke up first. "You feel guilty for the things you've done?"

Jessie clenched her hands together. "Yes."

"You want to stay with Draco?"

"Yes."

"Do you also want to stay with the three of us?"

She cringed. "Yes."

Jessie had been with multiple men at the same time plenty of times before in her life. She'd drank their blood when she finished with them and pulled their souls from their bodies so Duncan could gain more power, live longer, and get more full of himself.

How many souls had it taken for him to transform into that dragon thing? She still couldn't believe that was a card he had to play.

All that time. Right out from under her nose.

"You should go then."

"Carlton! Jesus Christ!"

Draco wasn't the only one who was shocked. Jessie couldn't believe he said that.

Well, actually never mind. She could.

"No, you shouldn't go if you don't want to go," Draco said, looking at Jessie as though she would disappear at any moment. "If you need to in order to feel better about all this, fine, that's all right. But don't go because this dick-head is going to chase you away." Draco threw a glare at Carlton one last time just to accent his point. But Carlton remained unfazed.

"I'm not saying it to get rid of her. That's not the point. She's not going to feel better about this by sticking around here and having us all staring at her like this, waiting for an answer. She thought Patrick and James took off on her yesterday. If she needs her space, then she should have it."

"Not saying she shouldn't have space." Draco clenched his teeth. "It would just be very nice if you would stop trying to make her walk away."

"Your alpha is right," Patrick said. "If she really wants

to stick around with you, then she'll come back on her own when she's ready. If you pressure her into staying, then she's not going to be happy."

Jessie thought that made sense, but it also shocked her that they seemed so calm about the idea of her leaving.

"Will it bother any of you if I go?" That probably made her sound a little too desperate, especially since none of these other men had to care about her the same way Draco did. They weren't made to her like Draco was. Still, she'd hoped that there would be *something* there. Maybe they would be a little concerned about the idea she would need to leave.

Yeah, she was definitely selfish. Even in her human form, she wanted her cake and to eat it, too.

Four of the most perfect men in the world? And they'd helped her kill Duncan and free her from his influence? Why *wouldn't* she want that?

Draco still seemed annoyed that she was being talked into leaving, but then he inhaled a deep breath and seemed to calm down. "If there's somewhere you want us to take you, we'll take you there. We won't let anyone hurt you. You can...do whatever you need to do and take your time deciding. I'll be here waiting, and you know these assholes will, too."

She didn't know that, actually, but a quick glance at James, his soft smile, brought her just the right amount of hope.

No one was asking her to go, or demanding it. They were just telling her that if she needed it, they would give her the time and space. The idea that she would be welcome to come back was the thing that got her the most. Even more so than the idea that Draco didn't want her to leave.

"I think...I'll go. I'll go, and I'll think and I'll...I don't know what I'll do, but if you really mean it, I might come back. To all of you."

It wasn't what Draco wanted to hear. She could see it all over his face.

He inhaled a deep breath. Clenched and unclenched his hands on his knees, then nodded. "I understand."

Maybe he did, but that didn't mean he had to like it.

But she needed this. She needed to be free, for a little while, for a long while, she didn't know, but somehow, staying with these four males, even if they wanted her to, without at least meditating on her future, and her past, seemed wrong.

She looked at James. "What about you?"

He tensed. "What about me?"

"Come on." She smiled, feeling something closer to normal. "You must be hoping I'll take off and never come back."

He crossed his arms. "I never said that."

She glanced at Patrick before looking back at James.

She wished she could have done more for the two of them, but...

No. Best not to dwell on *that* complexity.

She wasn't sure if she would be able to figure it out on her own, but part of her had hoped that, with her there, there might be something they could...

Nope. Not going to think about it. She didn't know either of them well enough to know if Patrick was attracted to other men. A kiss while in the heat of the moment hardly made for anything other than Patrick seemed to need a woman involved somewhere before he would look at his friend like that.

Then she looked at Carlton. Damn, she didn't even get in bed with him. That seemed unfair. The other guys at least got a lay out of the deal. He just...

Helped her anyway. Some of that was probably for Draco's sake, but she couldn't help but think he got the short end of the stick in all this.

Carlton seemed to take her staring for something it wasn't. "If there's something you want to ask me, go ahead and ask. I won't bite."

Jessie snapped her gaze back down to her hands. She shook her head. "No. There's nothing."

Another silence.

"Was there anywhere you wanted to go? Someplace specific?" Draco asked.

She shook her head. "I lived with Val...with Duncan for the longest time. I could always find a place of my own if he ever got on my nerves. He let me do that after a couple of years, but I was never allowed to go far."

"So you'll have someplace safe to be?" Draco asked. "A roof over your head? All that?"

He really did care. They all did.

He seemed to be feeling it the most.

"Yes, but, before I go, there's one more thing I want to ask all of you."

No jokes about how much she already asked of them came. They just waited.

"I know you were fighting for territory. If you could, don't do that anymore. Work it out, split the land if you can't stand each other that much, just...don't let me come back to find out any of you are dead. Duncan's killed a lot of people, and I don't want it to be anyone in this room."

Patrick and Carlton looked at each other. Both men's arms were crossed, neither just yet willing to make that first move.

"What do you say?" Patrick asked.

Carlton rubbed his jaw. "The injuries and two dragon deaths are enough that no one on my end is in the mood for war. They want to be with their families and recover." Carlton held out his hand. "I'm good for negotiating if you are."

Jessie sighed when their hands met.

Then she knew it would be all right.

She knew she could go.

43

DRACO

I<small>T WAS GOING</small> to be a while before he got used to seeing so many Goddamn wolves around his territory, not just the land that Carlton and Patrick had agreed to split that day Jessie left.

Left him.

No. The wolves were actually on dragon territory now.

Every once in a while, Patrick sent over some of his men to keep the relations going well.

At first, no one liked the arrangement. Any wolves on dragon land were eyed with little more than distrust, but the general population put up with them. Mostly because there were those in the clan who thought it was funny how the wolves struggled to get up and down the mountain.

It stopped being funny when Carlton suggested building a stairway for them.

Draco liked Patrick and James well enough, he supposed, but that didn't mean he wanted to boulder stairs for them.

James insisted he didn't need stairs either, which was the only reason why Draco still enjoyed his company, but that was it.

Just because they were working with the wolves now, farming the land they'd fought for, didn't mean everything was perfect. There were still those in the clan who struggled to recover. One male had to have one of his wings cut off. That devastated the entire clan.

No one wanted to be that guy. Even the wolves cringed when they heard it.

James had said he once knew a guy who'd lost his tail because he thought he could be smart and run through a sea of bear and coyote traps. Apparently, one of them had activated, jumped up and, snap, no more tail. Draco had laughed his ass off at that one, and so he told it to the dragon who'd lost his wing to cheer him up. The poor bastard had smiled a little, which was more than what anyone else had been hoping for at the time. It was something.

He hadn't heard from James in a while. He could check his phone again, but he didn't exactly get the best reception on this side of the mountain. The view was pretty, though. Made him think of her. The way the sun set just behind those trees reminded him entirely of the color of Jessie's hair.

He *missed* her.

He hoped she was all right.

She hadn't contacted any of them once since leaving, and three months was a long time to wait.

The worst part was how much longer he might end up waiting.

The sound of wings whooshing and flapping behind him caught his attention. He didn't turn. He was sick of Carlton's damn feel good, hopeful speeches. They didn't bring Jessie back, and it was starting to piss him off that Carlton was taking it so well Jessie had left.

"What do you want?"

"You need to cut it out with this mooning shit. It's not attractive."

Draco growled. "So? You're not the one I'm trying to impress."

"No, but when she sees you, she is going to smell the desperation in you. Women can sniff out that shit from underwater. She doesn't need to be a ghoul for that to be the case."

"Go away, please." Draco crossed his arms. "The last thing I need is for you—"

He stopped himself as he turned back, struck dumb as rocks as Jessie froze back.

She was bent over a little. Her hand reached out. As though she had been about to touch his shoulder before he saw her.

Draco launched himself to his feet. He looked at her, then looked at Carlton, who stood behind him with a smile. Behind him, James and Patrick were there. James smiled, waving his middle finger like the huge prick he was and ignoring Patrick's disapproving glare.

They had known, and they'd come here with Jessie to, what? Surprise him?

Those motherfuckers.

"Don't be mad. I went to see them first."

"I'm not mad." A bit of a lie. "Definitely not mad at you."

At least that much was true.

He drank her in.

"You look amazing."

Her golden hair was loosely tied and braided over her shoulder. She had on some kind of pastel pink top with loose sleeves and a scoop neck that accented her breasts and the gold chain she wore nicely.

Draco liked to think he knew a thing or two about women's clothes.

They all looked so good in them, after all, and he loved the skirt that showed off her beautiful long legs. Her flat sandals laced up her legs, giving off more of a girl-next-door vibe than the manipulative seductress he'd first met.

"You look like you've done a lot of thinking."

She nodded. "I have."

It was her hopeful expression that made his palms sweat, and now that he bothered to look, Draco was pretty sure he could see some of her pink lipstick on and around Carlton's mouth.

This might also explain why the wolves were here. James and Patrick did seem to be standing a little closer to each other than they normally did.

James in particular looked cheerier than Draco had seen since Jessie had left.

"Are you coming home?"

Jessie glanced back at Patrick, James, and Carlton before she took Draco's hands.

"Yes. We all are. If you're all right with that?"

His stupid heart wouldn't stop beating so hard. "All of us? You still want me to share you with those fools over there?"

"Screw you," James called.

Jessie smiled, clearly sensing his answer as he looped his arm around her waist, pulling her close.

And fuck did it ever feel nice to have the heat of her body pressing against his.

"Whatever you need, sweetheart. Your wish is our command."

THE END

NEXT UP: DARKNESS AWAKENED

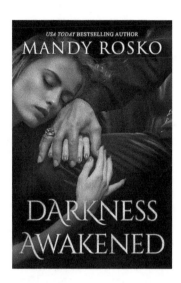

Awaken your inner wild side...

Lilac has led a picture-perfect life, not knowing that her life was bought and paid for long before she was born.

Her father sold his first born child to a vampire in a ritual for pure blood, and a lot of money and connections, and

Now, if Lilac wants to keep her lifestyle, and protect her father from bearing the brunt of his actions, she has no choice but to meet her secret benefactor, and find out what life will be like as a vampire's plaything...

Darkness Awakened
A Patreon exclusive until September 2019
Available everywhere October 2019

ABOUT THE AUTHOR

USA Today Bestselling Author Mandy Rosko is a videogame playing, book loving chick. She loves writing paranormal romances that range from light steamy to erotic, and has some contemporary and historical romances as well. You can find her on all sorts of platforms, including Twitch, Patreon, Wattpad, Radish, and more!

Get all the latest news from Mandy by signing up for her newsletter: http://eepurl.com/bQ8HvT

And get the most up-to date information on releases from Eighth Ripple Press by signing up for our newsletter: http://eepurl.com/gcUObH

facebook.com/MandyRoskoRomance

twitter.com/rizzorosko

instagram.com/mandyroskodraws

bookbub.com/authors/mandy-rosko

ALSO BY MANDY ROSKO

You've Got to be Shifting Me

Zero Fox Given

Howl Always Love You

Can't Bear to Be Without You

Alpha Bites

Alpha

Alpha Bear

Alpha Dragon

Alpha Wolf

Dangerous Creatures

Burns Like Fire

A Shock to Your System

As Cold as Ice

Gonna Make You Howl

Things in The Night

The Vampire's Curse

The Legend of the Werewolf

The Shepard's Agony

The Dragon and The Wolf

Stand-alone titles

Darkness Awakened

Jessie's Harem

Bad Boy Bear

The Wild Wolf's Wife

Vampires Don't Share with Dragons

Dangerous Guardian

Mate of a Dragon Villain

My Angel Lover Have Mercy on Me (M/M)

Bad Boy Billionaire Brothers

Arrangement with a Billionaire

Holiday with a Billionaire

The Billionaire's Fantasy

Learn more at mandyrosko.com